DEADLOCK

UNCOMMON ENEMIES: PANTHER FORCE (BOOK THREE)

FIONA QUINN

DEADLOCK

Panther Force

Uncommon Enemies

By

Fiona Quinn

THE WORLD OF INIQUUS

Ubicumque, Quoties. Quidquid

Iniquus - /i'ni/kwus/ our strength is unequalled, our tactics unfair – we stretch the law to its breaking point. We do whatever is necessary to bring the enemy down.

THE LYNX SERIES

Weakest Lynx

Missing Lynx

Chain Lynx

Cuff Lynx

Gulf Lynx

Hyper Lynx

STRIKE FORCE

In Too DEEP

JACK Be Quick

InstiGATOR

Uncommon Enemies

Wasp

Relic

Deadlock

Thorn

FBI Joint Task Force

Open Secret

Cold Red

Even Odds

Kate Hamilton Mysteries

Mine

Yours

Ours

Cerberus Tactical K9 Team Alpha

Survival Instinct

Protective Instinct

Defender's Instinct

Delta Force Echo

Danger Signs

Danger Zone

Danger Close

This list was created in 2021. For an up-to-date list, please visit FionaQuinnBooks.com

If you prefer to read the Iniquus World in chronological order you will find a full list at the end of this book.

*This book is dedicated to all of you who have faced your
monsters, stayed strong and found your way through.*

$$1$$

ROOSTER
Djibouti, Djibouti

"**B**EFORE WE BEGIN, I need proof of life."

The radio crackled with static in return.

Rooster scraped his teeth over his top lip, waiting.

"Mr. Honey." The buzzing and mechanical channel whines were replaced with the cheerful sound of lighthearted banter. "You know, every time I say your name, I laugh at the irony."

"How's that?" Rooster stretched his long legs out in front of him and crossed them at the ankle, settling into the conversation.

"Oh, if you knew, you would kick yourself." The man's accent sometimes rang with Arabic notes, sometimes with French, but his English was quite good. He had obviously spent time in America. "As for your proof of life, you must realize by now that I am an educated man. I'm not a Somali pirate raised with minimal thinking tools. I've done my research. I know your tactics. The Bowens are worth three million dollars. I will hold firm to that number. That number is *not* negotiable. The only things we are to negotiate are how the payment is to be made and how you are to retrieve your people."

Rooster was pleased. "Brilliant" had never strung so many words together at one time. Up until now, his responses had been monosyllabic, sometimes just grunts, since their communications had begun over a month ago. Rooster had made a career of hostage negotiations. It took him to some of the bleakest, most godforsaken parts of the Earth. Now, here he was in Djibouti on the Horn of Africa, sitting behind his radio set with a wet towel draped over his neck in a poorly air-conditioned rental house on the outskirts of the capital city. Djibouti was a country of dry scrublands, volcanic formations, the amazing Gulf of Tadjoura beaches, and temperatures that ran over a hundred degrees, day and night. *It's a dry heat*, Rooster reminded himself.

Though he drank water constantly, he hadn't peed in days. His clothes were covered in white scum from where his body's sweat had left its residue.

In hostage situations, when Rooster introduced himself as the negotiator, he used the radio call sign he'd been given way back in boot camp some twenty-odd years before, Honey. Well, he made sure to say *Mr.* Honey, so things didn't get weird. Not to say that most of the people he negotiated with were fluent enough in English to understand that the noun was often used as a term of endearment.

Most of the men who negotiated from the bad-guy side chose to be called names like "Big Man" or "Chief," sometimes "Boss." Rooster knew these were words they thought, in their limited grasp of English, gave them power. This was the first time an English speaker had wanted to be called "Brilliant." A narcissist. Someone whose ego swelled to cover up his lack of conviction, and probably the fact that he had a micro-dick. Rooster had steered his psychological tack accordingly.

Right now, though, Rooster needed to push things along. Time was the enemy. There was a statistical trajectory for good outcomes, and that section of the graph had come and gone. Hostage negotiation was a slow game. But they were now in the orange zone, the time when people without training, who were psychologically and physically unprepared for the challenges of captivity, folded under the weight. If the captors recognized their victims' decline, a deal was often possible. If they didn't, then Rooster's team would be trying to get the corpses back, so the victims' families would have closure.

Bad things could happen—did happen—to hostages held under kidnappers' thumbs. But so far, Rooster was batting a thousand bringing his clients home at least alive, if not always safe and sound. He reached out to knock on wood. He tended toward the superstitious when his ego bubbled up some wise-ass thought like good batting averages.

His teammate Randy sent him a chuckle when he did it, then refocused on his task at the computer.

Rooster pressed the comms button. "It's been a while since I heard from the Bowens. Before our conversation continues, I need proof of life," Rooster said, not a trace of emotion in his words. The captors wanted him to be passionate and work from the heart. Rooster knew the only way he could save these people was to keep an emotional distance. He had to think of these negotiations like a businessman buying office supplies: necessary supplies, but objects all the same. Compartmentalization was a honed skill set. Boxes were a handy tool. His emotions belonged to a different part of his life and not his career. Emotions equaled mistakes.

Brilliant laughed. "I am not stupid enough to be in the same area as my hostages. If you have some new communications tracking device, it will not work. I am a moving target."

Rooster rubbed at his chin, his focus sharp. "Okay, let's set up a time. I need to hear their voices. I need to verify that they are still the right people, and they're still safe and sound."

"Bowen is holding up under the strains of his conditions. His wife, on the other hand, is not. We believe she needs immediate medical attention. I am very worried for her."

"She has a heart condition. You know that," Rooster said. "Does she have her medication? Is there a drop point where I can provide supplies?"

"With a tracker attached? No."

"Can you tell me her symptoms?" The longer Rooster could keep this asshole talking, the better shot they'd have of picking up ambient noise—clues to his whereabouts.

"I believe the heat and stress, along with her particular location, are all problematic."

"She doesn't work for Hesston Corporation. Why don't you let her go? Call it a good-faith gesture."

"I would like nothing better. As soon as the payment is made, I will take her immediately to the hospital."

"Is the hospital a far distance? Should I arrange for a helicopter?"

"Ah, you think you can trick me into giving you information about where the Bowens are held. Listen to me. Anjie Bowen needs immediate attention. I want to get her that attention. It is you who prevents me from doing this." He let his words seep in. Waited for Rooster to panic.

Rooster knew all the tricks and traps. He sat silently, listening to the static.

"I realize how this works. It will not be Bowen's corporation that pays the ransom monies. It will be the insurance company.

You don't work for this man, Mr. Honey. You are paid by the insurers. But if this man or his pretty little wife dies, your reputation will be tarnished. The insurance contracts will go away, as will your paycheck." He paused. "Really, it's self-preservation that should make you wish to come to a happy conclusion."

Rooster leaned forward, his forearms on his thighs, staring down at the mic. He took a breath, making sure Brilliant had finished his communication before depressing the button to talk. "This is a business transaction. Your opening bid was three-million dollars, and you aren't coming down. I can tell you straight up, the insurers won't pay that. Not even close. And while Derek Bowen works for Hesston, Anjie Bowen does not. I'm sure you understand, from a businessman's point of view, why letting Mrs. Bowen go still gives you all the leverage you need." He paused to slick his tongue over his teeth. "And it shows everyone on this side of the table that you're acting in good faith. I need proof of life, and I need a more reasonable number."

Another man's voice could be heard in the distance—the sound of a car's horn. Then the crackle of radio static.

Rooster waited.

Brilliant gave no reply.

Sniffing hard, Rooster set the handset back in its indentation on the radio. He focused on the shadowy corner of the room. As he let his thoughts percolate, he reached for the jug sitting beside his chair. He upended it and chugged big gulps of the warm water. Swiping the back of his hand over his mouth to catch the drips, he turned to Randy.

"Almost ten minutes. That's an improvement," Randy said, sending the audio file back to Iniquus's Headquarters in Washington DC. "Still full of himself. He's convinced he holds a winning hand."

While Randy sounded like the name of a man raised on football and apple pie, he was actually from El Salvador. Randy was his call sign. He'd come to America over a decade before to put his considerable athleticism to the test, hoping to gain citizenship from his US military service. He'd served two rotations in the sandbox as a Ranger, tough as nails, with the brain and stomach for the hairiest of missions.

Now, Randy and he got their paychecks from the for-hire security complex, Iniquus, that worked civilian contracts as well as running black ops for the government. While Randy was a Strike Force member, commanded by Striker Rheas, and Rooster was on Panther Force, commanded by Titus Kane, those designations were often fluid. Operators went where they were told to go, based on capability and availability.

Randy had just finished up a close protection detail for an American businessman and put the guy on a flight from Kenya back to New York. The boarding call had sounded over the P.A. system, calling for Randy's flight to Tahiti where he planned to take his R & R. But Randy answered his phone and thus pulled the short stick. Now Randy was sitting in this rat hole with Rooster.

"Brilliant gave up some stuff this time," Rooster said. "Play that bit at the end again before the horn honk."

Randy tapped the computer, cocking his head as he strained to weed out what hid under the ambient noise.

"Do you hear that guy in the background? Can you isolate that voice?"

Randy fussed with his software, then hit enter, and they listened to the man's voice, free of distractions.

"I don't recognize that language. Any guesses?"

"Nada," Randy answered. "Let's see what I can find."

Africa was a continent rich in languages and cultures. Tradition. Segregation. And turbulence. If Randy's software could translate the sentence and give them a dialect, they might have something useful to work with.

Rooster pulled his headphones into place to listen to the recording. He believed what Brilliant had said about Anjie Bowen. She was in dire straits. With her medical history, extremes were perilous. Why she'd followed her husband on his boat trip along the coast of Africa at this time of year was a mystery to him. But it wasn't Rooster's job to second guess people's decision-making. It was his job to save their lives. And Anjie felt fragile to him.

Rooster knew that Brilliant had already figured out Anjie was disposable. It might even work in the kidnapper's favor to let her die. Rooster had hoped that Brilliant wouldn't realize that fact. But Brilliant's tone and word choices told Rooster Brilliant had already drawn that conclusion. He would use her as a bargaining chip as long as he could but didn't care one way or another whether Anjie made it home to her three young kids or not.

Word choices were everything. In people who negotiated in English as a second language, those word choices came from how deep their vocabulary well ran. This guy was fluent. That was a win for the good guys. It meant he had a wide range of phrases to use, and therefore specific meanings could be weeded out. Rooster moved the recording back to the beginning of their conversation when Brilliant had laughed.

"Mr. Honey. You know every time I say your name, I laugh at the irony."

The irony of my name. The irony *of my name.* He pressed play. "Oh, if you knew, you would kick yourself."

My name is part of the puzzle. Not Mr. Just Honey. Honey *is ironic.* Rooster stretched his arms above his head, laced his fingers together, and cradled the back of his head in the hammock they made, flicking his thumbs against one another as he let his mind wander. He worked to put a pin in the irony of "Honey."

"Got it." Randy's voice held a grin. It pulled Rooster's attention to him. "The man's speaking Afar."

"Translation?"

"He said, 'They bring the salt.' And that belching sound you hear isn't a man dying of indigestion. It's a camel's grunt."

Rooster tapped at his computer. His eyes scanned over the screen, then he leaned back in his chair and laughed with his hands covering his face. He scrubbed his palms up and down over his cheeks, around the back of his neck. "Oh, the irony," he said as he focused back on Randy. "The Afar tribe harvest salt spheres from Lac Assal. They bring them to the harbor on the backs of camels."

Randy waited patiently for the piece that made Rooster react.

"The Arabic name for that lake is *Buḥayrah ʿAsal,* which literally translates to Honey Lake. I do believe that Brilliant has failed to live up to his name."

2
———————

ROOSTER
Djibouti, Djibouti

NUTSBE, the Panther Force communications and analytics contact, was on the phone reading out coordinates. He had accessed military satellite imagery to find the temporary camp of the nomadic Afar tribe. They were an impoverished people, suffering from climate change, still clinging to their traditional land, hoping that somehow life would improve.

The good news was there weren't many tribespeople at the Lac Assal site. The bad news was, there was no road, no cover, and no high ground near the camp. There would be no stealth mode. Randy and Rooster would have to go in fully visible. And they'd also have to hope they could find one of the traders who could speak Arabic or French, the two formal languages of Djibouti, in order to communicate.

Randy and Rooster loaded twenty-gallon plastic jugs of

water into their 4x4, along with cases of a peanut paste with vegetable oil, powdered milk, sugar, and vitamins. This plastic-wrapped goo was used to treat acute malnutrition in countries facing famine. Rooster had found that tribesmen, hoping to save their children from starvation, were often happy to trade information or hostages for this portable food supply. In case they found the Bowens, Rooster also packed emergency medical equipment.

A helicopter from the naval ship, sitting off the coast of Yemen, was being worked out as their backup if the team got eyes on the captives. But Rooster couldn't wait for the thumbs up from Nutsbe. He thought Brilliant had probably recorded and was going over today's communications just as he and Randy had. Brilliant might catch his mistake, then he'd move the Bowens, and the rescue effort would be back to square one. Or less.

The Afar people who lived along Lac Assal survived next to one of the most salinized lakes in the world. They had been herders by tradition, but climate change had hit this region hard. With rainfall down to almost nil and the vegetation dead, the tribespeople turned to the one resource they had, salt. As the lake waters receded from lack of precipitation, they left behind massive salt deposits. Harvested and transported to market, the tribesmen earned about five US dollars per buoy-sized bag.

The problem with Anjie's heart was not just the stress she had undergone for over a month now, but how much salt was in her environment. Rooster had been in the salt flats of India, where people's hands and feet became so septic from salt absorption that when the families tried to follow the tradition of cremating their remains, their loved one's feet and hands wouldn't burn. It was that bad. If Anjie Bowen was being held in the Afar harvesting camp, the atmospheric salt could pose a unique and horrible medical problem for her, beyond the issues of water, food, and unbearable heat. Brilliant hadn't made an appointment for a proof of life call. If the Bowens were still alive, they didn't have the luxury of days. Maybe not even hours. He and Randy would need to do the thing that every trained operative works hard never to do, wing it.

THEY STAGED at the end of the last road heading in the general direction of the salt camp, waiting for the night to deepen. It was a full moon that didn't help matters. There was a wicked wind their landlady had called *Khamsin* that aggressively blew hot air in from the desert, lifting and carrying dust and sand with it, reducing visibility. That might give them a bit of protection. Both men were in their battle dress uniforms in a gray digital print that helped them blend into the barren landscape. Shemaghs —wrapped around their heads and faces—kept the debris from biting into their necks.

It was time. Rooster pushed down the clutch on his SUV and dragged the gear shift into first. They'd move fast until they were within a klick's distance, then creep in, hoping the engine noise would be lost behind the howl of the winds.

Rooster had the driver's seat pushed back as far as it would go. But at six-foot-eight, it was always like doing origami to fold himself into a vehicle. Randy had his chair pushed all the way forward, making room for the supplies that crowded behind them. He was just shy of six feet but was built like an anaconda, long, lean, and lethal. Randy sat with his knees nearly to his ears and grunted when their vehicle bounced over the rough terrain.

He gripped the computer in his hands, watching the feed coming from Nutsbe in the Panther Force war room back in the States. Nutsbe's voice periodically gave them information over the magnetic comms they'd dropped into their ear canals.

"I'm picking up heat signatures three-hundred meters from your location," Nutsbe said.

Rooster pressed his finger into the communications button resting on his chest so his voice could be heard over the satellite feed that connected him to Nutsbe. "What are they doing?" They'd been running with no lights, using their high-dollar, night-vision goggles with thermal overlay that got them as clear a picture in the pitch black as one could buy with existing technology. Iniquus didn't skimp when it came to top-of-the-line equipment. It often made the difference between success and a body bag. Iniquus operators were trained on Uncle Sam's dollar. They were culled from the ranks of retired elite soldiers—the SEALs, the Rangers, the Marine Raiders, and so forth. Rooster had been Delta Force, but he'd signed a stack of papers agreeing never to disclose that fact.

"Well." Nutsbe chuckled. "The set closest to you looks like there are probably three sleeping kids and parents working at making a fourth."

Rooster swung his night vision out of the way to focus on the computer screen perched on Randy's knee. It was insane how detailed pictures could be from images picked up in outer space. There was indeed a recumbent yellow and red length with another form on top. "That should keep his focus. Have you found our PCs?" Rooster used the shorthand for precious cargo, the people they were charged to protect at any cost.

"I'm going to put a circle on the hut. That's my best guess. My research says the housing is comprised of vegetation and skins shaped like igloos—one opening. Very flimsy construction meant to be taken down and transported to a new site, quickly and easily. None of these images look like peoples' hands, or feet are bound. I can't imagine how they'd attach them to the hut. I'm guessing the Bowens are held in place by their inability to navigate to safety. They probably believe that if they left, they'd die."

"And they'd be right," Rooster replied. "This heat and wind? They couldn't possibly carry enough water to survive the hike out. And the Bowens probably have no idea how to ride a camel. They're pretty shitty creatures. It's not like they'd be helpful to a couple of greenhorns."

The plan was to go in quiet. "If it's as primitive as Nutsbe says, I don't think they're going to have weapons, maybe some spears. When they see our rifles, they'll back down."

"You hope." Randy was unconvinced.

"Luck of the draw. Could be we can get in and get out without raising any suspicion."

Randy forced a breath through his nostrils that could be taken for a laugh. "Three-million dollars on the line? Don't fool yourself into thinking this is a cakewalk."

Rooster slowed the SUV to a crawl, traveling slow and steady. When they were a hundred meters out, they debussed. With these flatlands, it was as close as they could get without being a big neon sign saying trouble was coming their way. They pulled on their body armor and rucksacks, did a last weapons' check, and moved forward into the moonscape dotted with huts.

They were fully in the perimeter of the village, walking low and slow, swinging their heads, watching for moving heat signatures. Suddenly, from behind them came the sound of someone banging metal against metal. The clanging rode the wind, reached into each hut, and shook the inhabitants awake. More people rose, more clanging.

Though Rooster and Randy had the advantage of night

vision, sheer numbers could quickly overwhelm them. The village warriors surrounded them, their hands gripping their weapons. Randy and Rooster maintained their speed. Rooster in the lead, Randy keeping apace but walking backward. When Rooster looked left, Randy looked right. As the tribesmen closed in, the operators could make out spears and machetes in the warriors' hands. Rooster and Randy brought their rifles to their shoulders, ready to squirt out suppressing shots that would give them space.

Rooster stopped beside the largest hut. "I wish to speak to the tribal chief." He spoke first in English, then French, and then in Arabic.

The tribal warriors were just boys, really—Rooster would estimate between fourteen and twenty—the age when testosterone made them stupid enough to want to prove their courage in front of their fellow villagers. The warriors formed lines on either side of the largest hut.

An elder emerged, wearing the regalia of power.

Another man stood by the door. He crossed his arms defiantly across his chest and glared. "Speak," he said in Arabic.

Rooster responded in fluent Arabic. "I am here to negotiate with your chief. I ask that you translate with clarity and honesty as is required." Rooster had no idea if this was required or not. But it seemed like a good preface.

The man said nothing.

"You are holding two Americans in your village. I'm here to take them home."

The man translated, or at least he said something to the wrinkled man who stood in front of them with a swollen belly.

Rooster imagined the chief was a lot younger than he looked. Salt miners rarely lived to be sixty. "I do not come without gifts of thanksgiving for the hospitality you have provided. Water, food, Djibouti francs.”

When the man translated, there was a decided shift in the tribe's demeanor. Wariness. Hope.

“I have good news and bad news.” Rooster heard Nutsbe over his comms. “‘Copter's twenty minutes out, but fighting the wind. Bad news, there are five vehicles due west, thirty klicks and closing fast.”

Rooster tapped his communicator. “Roger that.”

“I'd get the PCs, get in your vehicle, and start moving. Let the heli chase you down.”

“Wilco.” Rooster looked up. “We're out of time. Give us the Americans now and receive our gifts, or we will take the Americans now, and leave destruction.” Rooster was going to have to remember that line. That wasn't half bad.

Nutsbe said, “Two o'clock, there's a hut with two adult-sized people. All the other huts seem to have emptied into your area.”

“Derek and Anjie Bowen.” Rooster's voice boomed. “American rescue is here, call out.” Rooster's sheer size won him some shock and awe in these situations. And the deep bass of his voice could leave people shaking with fear.

“Here. Here,” a man's voice called from the two o'clock position Nutsbe had advised.

Rooster and Randy made their way to the hut, where a man had pulled the door to the side and was craning his neck. “My wife is very weak. She can't sit or stand.” He gestured to the prone figure in the center of the hut, lying on a hide.

Rooster stalked to their position. “I need to verify identity. What's your full legal name?”

“Derek Matthew Bowen.” The man squinted and lifted his hand to protect himself from the high lumen glare of Rooster's mag light.

"Where were you born?"

"Richmond, Virginia."

"What is the name of your elementary school?"

"St. Chrispan's."

"And the woman?"

Bowen gestured inside the hut. "Anjelina Catherine Bowen, my wife."

Rooster's hands rested lightly on the rifle that hung from its sling. "Are you able to walk, sir?"

"I'll do my best. But I don't think I can help my wife."

"Put on your shoes. This is going to be a close shave."

"But…"

"I've got your wife." Rooster crouch-walked into the hut, dropping down to make a quick assessment of the diminutive woman sprawled at his knees.

Randy stood with his back to them, speaking to a tribal warrior. Rooster touched his comms. "What's up, Randy?"

Randy's voice whispered over the radio. "Near as I can tell, this guy wants to follow us to the payment that was promised to the chief."

"That's fine as long as he keeps up." Rooster leaned over Anjie Bowen. "This is going to be uncomfortable, I'm sorry. I'm going to carry you the way soldiers do in the movies. I'll be as gentle as possible, but we'll be moving fast."

She licked her lips and whispered, "Thank you."

Rooster pulled her to sitting, then shuffled to get a shoulder down to her hips. He drew her across the broad swath of his shoulders and the top of his ruck. Pressing effortlessly to a stand, he ducked out of the hut.

Rooster noted that Bowen had been equipped with a Glock from Randy's holster.

They set off.

Bowen stumbled out of the gate. Randy shot out a steadying hand. "Sir, you're going to have to dig deep. Pull up your will to get out of this alive. After we're out of the village, we can help you. But we have no time for any kind of coddling."

Rooster had one arm wrapped through Anjie's dangling legs, pressing her thigh to his chest with his forearm, and keeping her snug in place by pulling down her wrist. From this position, he kept his thumb available for his comms so Nutsbe could hear what was going on and advise. With his other hand, he swung his rifle left then right, making the nervous villagers take a step back. "Help is on the way, but we've also got the bad guys heading toward us," he said for the benefit of the Bowens.

"About twenty klicks," Nutsbe said from the safety of the Iniquus compound.

Rooster took off at a jog. Bowen was giving it his all. The Afar warrior ran beside them. He seemed to delight in being caught up in this adventure. He smiled broadly and waved to his fellow villagers as he ran by.

The Afar tribe gathered in circles, standing shoulder to shoulder, undulating their chests forward and up, back and down, dancing as the Americans hustled away. Rooster wished he knew the words to their song. It seemed to him that there was an African song for almost any occasion. He wondered if this one was, "You can run, but you can't hide. The bad men come skin you alive." Rooster didn't doubt for a second that Brilliant would exact a very painful price if he caught them stealing his treasure.

As they cleared the village, Rooster dropped his rifle on its sling, letting it dangle at his side as he grabbed hold of Bowen under the armpit, so the enfeebled man could lean on Rooster's bulk. Now that Bowen had support, Rooster pushed the pedal down. "Longest hundred yards of your life, Mr. Bowen, but you *will* run them."

Bowen was doing his damnedest, Rooster knew. What Rooster didn't know was how long ago the man had eaten his last meal, when he'd last had a sip of water. Rooster didn't want to drag this man to his death, but it was rock-and-hard-place time. They'd made the decision, and now they needed to see it through.

3

ROOSTER
Lac Assal, Djibouti

THE RUN WOULD BE perilous in full light; in the black of night, it was a fool's journey. The land had been formed into a rocky terrain by cooled lava. Djibouti sat at the confluence of three tectonic plates, which meant the ground beneath them was in a constant state of flux. Long fissures and gaps made footing tenuous. While Rooster and Randy ran with night-vision in place, Bowen was wholly dependent on Rooster's guidance. The Afar warrior placed a loose hand on Randy's shoulder and seemed to be skipping along as if they were going to pick daisies, not running for their lives.

Anjie's soft groans sounded like they were pushed through gritted teeth. Rooster barely registered her weight on his shoulders.

"They're in the village," Nutsbe said. "I can see two men

descending from their vehicle. The tribe seems to be getting between them and the chief."

A burst of gunfire cracked the air.

Bowen suddenly found a little more adrenaline to pump into his leg muscles. Rooster adjusted his pace to match that of his precious cargo.

"The Afar are scattering. I'm guessing that's the chief and his warriors that are lined up and holding position." Nutsbe said. "The one in the middle—I'll just call him the chief—is pointing. The direction he's indicating is slightly south of your trajectory. Smart move on his part. They don't want to piss these guys off, and they don't want to miss out on their water and food. There's a chance it'll work."

Rooster had learned long ago he couldn't afford wishful thinking. If shit could happen, it sure as hell would. He always assumed worst case. Tonight, he only had a Plan A—get to the car, get out of Dodge, and hope to hell the helicopter showed up.

As he thought those words, his hopes were filled and dashed at the same time. *Damn it.*

A helicopter's blades whipped through the hot air, churning the debris and making the team wheeze and cough. Its searchlights panned the area. Their SUV was lit up like a rock star on stage. The light, filtering through Rooster's night vision apparatus, burned his eyes and left him momentarily blinded. In the flat landscape, the enemy could see them from long distances. That light beam made them easy targets.

Sure enough, from behind them came the rat-a-tat-tat as a rifle opened up. Bullets tap-danced and pinged over the rocky terrain, leaping up, and ricocheting. Rooster's sheer size meant if these guys could hit the broad side of a barn, they'd have a good chance of taking him down. His bulk was sometimes a blessing, sometimes a curse. Rooster swung his head and saw the warrior had lost his happy grin. His eyes were held round and wide.

"Go! Go! Go!" Rooster yelled past the deafening sound of the rotor blade.

When Randy sprinted forward, the warrior never moved his hand off Randy's shoulder. They were stride for stride as they hauled ass to the SUV.

Rooster pressed his knuckle into his comms. "Get that fucking light off us!"

Seconds later, the heli banked right. Rooster ran to the far side of their vehicle, dropping the desperately heaving Bowen to the ground behind the protective bulk of the engine block. He opened the back door and lay Anjie in the space made by Randy and the warrior as they threw the provisions out the back hatch onto the ground. Randy made his way to Bowen and yanked a bulletproof vest into place, then gestured him through the driver's side door over to the passenger seat. "Head down. Head down."

Rooster draped a ballistic vest over Anjie's prone form, then leaped behind the wheel. He slammed the gear into place and took off with a lurch. Randy jumped over the open tailgate, scrambling into the cargo area next to Anjie, and lay on his belly. Knees bent, boots in the air, Randy lifted his torso onto his elbows and fired off his own rounds toward the headlights bumping and bobbing their way toward them at reckless speeds. The enemy bullets, now coming from a closer range, were finding their target and popping holes in the SUV's frame.

Rooster turned with quick glances to watch the helicopter swoop low. Human forms, glowing orange and yellow in his thermal goggles, seemed to dangle in mid-air from the helicopter's runners. The bright red explosions from their automatic weapons showered down on the convoy below. The tangos pursuing the SUV killed their lights and fanned out to make their positions a harder target for the copter, fighting the winds overhead. But the convoy kept coming for them.

Bouncing his vehicle along the barren landscape, zig-zagging his path, Rooster raced along. There was a hairsbreadth between the speed that might save them and what would imperil them further. A high-caliber bullet zinged through the SUV's interior and burst out through the windshield. Bowen screamed and threw his elbow up to protect his face as the safety glass splintered into a spider web of lines, dropping visibility down to zero. Rooster tacked left. One hand on the steering wheel, he wrenched his Glock from his side holster and beat a hole into the window.

Randy continued to lay down a hailstorm of bullets with minor breaks of silence as he changed his magazines out.

Peeking through the small visual he'd acquired, Rooster yelled over the noise, "Bowen, grab the rifle. Use the butt to clear this glass."

Bowen hunkered against the door, pulling his knees up until he'd curled into a protective fetal position.

Rooster slapped his hand out, catching the guy on the side of the head. "Grab the rifle and get this glass cleared away. Now!" His voice roared like God Almighty making the command.

Bowen fought against his shaking hands as he complied.

"Honey, the helicopter requests you stop pussying around," Nutsbe deadpanned. "They can't use their hellfire missiles. You're at risk for collateral damage in the strikes. Suggest heading to your two o'clock. There's a rock outcropping that could give you some cover."

Rooster wrenched the steering wheel to the right.

"Hold steady. Fifty meters and closing," Nutsbe directed.

They went over a bump that threw the occupants into the air, hitting the ceiling, only to land and be thrown again.

Rooster sensed rather than saw Randy hunkering over Anjie Bowen.

With another vertebrae-dislocating lurch, Rooster maneuvered behind a barely visible boulder. He wrenched his night-vision goggles away from his face just as the atmosphere was painted bright gold. Four earth-shaking explosions followed the first in quick succession.

The air grew heavy from the smoke and fumes billowing from the incinerated cars dotting the horizon. By the light of the fires, Rooster did a quick assessment of Derek Bowen. Randy was doing CPR on Anjie from a claustrophobic crouch in the back.

***

FLYING over the Gulf of Aden in the copter, Rooster was strapped into place next to Derek Bowen, who had fallen asleep with a rehydrating IV dangling from his arm. It was the sleep of the nearly dead, his reserves depleted.

Adrenaline still charged through Rooster's veins, making sitting still a challenge. He watched the lights of the naval ship blinking closer.

Randy sucked water from the blue tube of his camelback in his rucksack.

Anjie was going to have a hell of a bruise, but the defibrillator had done its job. She breathed rhythmically with an oxygen mask over her mouth and nose. Her IV line swung with the motion of the heli. Rooster knew that once they were on board the destroyer, some of the best medical attention available in the world would be focused on keeping her alive.

His precious cargo was back in US hands. His job done, Rooster only gave a glancing thought as to whether Brilliant had been exploded in the fireworks show or whether he was off somewhere contriving his next scheme. It was a game of whack-a-mole. If they took Brilliant off the playing field, there was always another bad guy ready to hustle up and fill the void. It was just a matter of time before Rooster would be called to save the next victim.

4

ROOSTER

Djibouti, Djibouti

"Yo, you serious?" Randy swung his heels off the tabletop in his Djibouti hotel room and sat tall with the phone pressed to his ear. His gaze focused hard on Rooster until his partner turned to look at him. Randy bobbled his brow to let Rooster know something was cooking. "Hang on. Let me find something to write with." Randy patted his chest then stood.

Rooster picked up the pad and pen from the nightstand and stretched to hand it to him.

"Go." Randy scribbled the incoming details across the page. "Yup. I'll be there as soon as I can get a flight… Yeah, I've got someone with me." He lifted his chin toward Rooster. "Me too. I'll call you back when I have details." Randy slid his phone into his pocket. "Cool."

Rooster waited.

"That was Meg. She's hanging out on the beach in Zanzibar."

"Sad life." Rooster sprawled out on the bed, crossing his arms under his head, his legs sticking a good five inches off the end.

"Yeah, I feel for her." Randy took a swig of water. "She says a couple of the scientists that were heading in for a meeting are running a few days late, and she wanted to know if I wanted to fill their shoes."

"You have a science degree?"

"Nah. I have tourist skills, though. They're heading to the Ngorongoro Crater tomorrow, and then they're going to climb Mount Kilimanjaro the day after."

"The scientists are up to that?"

"I doubt it." Randy opened his laptop to do an airline search. "They'll probably hang out at the lodge, drinking. Meg'll go for sure." He pulled up a screen and ran his finger over the details. "You heard Commander Kane. We're on required R & R."

"Nice of him to call at zero dark thirty with the news."

"He doesn't give a shit about time zones. You in?"

"Me in what?"

"Zanzibar and Tanzania. Watch some hippos humping, giraffes wandering in the trees through our binoculars. Change it up from the usual guerillas."

"What kind of science?"

"She's a wildlife migration specialist, part of some big multi-disciplined study funded by the Gateways Foundation. They're supposed to figure out how to save endangered species and indigenous tribes from the changes in weather. Why would that matter?"

"It doesn't. Fuck it. Let's do it."

The men stuffed their clothes in their duffels. They gave Iniquus their flight itinerary and got in touch with a local contact that Headquarters provided to pick up their communications and tactical equipment to send back stateside. Tanzania had laws that prohibited handguns, and while they could bring up to three hunting rifles, now that the dry season had begun, it might be hard to explain the special configurations of their weapons. It was extra weight and a theft concern. No big deal. They kept their night vision and cameras, though. Out in the crater, they might prove to be cool toys to play with.

THE FLIGHT WAS GOING to be a long one. Three layovers meant that if everything ran on schedule, they'd get to their Zanzibari hotel in time to shower for dinner. So far, so good. At least they'd made it out of Djibouti.

Rooster had given up on the red vinyl seats in the boarding airport lounge. The security dog gave them a wary eye as he panted his way down the aisle. Rooster hadn't shot a gun or handled explosives since he'd been to Africa this go-round. But that didn't mean his clothes weren't full of gunshot residue. Yeah, soap and water were supposed to take it out, but dogs' noses and human noses were on different ends of the spectrum. Last thing he wanted was to get dragged into a room for a chat with some uniformed guard.

His back pressed against the wall, Rooster had stretched his legs out on the cool floor and watched the comings and goings while he and Randy waited for their flight to be called. He finger-waved at a little kid clinging to his mother's hand, being dragged past them; the boys' eyes wide with astonishment. It was a normal kid reaction. At just shy of three-hundred pounds, Rooster had decided pro-ball wasn't his gig. If he was going to take someone down, it wouldn't be well-padded players on the football field. He was going after the worst the world had to offer. While his size made some things a challenge—like sitting in chairs—for the most part, he wouldn't give up an inch of his height. "Okay, so now that we're on the way to Zanzibar, tell me, who's this Meg science person? How'd you get on her fast dial?"

"Meg Finley?" Randy raised his eyebrows. "You know her brother."

Rooster canted his head. "Yeah? How's that?"

"Special Agent Steve Finley, FBI, terror."

"Son of a fuckin' gun. You shitting me?"

"Small world, huh? All of the Finley kids have got the same makeup—smart as hell, athletic. Do-gooders working to make the world a better place. Three kids. Meg's the oldest. I hung out more with their youngest girl, Kelly." Randy scratched the back of his neck. "Kelly's back from her stint in the Peace Corps. She just had a kid."

"I thought you went right from El Salvador to boot camp. How'd you come to know the Finley's?"

"I got a scholarship to come to the US my senior year. They were my foster family. I still call them Mom and Dad. Meg is my American sister."

"And once you got to the Finley's house, you decided you liked toaster waffles so much you were willing to risk life and limb to stay there?"

"After I developed my toaster waffle addiction, there was no going back." Randy let his slow smile slide across his face. "I only saw Meg that first summer, then on holidays. She was working on her Ph.D. But we've always gotten along and stayed in close touch."

Randy lifted his phone and scrolled through his pictures until he found one of a woman with her head thrown back in a full-body laugh. Strands of long, strawberry-blonde hair blew across her face as she gripped her stomach, her knees pulled up.

The picture surprised Rooster. He took the phone in his hand and drank it in like she was water on his thirstiest day.

Randy took the phone back and gave it another swipe that brought up a picture of Meg holding a baby orangutan on her hip, her emerald-green eyes sparkling with amusement. She looked like a doting mother. No makeup, freckled nose, sunburned forehead. The body of an athlete. Yeah, Rooster could see this woman climbing Kilimanjaro. Randy swiped again, and Meg was squatting next to an African elder. She had a no-nonsense, "what you see is what you get" feel. And Rooster found himself impatient to get to Zanzibar.

Rooster pulled the phone away, then tapped and scrolled through Randy's phone.

"Careful there, brother. I have pictures on there that are private."

Rooster handed the phone back to him. A new picture filled the screen. "Familiar?"

Randy looked down at the photo of a man standing in the shadows behind them. "Yeah. He was in the neighborhood around our safe house in Djibouti."

"And now he's flying Ethiopia to Kenya."

"Was he on our flight this morning? I didn't spot him."

"Nope." Rooster pulled his bag into his lap and rifled through it, using the distraction to watch the guy pretending to not watch them. His nonchalance seemed contrived.

"Odd coincidence."

"Yep." Rooster didn't believe in coincidences. He pulled a box of Altoids from the bottom of his bag and offered one to Randy.

Randy shook his head. "I'll send this to Deep back at Iniquus, see if he can put a name with the face." His fingers tapped at the screen.

"If this guy ends up in Zanzibar, we'll need to have a chat with him, regardless."

"Roger that." Randy paused while a disembodied voice spoke over the loudspeaker in Amharic. "That's us." He swatted Rooster's leg.

The men got to their feet and made sure they were the last to board. Rooster wanted to keep his eye on the stranger with the black hair.

5

———————

MEG

International Airport, Zanzibar

MEG'S EYES stretched wide as she watched Randy elbow the guy beside him, then raise a hand to wave at her. Randy looked like a child standing beside a man-mountain. The guy nodded as she waved back at them. She flicked her hair out of her eyes and tilted her head up with a smile. As they moved forward in line, Meg sidled over to stand with the others outside of the secure area as Randy, and the mountain made their way through customs.

Watching Randy approach, Meg bounced up and down, clapping her hands like a little girl who was about to receive a gift. They were both laughing as Randy ran toward her, scooped her up, and swung her around. When he set her back on her feet with a loud kiss on her cheek, Meg looked over Randy's shoulder to find the mountain studying them curiously.

Randy turned to see what had caught her attention. "Hey, Honey." He gestured the guy over. "Come meet Meg."

It only took the mountain three strides to reach them, where a normal human being would have taken six. When he towered above her, she was almost as shocked at his height as she had been that Randy had called this guy honey. "How tall are you?" popped out before she even said hello. Meg clapped a hand over her mouth. Someday she'd get control over the braking mechanism that held back her words. "Think before you speak," had been the childhood admonishment that her mother most wished Meg could master.

The mountain sent her a wicked grin. "Six-foot-eight and worth the climb." He winked, and Meg's face heated to what she was sure must be flame-red at the mental picture of this guy lying naked and ready on her bed. That kind of bawdy imagery wasn't something she normally conjured. It shocked Meg, and she stood there feeling off-kilter and not quite able to breathe.

Randy backhanded the guy's chest. "Cut it out."

The guy spread his arms and herded them out of the stream of people passing on either side.

When they reached the wall, Meg said, "Welcome to Zanzibar." She stretched out her hand for a shake, trying to reset the introduction. "I'm Meg Finley."

"Rooster Honig." He wrapped her hand in his with gentle pressure.

Meg thought that if he wanted to, he could pulverize her bones. "Rooster's an unusual name. Is that like Eduardo being rechristened Randy by the army?"

"Rooster's not a call sign. I ticked my mom off when I was a fetus, and that was her idea of payback."

Randy tipped his head down the hallway. "Let's keep this

conversation going in the cab. We need to catch a shower back at the hotel."

"And get to dinner. I'm hungry as a bear." Rooster looked down at Meg when he said it and gave her a smile. That must be some kind of private joke unless he was teasing her about her gaffe when they met. She sent him a tight-lipped smile in response. Something about Rooster Honig was throwing her off-center. Short-circuiting her brain. She felt a little dizzy and a lot ridiculous. They came to a halt in the baggage area.

"How long have you been in Zanzibar?" Randy stood next to the conveyor belt, watching the luggage stream past.

"A few days. I've been over in Tanzania trying to put together this conference. The touristy part—the crater and Kilimanjaro—is supposed to be the icebreaker. Give us a little group history and adventure together. Hopefully, when we pull our chairs around the conference table, we'll be able to communicate effectively during our strategic planning."

Randy reached out and picked up a hard plastic case with metal corners. It looked like if a bomb were to explode and take down the building, this case would be the lone, undamaged survivor. "Here, Honey, take this," he said, handing it off.

Rooster reached for the box, then set it between his feet.

When Meg had seen Rooster standing next to Randy, her first thought was that here was a man's man. The rugged individualist type that she'd often seen on conservation hunts put on both for population control and tourist dollars by the Tanzanian government. What she hadn't suspected was Rooster was also a "man's man."

She thought back to any time that Randy had told her about his love interests, but Meg could only remember them being women. Gorgeous, voluptuous, accomplished women. Randy was handsome and smart, an American hero, and all that. But still, it always seemed to her that he was hooking up with girls who were out of his league. She wrinkled her brow and considered Randy. He *had* signed on to the military before the ban on gays and bisexuals serving was lifted. And he had tried out for the Rangers as soon as his citizenship papers were signed. Was there something in that ultra-manly world that would make being "out" a problem? She tipped her head. Well, Randy was working for the security group Iniquus now. Maybe this was the first time he felt comfortable sharing this kind of relationship publicly.

"*Meg*," Randy called loudly.

She jolted herself back to present moment. "Sorry, I was in la-la land. What were you saying?"

He flipped something toward her, and Meg reached up to snatch it out of the air. It was one of the little wooden puzzle balls that Randy liked to whittle to beat the boredom on his missions. "Aww, thank you, I love these." She looked over to Rooster. "I have a wonderful collection that Randy keeps adding to. They keep me company when I'm in waiting mode out in the bush." She reached into her bag and pulled out a similar puzzle. "This was the last one. I still haven't figured it out."

"Glad you still like them. This is all of it." Randy pointed to their duffels. "Which way to the cabs?"

<hr>

MEG TOOK the front seat to allow Randy and Rooster to sit together in back. They must have been a couple for a while now. Even in the short time she'd seen them together, she noticed how they could communicate by catching the others' eye or giving some small sign—a tilt of the head, a lift of the chin. It was sweet, really.

Even with her seat pushed forward as far as it would go in

the SUV, Rooster still had trouble getting himself into the car. Meg could feel his knee pressing into the seat, hitting her mid-back. She leaned into the car door, energetically dismissing the weird rush that the contact had given her. God, she needed to get out more. Her dry spell was obviously wreaking havoc with her libido. She rolled down the window and let the velvety warm air waft over her face. She breathed in the scent of cinnamon and lemongrass mingling with the pungent ocean salt air, trying to center herself.

Rooster was off-limits. She wasn't his preferred gender, and he was in a relationship with her brother, for heaven's sake. Meg truly did think of Randy as a brother; the Finley family made no distinction between the children they fostered and the three biological kids. She scooped up the hair that flew into her face and pulled it into a makeshift bun that she held at the nape of her neck. "Is the window being down okay for you back there?"

"Definitely," Randy called to her. "Man, what a difference a slight change in geography can make. This feels like spring."

Meg looked back over her shoulder, lifting her voice above the noise of the road and wind. "Where were you?"

"In the pit of hell, for about a month." Randy lifted his arm and sniffed. "You can still smell the sulfur on my skin."

"Ah, okay." Meg knew better than to ask for specifics when Randy was an Army Ranger. She guessed that would apply to his work with Iniquus too. "Well, seems only right that you should end up in paradise." Meg used the side mirror to see Rooster's face. "You said you guys were hungry. What are you in the mood for?"

"This is an Islamic island. Do they allow beer?"

Meg smiled broadly. "Oh, do they ever. How about some street food and then a bar? I can take you on a tour of some of Tanzania's finest brews."

. . .

THE TAXI PULLED to a stop in front of the Seraphina Hotel, its enormous white edifice sitting regally across the road from the turquoise waters of the Indian Ocean. A valet opened their doors, and Meg stood back to watch the man's expression as Rooster unfolded himself from the back. She found the valet's drop-jawed response to Rooster at full height highly amusing. That was probably what she'd looked like when she had seen him at the airport. Meg's face heated as she remembered how crass she'd been before they were introduced. She looked up to find Rooster watching her with that curiosity she kept finding in his eyes.

"Well, then," she said as they moved toward the lobby, "I put you in the rooms that Dr. Clemson and Dr. Lemmings would have had." She flipped her hand back and forth between them. "I don't know how you two want to work things out. But they're side by side."

Rooster and Randy took their key cards, and a plan was made to meet up in the lobby later. The three headed across the lobby to go to their rooms when Randy strained his neck. "You see that, Honey?"

Meg glanced up to catch Rooster's gaze hard on the elevator bank. The elevator door was just sliding closed. Both men whipped their phones from their pockets.

"Go," Rooster said.

Randy dropped his bag and moved toward the stairwell with long strides.

Rooster was watching the lights above the elevator moving up. Up. Up. Meg shifted from foot to foot. She wondered what the men had seen, but she also realized this wasn't the moment for questions.

"Fifth floor," Rooster said into his phone. A moment later, he said, "Eighth floor," as the light lit up in the very last spot then moved slowly back to the left. "Seventh floor," he said as the light held then steadily descended back to the lobby.

After a moment, the elevator slid open in front of them. Rooster made no move toward it, though Meg would have been happy to help with the luggage.

Rooster held the phone to his ear as he scanned the lobby. Finally, he said, "Okay, I'll meet you at our rooms."

A bellboy came over with his trolley to assist them.

"That's okay, I've got it." Rooster reached down and gathered the duffels by their slings and draped them over his left shoulder as if they were weightless. With the same hand, he reached for the plastic case, then gestured to Meg with an open hand toward the elevator bank.

"What's in the case?"

"Night vision equipment and cameras."

"Oh, that'll be good to use in the crater, come nightfall, though I think they have rules against wandering at night."

"Rules or laws?" Rooster asked.

"That makes a difference to you?"

Rooster smiled.

"Who was Randy chasing up the stairs?"

"His shadow," he replied.

Meg wasn't sure if that was a proper answer, a dismissal, or him being poetic, maybe ironic. She leaned against the wall in the elevator as Rooster moved through the doors on the fourth floor. "I'll see you two downstairs in an hour. Enjoy your shower." And then another unbidden visual sent color rushing to Meg's face.

6

———

ROOSTER

Stone Town, Zanzibar

ROOSTER STOOD BY THE DOOR, leaning into the wall as Randy pulled a belt through his pant loops and checked his image in the mirror. "Okay, pretty boy, so tell me about you and Meg."

Randy unscrewed the top of his cologne. "I knew you'd like her." He smiled into the mirror. "She likes you too. Did you see her blushing?" He sprinkled a few drops into his palm. "And since she's my sister, I'll give you two my blessing." He turned to look Rooster in the eye. "And I'll also warn you. If you're a prick to her, you'll be answering to me." His point made, Randy turned back to the mirror as he patted the scent over his cheeks and neck. He looked up to find Rooster's scowl reflected back at him. "It's time, my friend," he said in all seriousness. "Maria would want you happy."

Maria *would* want him happy. She had said so, time and again, as he held her hand in the oncology ward. But he hadn't thought in terms of a relationship in the ten years since. "That's quite a leap. All I asked was for you to tell me about you two."

"And that speaks volumes." Randy slid his phone and wallet into his pockets. "Come on, she'll be waiting for us."

The two men moved through the door and saw Meg walking toward them. She nodded her head as if confirming something to herself, then held out both her hands to Randy. When he took them, she lifted onto her toes and kissed him on each cheek, holding longer on the last kiss. "Mmm. You smell good."

Meg didn't look much different dressed up for the evening than she had at the airport. She'd changed her jeans and blouse for a long dress made of floaty material that curved over her figure and clung to her thighs as she walked. Any man was sure to enjoy the tease of her long shapely legs hidden just out of sight. She'd curled her hair and put on a touch of makeup, but she let her beauty shine from the inside. Rooster liked that. A lot. It had been a while since he'd felt this kind of buzz. He wondered if Randy was right, and Meg felt it too.

Meg reached her hands to Rooster and rose higher on her toes as he leaned down to receive his kiss. The look she sent him as she lowered her heels was one of sisterly affection. Shit. She didn't feel it. He was an extension of Randy. Friend-zoned.

"Ready then?" She turned without waiting for an answer. "We could go and sit at a restaurant if you're tired, but with only one night in Zanzibar, I'd hate for you to miss out on experiencing the street food."

Outside the hotel, Rooster did a sweep of the area. It was as natural as breathing for him to assess and discern possible threats, but tonight he was on the lookout for the man from Djibouti, who might have been on the elevator back at their hotel. Rooster thought they were overdue for a conversation with the guy.

Meg led the way down the road. A stream of people moved in an ebb and flow along the sidewalk with an ease that said they'd get to where they were headed when they got there, no worries. It was a pace that most Americans would find frustrating. The locals were dressed in Muslim-style clothing—the women, even the girls, covered their hair with hijabs and the men with kufi caps, the brimless, rounded cap worn by men in much of Africa. Tourists and locals alike modestly covered their shoulders and knees. Rooster's dark-blue dress pants and white silk button-down shirt fit in just fine.

Meg opened her bag and pulled out a scarf, which she draped over her hair, flinging one end over her shoulder to keep it in place. Normally, Rooster took in details, and if they didn't have anything to do with survival, he discarded them just as quick. But this picture he'd hold on to—Meg looking up at him with her bright green eyes, the shiny copper of her hair, the sapphire of her scarf, and behind her head, the sky was on fire in a blaze of orange, yellow, and purple. It was almost too beautiful to take in. Rooster felt his heartbeat pounding in his chest. He offered her his arm, and she glanced over at Randy before she took it. Maybe Randy needed to have that blessing conversation with Meg too. Maybe she had a policy of some kind about Randy's friends. Bros before beaus, or some such code.

They were on the outskirts of Stone Town, which took up the center of the island. The white sand beaches on their right were empty now. Meg seemed to know where she was headed as they walked past the people—some speaking Arabic, others English, some Kiswahili. Rooster's ability with the Swahili language was conversational, but he was clearly missing something. Something they were saying tickled Meg. She tried to stifle her laughter, but she was lit up with amusement, turning her bright smile toward him. Rooster thought that the next two days were going to be long and painful. He really didn't need the aggravation of what he'd describe as unrequited "heightened awareness" working at him when he just wanted to unwind and watch some critters up close and personal, let go of the stress he'd packed on during that last race to safety with the Bowens.

They moved through a tangle of architecture. Centuries-old buildings dominated the city. The carved stone reflected the Arabic influence. They walked past wooden sawhorses where oriental carpets were draped to dry after being cleaned outdoors.

"This reminds me of Ali Baba and the magic carpet rides. It's enchanting being here." Meg ran her hand along one of the rugs. "This city is on the UNESCO World Heritage List." Her arm swept out to take in the buildings. "I love the mishmash of architecture—European, Arabic, Indian, and African. Lots of the buildings are renovated, though you'd be hard-pressed to find a single one with a fresh coat of paint." She pointed at the mansion across the street. "This one belonged to a guy named Tipu Tip. It hasn't been restored."

"He had bucks," Randy said as he took in the expanse of the house.

"Tipu Tip was a horrible man who got his money from the slave trade. He'd send his servants out to capture people and bring them here to the slave market. Zanzibar has a dark history in the sale of humans." She pointed to the muddy ground surrounded by wrecked boats exposed by the low tide. "That's the fish market. When the tide is out during the day, the fishermen sell their catch right there in the mud. When the tide rises, they go out to sea again." She looked across Rooster to Randy. "Unless I know and trust the vendor, when we get to the street food, even though it looks wonderful, I'd steer clear of the fish. Sometimes they were caught in the morning and have been laying out all day. They don't refrigerate ingredients between purchasing and cooking them." She shifted to look at Rooster. "Most of the food is absolutely fine, but since we have a long day of traveling tomorrow, it's good to be cautious. Here, just up a little farther." Meg let go of Rooster's arm and skipped forward with excitement. "I want you to see the tortoises."

A park opened up near the houses. They found an empty bench and sat. Randy pointed. "One o'clock," he said as a gigantic tortoise lumbered toward the old man who had pulled a head of lettuce from his pocket.

"Aren't they amazing?" Meg asked. "Sometimes, Zanzibar is called Turtle Island because of them. Scientists believe that some of the tortoises have been here for over two-hundred years."

"This is a very different Africa than the one we just came from." Randy relaxed, leaning back with his arm stretched along the bench.

"Yeah?" Meg asked. "What was that like?"

"Salty," Randy replied. "Different architecture."

They sat in silent respect for the Maghrib, the Muslim sunset call to prayer.

"God is the greatest. I bear witness that there is none worthy of worship except God... Hasten to the prayer. Come to Salvation. God is the greatest."

As the last note rode the wind out over the Indian Ocean, Meg sighed. "Just beautiful. His voice is amazing, the way it resonates through the stone architecture," she said with her eyes closed as if to savor it. Meg's eyes flashed open, and she turned to Randy. "Can you hear that? My stomach has been rumbling ever since I talked about the street food." She laughed as she stood up and led them back into the labyrinth of buildings.

Rooster and Randy both had their heads on a swivel. The tight streets, with plenty of shadows and hiding places, made Rooster uneasy. He could feel eyes on him, and they weren't the usual curious ones that followed him because of his size; they were the kind that were keeping track. Rooster knew Randy had picked up on it too. "Any word from Deep?" he asked over Meg's head in a tone that was meant to stay private.

"Nada," Randy said as he tucked Meg tightly between them.

Walking too closely in the alley, they couldn't swing their arms. Meg slid her fingers into the crooks of their elbows. Rooster resisted reaching across to hold her hand. The reflex made him remember the last time he'd felt this way with a woman on his arm. Randy was right; Maria would want him happy. Rooster knew Randy wasn't accusing him of living a sad life; things were good. He was fulfilling his life's purpose. But in the long days of sitting and waiting for the radio calls from Brilliant, there had been some soulful discussions between the two men.

Rooster had to admit that having Maria in his life had given him more dimension. Despite his world view—you had to embrace the light and the dark. He'd been focused almost uniquely on the dark side of things lately. As Orwell said, "People sleep peaceably in their beds at night only because rough men stand ready to do violence on their behalf." They needed to be every bit as willing as the bad guys to bring destruction. He was that guy. He lived in that world. But when he had Maria, he had someone who reminded him that he was whole. He was also the poetry he loved, the art he used to paint, a man of contemplation and philosophy.

With Meg on his arm, he felt different than he had yesterday, he mused. How so might take some time to put his finger on. It was a good different, though.

They strolled onto a road that was full of color and had the carnival atmosphere of people enjoying the cool evening and each other's company. Men played mancala at small tables outside of the carved wooden doors that were famous in Zanzibar. Meg caught Rooster focusing on them. "The carved teak and mahogany doors tell the tales of the early island dwellers," she explained. "The patterns tell the story of that house's ancestry and professions. Brass spikes, like the ones at this house, meaning the family was originally from India."

"Did they serve some kind of purpose?" he asked.

"They were supposed to keep elephants away, by tradition, though there were no elephants on the island. The lotus flower—a historically Egyptian symbol—was carved to promote fertility. Other doors depict chains. A sad reminder that this was once a central hub of the slave trade."

The women walked past in gaggles, their children clutching at their skirts. They filled their baskets from the pyramids of fruit that were arranged on cloth-covered tables—pineapples, papayas, jackfruit, and mangoes.

Meg stopped mid-stride, tilted her head back, and sniffed the air. "Mmm," she hummed, then opened her eyes to look at Rooster. "Where else in the world can you experience a sensory riot like this? Ylang-ylang and cinnamon—it's like living in the bottom of a genie's bottle." With a laugh filled with joy, she turned her focus down the street. "Just around the corner now." They had to release their hooked arms, but Randy grabbed at Meg's hand, and Meg, in turn, reached for Rooster's as they made a human chain and wove their way around the crowd moving toward the nearby open grills.

"*Jambo!,* Jooma," Meg called.

"*Jambo!,* Dr. Meg. What can I get for you and your friends tonight?"

"When was your fish caught?"

"Last net of the day. Fresh."

Meg smiled. "Could we have an order of coconut rice and curried fish soup?"

"That is all for you tonight?" He frowned up at Rooster.

"Yes, thank you. We're on a tasting tour. And of course, I brought my friends to try your food first."

"Thank you, I hope you will enjoy." The man handed them a bowl of tilapia broth that he had topped with garlic and lime. It came, as was tradition, with another bowl that held a salad of eggplant and tomatoes topped with thin bread meant to be used as an eating utensil.

They moved to the side to taste, sipping the soup from plastic spoons that Meg carried in her purse, then returned their empty plates to Jooma before proceeding through the market area.

Meg waved toward the end of the street. "Two more things you must try, then I'll buy the first of what I'm assuming to be a well-deserved round of beers." She stopped and ordered them a heaping box of fries that the vendor doused with hot sauce and tamarind. A combination that had Rooster wary but willing to try. *Once*.

"No?" Meg asked with a little laugh.

"I'll pass, thanks." Rooster noticed that Randy was hanging back, letting them have some space. It was a nice gesture and all, but there was no spark to fan on Meg's part. She was just excited to be sharing her discoveries.

"All right, well, maybe the next dish will taste better to you," she said, popping a fry in her mouth.

Rooster smiled as he reached out and rubbed his thumb over the corner of her lips to capture the drip of sauce left there.

Randy moved up to their side, relieving Meg of the box as he wolfed down the rest of the fries. "This is so much better than Honey's cooking. You have no idea."

"Yeah? What do you cook, Rooster?"

"MREs, mostly."

"Ah well, I could see where Randy would have room to complain. What is it exactly that you do for Iniquus?"

"Hostage negotiation."

The smile slipped from Meg's face, and she put both her hands on his forearm. "Oh. My. That's—that must be a difficult thing to work through. I wish you every success." She gave a shudder and whipped her head around to look behind her. "Ha," she said, turning back to him. "Someone must have walked over my grave."

It was an old saying that Rooster hadn't heard in a while. Something about the way she said it worked a shot of adrenaline loose in his system. He took a moment to do a thorough scan of the area. Randy caught the move and added his eyes to the search pattern.

Meg seemed oblivious of the sudden tension as she tucked her hand around Randy's arm and started down the street. "What led you to that kind of work, Rooster?"

Randy twisted his weight to glance back at Rooster. "He fell into the job, literally. That story is classified, but I can tell you he has an uncanny way of knowing things about people. Don't you, Honey?"

Rooster thought Randy was trying to sell him a little too hard.

Meg spun toward Rooster and stopped. "Is that true? I challenge you, then." She grinned. "Tell me three things about me that Randy couldn't possibly have told you."

Rooster sent her a long, speculative glance. "And if I get all three right? What's my prize?"

"Round two at the pub."

"Fair enough." Rooster ran an assessing gaze down her body to the pink paint on her toenails, up the length of her dress—

making sure not to stall at her breasts—then up her neck to her hairline, and back down to her eyes. She was blushing again. Randy thought that was her "tell" that she was interested. Rooster read it as modesty. He rubbed his thumb along his jawline. "One, your mom put you in dance class as a little kid even though you preferred climbing trees with the boys."

"Yes." Her smile held as she looked up at him expectantly.

"The first time you fell in love, it was with a horse."

"Yep."

"Your father was left-handed." That one slipped out. He hadn't meant to say it out loud. It was unlike him to throw words around. Words were tools. You picked the right tool for the right job. If his job was to wrangle himself out of the friend-of-my-brother corner, he shouldn't pick up a crowbar and start prying when a little oil would do him better.

Meg's smile turned lopsided as she looked up at him.

"Ha," Randy chuckled. "You got that one wrong. Jim is right-handed."

Meg held Rooster's gaze; a spark of curiosity lit her eyes. Rooster realized that the green in her iris was broken up with flecks of blue, changing her eye color like those mood rings the girls wore back in high school.

"No, Randy, he's right. He said my father was left-handed." She pulled her gaze away from his to focus on Randy. "Jim is my adoptive-dad. My biological father, Paul, was left-handed. A southpaw pitcher in the farm leagues." She took a step back. "Wow, that's…amazing. We don't really talk about Paul around our house, so I seriously doubt Randy knew that one." Her eyes back on Rooster, she tilted her head. "Are you a bit psychic?"

"I think every soldier in a war zone develops their sixth sense to some extent."

"I agree. Anyone who's in survival mode over a period of

time does." Meg adjusted her scarf over her hair. "Well, I am duly impressed, and it will be my honor to buy the first round that I promised for your work just completed, and my pleasure to buy the second round that you just won so handily. But first, you have to try the famous Zanzibari pizza."

"What makes it famous?" Randy asked as they started off in a different direction.

"You have to see for yourself." They moved toward yet another table, prepping street food. Meg ordered three chicken pizzas. The cook spread three very thin pieces of dough. With the knife skills of a martial artist, he chopped an onion. Rooster watched Randy's face with amusement. Rooster? He'd eaten everything from slugs he pulled from under rocks in the South American jungle, to Balut—an aborted duck fetus—in the Philippines, to scorpion in Beijing. He could and would eat anything required for survival or to honor his host. Randy's tastes tended toward the more delicate, even in his MRE choices.

The dough went onto the hot griddle; chicken, onion, processed cheese, mayonnaise, and a raw egg were added and swirled together. Meg was delighting in the whole event, and Rooster thought she had brought Randy there specifically to tease him about his refined pallet. Randy wrapped his arm around Meg and pretended to weep into her shoulder. "You are so mean. Raw egg?"

Meg swatted him off. "You'd never guess that such a wimp was a Ranger."

"I did my stint eating crap for Uncle Sam, and I swore to myself that when I finished my stretch, I'd eat only good things, like your mama's peach cobbler."

Meg closed her eyes. "Mmm, that is so good." With a sigh, she opened her eyes. "If you think this is challenging—and it's not, it's actually really good—just think how bad tomorrow will be."

"Why? What's tomorrow?"

"Tomorrow, when we visit the Maasai, you'll probably be offered some warrior soup."

"Which is what?"

"The main ingredient is blood." Meg reached out for the first paper plate being handed to them and passed it to Rooster. "You'll have to be brave and be the first to taste test."

She handed another to Randy, then gathered one for herself. They moved to the nearby benches to sit down.

"Okay," Randy said as Rooster pulled his phone from his pocket. "It should be disgusting, but it's actually pretty good."

Rooster glanced up to catch Randy's eye then turned to Meg. "You'll excuse me for a minute? This is Headquarters."

7

ROOSTER

The Streets of Stone Town, Zanzibar

"HONEY HERE." Rooster moved to the side of a building, tucking himself into the indentation. He had a good view from this position and was out of the stream of traffic.

"How's the R & R going?" Nutsbe asked.

"So far, so good. We just got in and hooked up with Randy's sister. What've you got?"

"Two things. First, the Bowens. They're in Germany at the Army hospital. Mr. Bowen was released. His wife is stable. The doctors are saying you got her out of there in the nick of time. Anjie Bowen's got a shot at surviving her adventure."

"Good to know. What's the second thing?" Rooster had his eyes on Meg. She had gone to toss her plate into the trash when the wind had kicked up. It tugged at her dress, plastering it along the smooth curves of her body. She turned to face the gust, her fingers catching hold of her scarf, letting it fly out behind her like a kite as it whipped from her hair. Copper curls blew around her shoulders. Her head was thrown back, and she was laughing like she was in the picture Randy had shown him back at the airport. He caught himself smiling at her antics.

"I'm still on the first topic." Nutsbe's tone refocused him. "We forwarded the last audio file of Brilliant to the CIA since he spoke in actual sentences this time. Their chief of station in Djibouti says he knows the voice. It's a guy by the name of Momo Bourhan. That's: bravo, oscar, uniform, Romeo, hotel, alpha, November."

"Got it."

"After the spook heard the tape, he went looking for Momo. He was safe and sound at the airport, heading out of Djibouti. He wasn't part of the group who went to move the Bowens from the Afar camp."

"But the CIA knows his affiliations?"

"Low-level Al-Qaeda."

"Well, shit." Rooster stabbed a hand onto his hip.

"I'd say that's about right. Ready for item number two that makes number one so much more interesting?"

"You have an ID on the guy hanging out with us in Djibouti?"

"Roger that. You sent us a crap photo, but the computers are giving it a good probability that your secret admirer is Hiram Follman. He was *Sayeret Matkal*."

"Israeli Special Forces? You're speaking past tense. What's he doing now?"

"Moldering in the grave. He was blown up in an explosion targeting a fair number of the Israeli elites."

"Are you kidding me? Is this the same explosion that gave us the Rex Deus band of kidnappers in DC, trying to get hold of Zoe Kealoha and her micro-robotics research?"

"One and the same. Seems that explosion helped move a shit-ton of Special Forces guys off their census. They're ghosts."

"So how are we classifying them?"

"Consensus has it that they're now a Mossad black ops group. Complete disavowal. They'll probably work with the US if it serves their present purpose. But you never know what their long game is. Did you catch a look at the guy's left wrist? He got the tattoo?"

"I wasn't close enough to pick up details in Ethiopia. Randy and I think we spotted him at the hotel when we got in. How he beat us here, I can't figure. But the hair on the back of my neck is telling me that someone's got us on their radar. Any clue why Mossad is interested in Randy and me?"

"Kane and Spencer had a powwow over at Langley. They're speculating that Follman had his eyes on Brilliant and found you as a by-product. There's concern in Israel about the spread of extremism in East Africa. Things have been nervous ever since the El Adde attack on Kenyan soldiers in Somalia. So far, that's been tied to Al-Qaeda, but as the US and our allies are stripping Al-Qaeda of power and prestige, there's intel that says ISIS might be stepping into the game."

"Why is this Momo guy picking up American executives in the Red Sea?"

"Terrorism is expensive, man. They need money. And if that doesn't work, then there's always video footage of American deaths for propaganda. They're probably pissed as hell that they got neither out of this deal."

"Follman isn't targeting us in retaliation for Panther Force taking twelve of their operators off the playing field?"

"They were all returned—both the warm bodies and cold ones—with a bow on top as a gift from the CIA to the Mossad. To answer your question, we don't know what this guy's up to.

Could be he's gathering intel. Could be he thinks that, now that you've saved the hostages, you'll press on, maybe lead him to bigger players. Could be he's gunning for you guys. Could be none of the above. It's a coin flip. The CIA reached out to Mossad for answers. I don't have anything for you yet. I'll get hold of you or Randy as soon as I do."

"Should Randy and I head out?" Rooster rubbed a hand across his forehead. "There are civilians who could be at risk if we stick around."

"If Follman comes for you, it won't be public. I don't think your presence puts civilians at risk. The reigning theory at Langley is that Follman is on his own assignment, and he's finding it curious that there's an Iniquus team on the same route. He might be trying to figure out what you know that he doesn't. And he could also be making sure that you aren't stepping on his toes. He might even reach out to you. And the CIA would appreciate it if you'd have that conversation."

"Understood. What I'm hearing is that you all have a lot of speculation, and you don't know what the hell's going on, but we should enjoy all this rest and relaxation and maybe make a new friend along the way."

"Your call if you stay in Tanzania. But Randy said you all are headed to the crater in the morning and then Kilimanjaro. Small groups with arranged guides, remote hotels that cater only to tourists, you're taking two other people's places, and your names aren't even on the rosters, how the hell could he follow you without you being abundantly aware?"

"All right, we'll stay on course. Call me if you get anything new. If we see this guy again, we'll check for a tattoo."

8

———

Overlooking the Indian Ocean, Zanzibar

Randy slid onto the barstool at the round table they'd picked in the corner. Meg knew very well that he'd position himself where he had the widest view and nothing obstructing him from seeing the exits. She also knew that by the time she climbed onto her own stool, he would have mapped six different escape routes and had a plan for how he'd get her out safely. She never worried about her well-being when Randy was around. And with Rooster thrown into the mix, it would take a car bomb barreling through the front door to put her in harm's way.

Meg slid onto the seat with her back to the room.

"What was that stupid song your sorority sang, Meg? Drink beer, drink beer, drink beer, God—"

Meg put her hand over Randy's mouth. "I'm not singing the song in public, and I'm certainly not cussing in a bar in a Muslim country."

Randy looked over at Rooster. "She won't drink beer here either. I bet you ten dollars she'll order wine."

Rooster looked at Meg for an explanation.

"When she drinks beer, she belches like a sailor," Randy said.

Meg's eyes rounded. "Randy, that was one time. I burped one time ten years ago. Why would you say something like that to Rooster?"

"I wanted him to see how fiery you can get." Randy looked over at Rooster. "Born redhead with the temper to match."

Meg swatted at him.

Randy caught her hand and held it to his chest. "See what I mean, Honey? Vicious. And they say that Latin blood runs hot? Nothing like a redheaded woman."

Meg turned her attention to the waiter who had moved toward them with his pad, and Randy released her hand. "*Jambo!* I think we'll start with three beers, please."

The man nodded and went off.

Meg turned back to the guys. "And while you guys can probably drink a swimming pool's worth of alcohol and still recite the alphabet backward, I can't hold my alcohol very well anymore."

Randy chuckled. "That wasn't always true, I remember when—"

"You remember when I was in college. Now I'm older and wiser, with a lot less tolerance. I'll probably be mostly a tour guide on this bar trip."

The waiter brought them three bottles and set them down.

"Cheers."

Randy clinked her bottle then took a long swig. "That was a bit grim."

"Says the Ranger. Did I make you worried about the safari

tomorrow?" She patted his arm. "Speaking of which, we need to be out of the hotel early. We'll be flying to Arusha at the crack of dawn."

"Crack of dawn means different things to different folks," Rooster said.

Meg grinned. "I can't tell you how funny I find it that a man named Rooster is asking me to define crack of dawn." She propped her elbows on the table and squinted her eyes. "If Rooster isn't your call name, there must be a story behind it."

"My mom has a weird sense of humor. The story goes that before I was born, I used to wake her up every morning at the break of day by kicking her in the bladder. One day she got pissed off—pun intended—and said, 'I swear to God if you do that one more time, I'm gonna name you Rooster, and you'll have to explain yourself for the rest of your life.'"

Meg chuckled. "So you did it anyway. You kicked her again."

"Seems so, and she's a God-fearing woman. If I got her to the point of swearing, she was darned well going to follow through."

Meg looked from Randy to Rooster then back to Randy. "He's lying."

Rooster grinned. "Rooster is a family name. On my mother's side of the family, they follow the old southern tradition of the firstborn taking the mother's maiden name as a first name. Lucky for my sister, I got there first."

Meg peeked over to Randy to see if Rooster was telling another tale. Randy sat there, blank-faced. Rooster's name was actually Rooster. "I've heard about that before. Langston Hughes's mom was Caroline Langston. What's your sister's name?"

"Mary Margaret. Another southern tradition. Why give a girl one first name when two would be twice as nice?"

"Rooster. Huh." She slid her bottle back and forth between her hands. "Did you get teased as a child?"

"I was always pretty big. People didn't tease me much. Rooster isn't bad. I have a female cousin whose name is Stanley."

"Seriously?" Meg looked at the men's bottles. Both were empty while she was still on her first sip. She glanced over at the server with a little wave.

"She decided to go with Ley so people would stop asking."

"I would." Meg caught the eye of the server who had made his way over and was gathering the men's bottles. "Can you bring them some banana beer, please?"

"Nuh-uh." Randy waved his hands in front of him. "This is supposed to be Rooster's prize. You have to pick something good, not beer that tastes like a fermented banana."

"One sip. If you don't like it, I'll order something else." She held up two fingers to the waiter, and he moved toward the bar. "It tastes more like hard cider than anything else. I have to warn you, though, it's about twice the strength of most beers."

Rooster crossed his arms and rested them on the table, leaning in. "Tell me about your project. What's it called?"

"The Key Initiative—we're trying to facilitate conversations between scientists and those people our findings will impact on a day-to-day basis. There's anger and fear and entrenchment between modern and traditional, science and myriad belief systems, old and young, and most importantly, survival in the moment and survival over time. Right now, we're at a deadlock. Emphasis on the *dead*. Species and cultures are dying out faster than predicted." Meg looked down at her bottle, spinning it in her hands. In that moment, she felt the pressure, the panic that went along with this task. Her newest satellite photos of the great migration—where millions of animals moved with the rains during the wet season to fresh pastures—had been dire this year. Again.

"Are your efforts focused on Tanzania?"

Rooster's voice brought her head up. "Well, we're starting here to try out different ideas and see how we do, then we hope to expand. We chose Tanzania because it's relatively stable politically, and they have the crater that is the Garden of Eden, one of the spots that have the most diversity in flora and fauna. Many of our endangered animals live there. It's an important place to put our attention."

The doors burst open with the wind, and the crowd at the bar all turned to watch the bartender wrestle it shut. Rooster stood up to help the guy. That was nice of him, she thought. Gentlemanly.

"Big storm tonight, tomorrow all better," the bartender said. "It's good inside. We drink and enjoy." He raised his hands like he was conducting an orchestra. The men at the bar moved back to their conversations.

When Meg traveled, she didn't think she could get the flavor of the area if she went to places that catered to tourists—spots where it was in their best interest to provide her with what they thought she was looking for. What Meg was looking for was authenticity. At this bar, there was a mix of tourists and non-Muslim Zanzibaris—it was one of the few places that sold alcohol on the island. Meg was one of only a sprinkling of women in the room. She tried not to feel intimidated by the eyes on her. Being with Rooster and Randy helped.

"This deadlock isn't just an African phenomenon," Randy said as Rooster rejoined them. "Just look at what's happening in America today. There are groups of people who live in areas where their families have traditionally lived, following the careers their families have traditionally followed. Families who are fighting to keep mining coal in West Virginia, factory workers in the rustbelt—those jobs are going away. That way of life. American traditions are dying, and people are fighting to keep them in place. I obviously don't feel that way. I left my homeland for a better life."

"It's completely understandable why people would want to preserve their heritage." Meg tucked her hair behind her ears. "Things are changing everywhere. I think people are struggling with the idea of day-to-day survival. All over our country, all over the world, things are changing faster than they ever have. The industrial revolution was more than a hundred years of shift and change. The technology revolution changes daily. If folks want to survive, they have to keep up. Even if they keep up, computers are taking over blue-collar jobs. White-collar. Even scientific jobs. Take the CRISPR, for example. Have you heard of it?" She glanced between the two men.

"Fighting insects spreading disease? They have some kind of way to mutate the males?" Rooster asked.

"Well, yes, that's one application. CRISPR is a gene-splicing machine. It works sort of like a word processor. The scientist identifies a sequence that they think is problematic, and they decide how they would like to fix that sequence. Sort of like the find/replace command on your word processor, the computer will search out all the times it finds that sequence in a gene and do the exchange. Fast. Easy. They're hoping to apply that knowledge, not only to pest insects but to malaria-causing mosquitos here in East Africa."

"That would be a huge success story," Rooster said.

Meg shrugged. "Maybe. Maybe not. We don't know the effects of our interference. It's hard to predict because, frankly, we don't have enough of an understanding of how the whole interdependency works. The wrong move could have unexpected and maybe devastating outcomes. These kinds of questions are being thought through by medical ethicists. But let me tell you about the CRISPR and cancer. It used to be that in order to study cancer, researchers had to develop a strain of mice with a type of cancer that they thought might mimic the cancer in a human and then experiment on that strain of mice. It could take years to develop that colony. Maybe they'd need to hire nine or ten graduate students for the project. Now, CRISPR can do the same thing in just days at a very low cost—a win for cancer research. But because it can be run by a single graduate student, eight have lost their jobs. *Everything* is becoming mechanized, from picking crops to robots that are being developed to monitor and socialize our elderly populations."

"What? Buy a robot and let it take care of Memaw?" Rooster leaned back and crossed his arms over his broad chest.

It took Meg a second to pull her eyes away from the expanse of his shoulders, the size of his biceps. And to push down her guilty feelings for eyeing her brother's boyfriend. She wondered if the bar was dark enough to hide her pink cheeks from Randy. "Wouldn't it be easier to buy a robot and program it rather than hiring a caregiver?" she asked. "Possibly more reliable. Possibly a cheaper alternative with no employment documentation or taxes. No concerns about elder abuse or theft. Some countries are beginning to see that. Soon, there will be little reason to work. And they're the ones who are considering paying everyone a living wage. Finland's experimenting with it now. You get a paycheck just for citizenship. Now, that hasn't passed anywhere, but it's on the horizon. Something like it, anyway. What will people do with their days? How will they gain esteem and be self-actualized? Here in Africa, it's a petri dish. It's happening here and now. The Maasai can no longer gain prestige by hunting lions. The El Molo tribe in Kenya proved their worth on alligator hunts. Now, that's illegal. There are no new rites of passage—

nothing that can take the place of their ancestral rituals. A whole generation of tribal men have missed out, and they're angry about it. Angry young men with no good alternatives can become dangerous."

Rooster nodded. "I've seen some extremist tactics that are taking advantage of the changing circumstances. With tribes' traditional ways of living, herding, and hunting disappearing with the changes in climate, relief workers are sending supplies to help the transition—food, medicine. The militants steal the supplies and then use them as recruiting tools, incentives to get the men to join their ranks. That, or they keep the resources away from the people, so they become desperate. When that's the case, if the UN declares an area of famine, they say it's an exaggeration, and they ban help from coming in. Once the people are desperate, their leaders start blaming others, mostly the US and the EU, giving the people an enemy to hate and a desire to fight."

"I've seen this. And it needs to be stopped." Meg's tone was adamant. "There are thousands of people suffering—children."

Randy chuckled then upended the last of his beer. "Sounds like you'll be running for political office when you get back to the states." He waggled the bottle in the air, and Meg saw their server nod in response.

"Never. Washington gridlock just exacerbates the deadlock. I'm choosing my words very carefully there. This is it. This is all about survival. All animals fight for survival, humans included. As humans, though, we have the unique ability to see the effects of our actions and make decisions. Washington can be very myopic—looking at what will get someone more money in their campaign chest, get them a few more votes. I take the long, long, long-range view. The one I get from looking at satellite images. Comparing them year to year. I'm telling you, we're at a tipping point. People are dealing with survival *this* day, maybe even *this* minute. I truly understand that. Here in Africa, it's so obvious. I was just out talking to the Afar tribal elders about it."

Rooster canted his head. "In Djibouti?"

A wrinkle creased between Meg's brows. The Afar had a larger population in Ethiopia, or even in Eritrea to the north of Ethiopia. It was odd to her that Rooster knew that there were Afar tribespeople in Djibouti. "Yes, you've heard of them?"

"Salt, right?"

Something tickled at the back of Meg's memory…something Randy had said, but the beer was working on her. God, she was a lightweight. The server stood beside them. "Did you guys like the banana beer enough to want another one?" she asked. "Or would you like to try something else?"

"Something else would be nice, to get a better tour of what Zanzibar has to offer," Rooster replied. "Go on, about the Afar, you were speaking with the elders…"

"Right. They're gathering salt now to make money. They are herders by tradition. No rain in the Djibouti region means there is no vegetation, nothing to feed the herd. The lake where they live is highly salinized. There's no fresh water to drink. They must buy everything, and they raise the money to do that by digging up the salt left by the evaporating lake or wading out in the water to gather the salt spheres that float there. They will die off very soon if they don't move. Change is imperative. But right now, they won't. Initiatives are being tried—tourism, though it's one of the hottest places in the world. Wind farms. They have crazy high winds that blow through the region. Momo—one of the men who is interested in shifting the tribes to adapt to the new realities—wants to spread the work that we are focusing on here in Tanzania and Kenya and bring it up to Ethiopia and

Djibouti. We need that kind of grassroots push to make things expand quickly."

"Momo?" Rooster asked. "I knew a guy by that name. He was educated in America. Momo Bourhan."

Meg smiled broadly. "Small world. Yes, it was Momo Bourhan."

"So he was with you when you went to visit the Afar tribe? When was that?" Rooster slowly peeled the label from his bottle.

"Early June, about four weeks ago. I have his contact number if you want to get in touch with him."

"Yeah, that would be great." Rooster pulled out his phone. "I'm wondering how common that name is in East Africa. Did you take any pictures with him? Or better yet, any video?"

"Yeah, sure, let me see." Meg scrolled through her phone. "He's going to be a good resource, I think. He travels a lot in this region and has political connections."

"What was he doing out in the salt beds?"

Meg glanced up. "Reaching out to start a dialogue with the tribe. There are people who understand the idea of short term/long term survival. Laws that limit and destroy indigenous cultures create a lot of anger. We don't want a fight—we need results." She focused back on her phone. "He and one of my colleagues, Abraham Silverman, are trying to be inventive. If the people can get what they need to survive and incentive to protect rather than destroy, then it's a win-win. I want that for every living thing. I want us all to win." She scrolled further. "That's what Momo is trying to figure out in Ethiopia, a way to bring hope and power to the people, so they can survive both short term and long." She held out her phone. "Here he is."

Rooster took the phone from her hand and tapped the play triangle. Randy hunkered head to head with Rooster so they could both see.

When Momo began to talk, Randy's body gave a jerk, and his face tightened. "You were at the Afar camp four weeks ago with this guy?" he asked. "Was there anyone else there besides the Afar tribespeople? Those tourists you mentioned, maybe?"

"I wasn't allowed to go into their camp proper. I was only allowed to go out to see the lake—Lac Assal—and meet with the elders. Are you okay, Randy? You don't look well." Her frown deepened with concern.

"I'm good. Shocked that you and Momo were in the same place, same time. Like you were saying, small world."

Rooster put Momo's contact information into his phone. "Mind if I forward this video and his photos to a friend of mine? He'll be interested to see Momo looking so well."

Randy caught Rooster's gaze. He and Randy had a full conversation without saying a word. Meg sighed. She wanted to have that kind of connection. It had been a long time since she'd had a partner for anything besides sex. Sure, sex was stress-relieving and fun. And sex-centered relationships left her with zero in the way of guilt when she had to pack a bag and go. But she longed for intimacy. She just wasn't sure how she could work that out and keep her career. Meg nodded her thanks to the server as he brought their Kilis. She lifted the bottle and let the yeasty bubbles slip down her throat.

Rooster slid his glance back to her and raised his brows, looking for his answer.

"No, that's fine. Send it to whoever you want."

"You told him about your conference?" Randy asked. "Your plans with the other scientists?"

"I don't know. Maybe? Why do you ask? You're both acting weird. What's going on?"

"Just wondering if I might get to see him again tomorrow," Randy said.

"No, I'm sorry. He's not on our roster. We'll be a small group of twenty."

Rooster handed her back her phone. "Since we're talking old home week, Momo and I had some mutual friends. Derek Bowen and his wife, Anjie Bowen? They were headed over to the Red Sea on vacation. Did Momo mention them to you?"

"Well, no. I can't imagine why he would tell me about them. I don't know the Bowens personally, but I do know *of* Derek Bowen. He's an executive with an American oil company, Hesston. He's coming here to Zanzibar sometime soon, this week, I think, to talk about offshore oil. It's creating problems for us in the adaptation/survival field. Here we are, asking people to change, and then in comes big American oil, putting these beautiful waters at risk." She gestured out toward the ocean. "The tourist industry, the fishing industry. All on the line. Again, personal prosperity and survival in the now, but the potential is there for catastrophic outcomes, even if it's just putting more fossil fuels in the air. Regardless of your stance on that industry, there's no denying that it's increased anti-American sentiment and making the Key Initiative's job harder, though there are only two of us who are American on the team. Lucky for me, I'm an animal migration specialist. The wildebeests don't care where I come from."

Rooster's phone buzzed. "Sorry," he said, looking at his screen. "Headquarters. They've identified a threat we're keeping an eye on."

9

MEG

 Poseidon Bar, overlooking the Indian Ocean, Zanzibar

RANDY WATCHED Rooster head out the door into the storm winds, then turned his attention to her. Leaning his weight onto his elbows perched on the tabletop, he cocked his head to the side. "What do you think of Rooster?"

"Besides big?" Meg took a swig of beer to realign her thoughts from the inappropriate place they had meandered. "He seems like a great guy. I think he's charming and smart. Are you two partners now?"

"He's a straight shooter. You have to like that in a guy."

"With a gun and in his personal life?" Meg grinned. "When did all this happen?" How did she fall out of the loop? Meg was a little hurt. She had thought she and Randy were closer than that.

"This last time? Just over a month ago."

Meg slipped her hand over Randy's and gave it a squeeze.

She was sorry to hear that. Things must not have been going smoothly for them if their relationship status was clicking on and off. Randy deserved to be happy. He'd fought hard for what he had in life. Meg wished at least his love life came easily. Well, there was nothing more romantic than an evening in Zanzibar, seconded only by the Tanzanian wildlife. It could be the perfect lovers' getaway for them. Maybe she should go back to the hotel and leave them to their own devices. Before she could say anything else, Rooster blew back into the bar. He sought out Randy's eyes first thing and held them for a long minute. Meg sighed. She really needed to do something about her dry spell; she missed that kind of intensity and connection.

"All good, Honey?" Randy asked.

"Interesting, at any rate. It's been a long day, and I'd like to get to bed," he said with a significant look at Randy.

Okay, Meg was jealous. She'd just flat out admit it to herself. As much as she loved hanging out with Randy, and as much as Rooster… She stopped herself from forming that sentence in her mind. God, these next two days as a third wheel were going to feel long.

10

———

Seraphina Hotel, Zanzibar

THE THREE ARRIVED at Meg's door, and Randy reached for her key card. "Old habits die hard. Let me do a quick sweep."

Meg laughed. "Sure, if it makes you feel better. But I'm not expecting a boogeyman under my bed."

Rooster watched her face go from grin to grim. He wondered what thought she'd just landed on. Before he could ask, Randy was back.

"All clear." He handed her the card. "Hey, do me a favor, if you're planning on leaving your room tonight, give me a call. We're just up one flight."

"You do realize I've traveled all over the world without a private security detail? I can handle myself."

"Handle yourself, as in fight your way away from a predator? Or handle yourself, as in you've been lucky enough never to have faced an attacker?"

"Don't jinx me." Meg reached over and knocked on the wooden door. "If it means that much to you, I'll call. But you're only with me for a few days. I'll be on my own again very soon."

"Indulge me." He bent to kiss her cheek.

Meg gave Rooster a wave as she shut the door.

"What was that about?" Rooster asked as they moved toward the stairs.

Randy reached up and rubbed his neck. "I've got eyes in the back of my skull, man. I can't figure out where they're coming from. What did Headquarters say earlier when we were at the bar?"

Rooster tipped his head toward the stairwell. Normally, he would have liked to have a walk and talk about the subject, but given the windstorm outside, Randy would never hear him. They'd have to keep it to low tones in his room.

As they passed through Rooster's door, the men moved to give it a quick once-over. They sat, heads side by side, so they could speak softly into each other's ears. "Momo is an up and comer in Al-Qaeda, the African branch. Meg is lucky she walked out of there."

"Why do you think they let her go?" Randy rubbed his palms down his thighs and planted his elbows on his knees.

"My gut says they didn't think she had the financial connections to be of any use. Either that, or there was something about Meg's translator that pulled her out of the net. Maybe his tribe and the Afar tribe had agreements for safety and hospitality like *Pashtunwali* in the Middle East."

"Or maybe his tribe would have retaliated had anything happened to him or Meg. Jobs in the area are few and far between. They start capturing tourists, and there'll be no more tourists a nanosecond later. The Bowens were nabbed off the seas."

"Fair point." Rooster paused as he let his thoughts settle. "We don't know what leverage Momo had over the Afar tribe. I agree with you. Meg walked into the lion's den. The only thing that gives me any peace about that is, we'd have found her and gotten her out with the Bowens."

"That doesn't give me a lot of relief. We only got out of that scrape with the help of the Navy." Randy screwed his brows together. "Go on, what else have you got on Momo?"

"The CIA has signed a contract with Iniquus. Panther Force is mobilizing."

"My team's already in Afghanistan."

"Strike Force is wrapping up their assignment. You're still on loan to the Panthers. We'll be with Meg through Kilimanjaro and the flight back to the capital. After that, we'll go to a rallying point for a debrief, then we're to leave Africa to start our R & R."

"R & R hasn't started yet? We're on guard duty for The Key Initiative?"

"Keep eyes and ears open for the scientists' safety. There's no reason to think they've been targeted. The CIA tracked Momo's movements into Tanzania the night the Bowens' got rescued. There's been a lot of rattle in the last couple of days, something ramping up in Tanzania. CIA and Mossad had a chat. There's someone Mossad would like us to meet tonight." Rooster checked his watch. "Fifteen minutes, downstairs."

"Is this our ghost?"

"That'd be my guess. They gave me a countersign, so this is a clandestine meet and greet. Might as well get in place."

Both men moved toward the door. Randy opened it and did a quick sweep of the hallway, then Rooster followed him to the stairwell.

Rooster had a hard time doing covert. He just wasn't built for the job. Randy, on the other hand, had a stature and a skin tone that could adapt, chameleon-like, to most regions where he got to play. Here in Zanzibar, where various ethnicities had been steeped together for centuries, Randy's tanned Latino skin and his ability to mimic both the spoken and body languages of those around him meant no one looked his way when he walked by. Everyone looked Rooster's way. That was why Rooster preferred the stairs and why he trailed behind Randy a few good paces.

Rooster did his best to slip quietly into the gentleman's lounge, where deep leather sofas were scattered about in the low lighting. It seemed the host at the door was doing a good job dissuading women from going in. There were a few groups of men in tailored slacks swirling tumblers of scotch. The scent of cigars filled the air with pungent smoke. Rooster moved to the side of the heavily draped window and sat where he could keep eyes on the activity in the room. Randy sat at the bar doing the same. No weapons beyond their pocketknives. They shouldn't need them.

The Ghost walked into the bar, signaled to the host that he saw his party, and moved toward Rooster. A case dangled from his left hand, his right hand extended out. A "glad to see you again, old friend" smile on his face. Rooster stood and reached for the handshake—he had the guy by almost a foot in height and a good hundred pounds, maybe more. The Ghost didn't seem intimidated, though. Interesting. There was no attempted show of power with an aggressive squeeze. Rooster would have known he was talking to an amateur if he had tried to prove himself in such a lowbrow way. Professionals didn't do petty shit.

Rooster's focus dropped to the man's left wrist. The guy's watch had slid far enough down his arm that Rooster caught the swirls of the tattoo that it obscured. The circles and lines of the Sephirot, the tree of life. In esoteric Judaism, it was the central mystical symbol that originated in the Kabbalah. Different spheres, he was told, represented a different aspect of enlightenment.

Back in Washington D.C., Panther Force had taken down a dozen men with this same tattoo on their wrists. Iniquus had learned nothing about the tattoo in the interrogations. The CIA, if they had anything, wasn't sharing. But his commander, Titus Kane, brought a scholar in to teach them the basics. They'd nick-named the group the Rex Deus after what they'd learned from USIPAC —the United States Pro-Israel lobby—a group who tried to fight Jewish stereotypes in the United States. When they had seen pictures of the men's tattoos, the USIPAC folks had gotten riled up. It seemed the Rex Deus, sometimes called "Star families," was supposed to be the stuff of conspiracy theories and imagination. To have a band of men wearing the Kabbalist sacred symbol was a concerning thing. The Mossad seemed to think otherwise, or this man wouldn't be here representing them.

The group of twelve Rex Deus who went down in the US had illuminated the first triangle in the design. That highlighted aspect symbolized wisdom, understanding, and knowledge. That group had tried to kidnap a DARPA scientist building a micro-robotics WASP prototype.

Another man with the tattoo had shown up on their radar even more recently. Panther Force was protecting two archaeolo-gists who were helping to safeguard Syrian artwork. That guy had refused to talk about his tattoo, as well. But it was noted that his ink, unlike the other tattoos they had seen, had the sixth sphere illuminated, *Tiferet*. Their resource said this one had to do with beauty, balance, and harmony—that made sense.

Perhaps the Israeli elite warriors who were in the "explosion" that took their names off the military rosters had made decisions about what path they would follow once they didn't exist. It was a theory they'd thrown around in the Panther Force war room. But if that theory played out, this would be an interesting meeting. The sphere that this man had illuminated was *Gevurah*—an instrument God used to judge humans and punish the wicked. Rooster pinched his chin and gave The Ghost a surreptitious head-to-toe assessment to figure out where his weapons might be hidden. Since Panther Force had killed some of the tattooed group, Rooster wondered if he and Randy might be this guy's end targets. Why exactly had Iniquus agreed to this meeting?

"Lovely night for a stroll on the beach," Rooster said.

"The wind will fill the fisherman's sails," The Ghost replied.

"I walked by the dock and ate shrimp."

"The octopus is a treat." That was the last of the required exchange.

Okay, good. Now what? Rooster took his seat, careful that when his eyes scanned the room, they glided right over Randy. Of course, The Ghost knew Randy, probably had a few hundred photos of them from Djibouti. It was just part of the dance.

The Ghost moved his seat to protect his back with a wall, moving farther from the window. It put them at an acute angle to each other. They could speak quietly near the other's ear without looking at each other.

The waiter came over, and Rooster said, "Whiskey, please."

The Ghost nodded his head to ask for the same. "Congratulations on your recent success," he said as the waiter left.

"Which one would that be?"

"Momo Bourhan is a dangerous man. He has an enormous ego and equally large aspirations in Al-Qaeda."

"He's a true radical? Or is he using that as a vehicle?"

"As with many in the upper echelons, he is manipulating those around him to do his bidding with little personal conviction."

"How'd you get involved?"

"The Tanzanian government has been focusing their tourist advertising on Israel. They want to make Tanzania the preferred holiday destination of our citizens."

"Beautiful place."

"Possibly a volatile place."

"That's true most anywhere you go these days."

"We believe that Al-Qaeda is leaning on its alliances along the east coast of Africa, infiltrating the weak spots, and gathering members to the radical agenda."

"What makes these spots weak?"

He tilted his head from side to side—a non-answer to a too-complex question.

"You've had your eyes on us," Rooster said, wondering what was in The Ghost's case.

"Only to find out why you were in communication with Momo Bourhan."

Rooster looked up as the waiter moved toward them, balancing their drinks on his tray. He placed shell mosaic coasters on the table before he set their drinks down with a white-gloved hand. "You know," Rooster said as the waiter moved out of listening distance. "He introduced himself to me by the name 'Brilliant.' I only just identified him as Momo Bourhan."

The Ghost looked at his feet as he snickered. Then he rolled his eyes and tilted back to stare at the ceiling. After a moment, he shook his head. "My hope is that his ego will be his downfall." He lifted his glass in salute. "To his failure."

"I'll drink to that." Rooster took a sip. "So why are we chatting?"

"You seem to be friends with one of the Key Initiative scientists. I'm guessing that you'll be going with the group on their trip to the crater?"

Rooster had been playing poker with bad guys for a long damn time. When he was in dialogue, he was emotionless. Of course, the Key Initiative scientist The Ghost was talking about was Meg. Rooster wasn't about to verify anything. He would only give up as much information as it took to get the data he might need. "You're representing Israeli interests?"

"Exactly. The UN is warning that there's an escalation of attacks, grenades, and small bombs in Arusha as Al-Qaeda is encouraging their African brothers-in-arms to target westerners and keep them out of Africa. Already, many Israelis have lost life and limb. Tanzania, of course, is desperate for tourist money. The changes in climate are pressing down on the traditional ways of life. Suffocating the people."

"And you're here because there's an increased concern about Israeli citizens being attacked? Captured?"

"Exactly. We don't want Al-Qaeda to believe that they can attack Israelis anywhere in the world. One of our scientists works with your friend's initiative. I will be taking his place until they get to Dodoma to start their work. He will be given a security team and reintroduce himself once they are there. I knew you'd caught sight of my face in the airport and recognized me from Djibouti. It's important that I maintain my cover."

"And you thought we'd expose you?"

"Not out of malice, but out of curiosity." He gestured with his drink in his hand.

"Why the charade?"

He took a long sip. "Our scientist's name has been mentioned in Momo's communications."

"Specifically?"

The Ghost nodded once.

Rooster leaned forward, his voice a low rumble. "Anyone else mentioned by name?"

"No."

Was Meg at risk? "The name of the Initiative?"

"No."

"What's this scientist's specialty?"

"Renewable energy. We held him back once we heard the chatter about his trip to Djibouti. He was supposed to reach out to the Afar tribe. The tribe is in an area where they could generate a great deal of energy for Djibouti—geothermal and wind."

"But you didn't let him go to his meeting."

"We had information that the Afar were in communication with Momo. Your Dr. Finley went instead."

Rooster worked to keep the anger he was feeling pressed low in his gut where it wouldn't show. "And you let her go, knowing the circumstances?"

"Israel and America are allies. We arranged for a trusted interpreter to be assigned to her. We maintained surveillance of the situation."

Rooster sent him a long, assessing—it might have been interpreted as an intimidating—glare. "That was big of you. Did you also send word through American channels this was going down?"

"I don't follow the lines of communication. I can't tell you what happened."

"You communicated with someone, though."

He nodded slowly.

"Did you know Momo would be there?"

"I've been tracking him, trying to figure out what he's up to. Momo has big eyes and a small plate. But he is working to position himself for leadership. My understanding is that you took three-million dollars out of his pocket. I'd say watch your back, but I don't believe he put a name and face together. The Afar only know that a giant came into their camp. He had glowing green eyes and big guns, and they were frightened. They said that you put the Bowens on your heads like women carrying water. They've never seen anything like that before." The Ghost chuckled. "What I would have given to watch that scene."

"Do you think there's any kind of danger on this trip, aside from the obvious concerns of lions and such? Maybe the field trip should be curtailed. Maybe they should go right into their meeting and get security on everyone?"

"The hippopotamuses are more likely to kill you than the lions. And no. The target is our scientists for more reasons than one. The Ngorongoro Crater and the trek up Mount Kilimanjaro aren't good strategic places to take Silverman. They'll wait until he's in the capital filled with places to hide and without the fear of being killed by the animals." He shifted onto a hip and pulled a linen handkerchief from his pocket.

"Yet you're here."

"Excuse me." He turned away from Rooster and sneezed, rubbed his nose, and thrust the hanky back into his front pocket. "I'm sure you are contemplating the safety of your friend, especially since our scientist will not be showing up. The truth is that he was detained by his father's funeral. We would not force him to sit out this leg of the journey. I am simply taking advantage of the fact that there's an empty seat so that I can take a look at the other scientists on the off chance there's a mole of some kind."

"Care to elaborate on that? What would be the purpose of the mole? These are scientists."

Again, a tip of the head from left to right. A non-answer to a complicated question. Rooster didn't need the fine print on why the Israeli scientist was interesting to Momo Bourhan. But he damned well needed to make sure Meg was safe. Rooster was surprised by how vehemently that thought rushed through his system. He knew The Ghost had seen his reaction. Probably guessed at his thoughts. His emotions had taken him by surprise, and he hadn't had a chance to shut them down. He wondered if The Ghost would use that as some kind of ammunition against him along the way. Rooster slicked his tongue over his teeth.

"She'll have both of you there. I've been tasked to be at her disposal as well, should a need arise. For both of the American scientists, actually. I doubt seriously either of them will need my help other than, perhaps, to carry their bags to the shuttle." He offered a smile. His teeth were stained along the edges from tobacco and coffee. He was fit, but he had a balding head and the weathered face of a man approaching forty.

Rooster wouldn't let the man's age fool him, he'd met many an operative, and he'd learned to scent out the people with deadly skills. This man reeked of lethality.

"I consider this outing a perk of the job," The Ghost was saying. "And I plan to enjoy myself. In the event that this conversation has made you concerned about the situation, an arrangement has been made between our organizations for you to have what you might need for comfort's sake." His eyes fell to the case. He lifted his glass and took the last swallow. He clapped Rooster on the knee and stood. "Well, old friend. Always a pleasure to find time for a drink with you. Sleep well. We leave very early tomorrow morning."

11

ROOSTER

The Gentleman's Lounge, Seraphina Hotel, Zanzibar

"YOU GET ALL OF THAT?" Rooster asked.

"I sent the recording to Nutsbe. I'm waiting for an all-clear so I can erase it."

"I want to listen to it one more time before you do." He flexed his wrist. "This case feels like it's full of bricks."

Randy clenched his teeth, making the sides of his jaw bulge in a staccato beat, while he thought. "I'm not clear about our role here."

"We're eyes and ears until the Panthers are boots on the ground. But yeah, that info file is feeling kind of thin. Let's see what we've been handed, then we'll call Nutsbe."

Randy signed his tab, and they walked out of the bar one at a time. Randy took the elevator. Rooster pushed the door to the stairwell open with his shoulder, checked that it was empty, and jogged up the stairs, three at a time. He was already swiping the key card to his room when Randy moved up behind him.

Randy checked the room, pulled back the curtains at their window. "If this weather keeps up, the plane they chartered isn't going wheels up any time soon."

"The bar guy said it'll be nice by tomorrow." Rooster inspected the outside of the case. "Nothing ticking."

"There's a relief." Randy pulled his phone from his pocket. "Strike Force is out of the loop since Panther Force has this assignment?" He raised a brow.

"Nutsbe's running us for the time being."

Randy nodded and pushed eight on his quick dial. "Randy here. You're on speaker with Rooster and me."

"Lucky sons of bitches," Nutsbe said. "You're getting paid the big bucks to hang out playing Tarzan while I'm here punching keys in the war room."

"Haven't swung from a vine since we've been here. Did see a ghost, though," Rooster said.

"How'd the contact go?"

"Interesting. Rex Deus tat. I didn't see the whole thing, but the illuminated sphere on this one was *Gevurah.*"

"Serious? He's their punisher? And he's on your trail? I'm suddenly liking the fact that I'm tapping my keys here in the war room. Good luck with that."

"Yeah. Thanks," Randy said. He and Rooster sat on the bed with the phone between them, their heads lowered to keep the conversation from being heard by any interested ears on the other side of the wall.

"He said he's here because Momo Bourhan is showing an unhealthy interest in one of their scientists," Rooster said. "An Israeli who's involved in the Key Initiative. He's going to take the guy's place until the group is back at the capital."

"Roger that," Nutsbe replied. "He's playing the role of Dr. Abraham Silverman."

Randy sidled closer and leaned over the phone, laying on the bed. "Got any intel on the good doctor?"

"His specialty is renewable energy."

Rooster rubbed the back of his neck. "Well then, that explains that. The Ghost said that Silverman was supposed to be out at the Afar camp last month chatting with the elders. That region is sitting on a geothermal hotspot, and they've got a wind blowing so hard it could probably power half of Africa. Wonder why he had Meg Finley take his place?"

"My guess would be that Meg was already in Tanzania doing the legwork for the group, setting up the meetings," Nutsbe said. "She could have easily taken a quick flight to Djibouti when Silverman's father was hospitalized. I've followed that trail. It's legit. Silverman's dad kicked the bucket. The funeral's scheduled for tomorrow."

"That's what The Ghost said. But he also said that they pulled their scientist off the Afar trip because they heard Silverman's name on Momo's channels."

"Noted. I'll do some digging."

Randy leaned closer to the phone. "Where are the other scientists on this gig?"

"They had a pre-meeting gathering of those working in Tanzania. There were supposed to be four, all told. Silverman, Finley, and the two who got hung up with visa issues. You're filling their shoes until they get back to the capital. Those two plan to land in Dar es Salaam Monday."

"And the ones not assigned to Tanzania?"

"The others are gathering at the airport tomorrow morning to fly out on the private charter to the crater. You three will be taking a puddle jumper over to Dar es Salaam in the morning to meet them, but you know that already."

"I have a package from our new friend," Rooster said. "You think I should open it or wait for Christmas?"

"You sent your equipment back with the courier. Iniquus said you'd be uncomfortable with a plan that put another country's operative on the tour bus with you when you weren't comparably equipped."

"Tell me about that contact chain." Rooster ran his thumb over the latch of the case.

"Assumed operative contacts their mothership, the Mossad. CIA contacts the Mossad. Mossad says they'll make an asset available for a meet and greet. CIA hires Iniquus to go to the party. Iniquus assigns Panther Force. Panther Force is going wheels up. You and Randy got tapped to keep eyes and ears as things unfold—or don't unfold—since you're our closest operators. And it helps that you know Dr. Finley and are already heading in the same direction."

"Okay, the case then." Rooster moved off the bed to squat. "If Randy and I take a free flight to the Pearly Gates, you know whose neck to break in retaliation." He pushed his thumb in. *Pop*. He pushed the other lever. *Pop*. He lowered to his knees to be eye level with the seam. If this thing was going to explode, he might as well have a front-row seat. He cracked the lid a millimeter and ran the pad of his thumb along the groove. He didn't feel any catches that might signal a booby trap. He lifted the lid.

Randy jumped forward, his hands spread. "Boom!" he shouted.

"Jackass." Rooster hadn't flinched, didn't even look up. He was much more interested in what The Ghost thought to equip them with. Two ankle holsters with pistols all ready to go with full magazines and one in the chamber. Seven bullets in all. There were two in-waist holsters with pistols, six extended magazines, two suppressors, four boxes of .45 caliber hollow-point bullets. He pulled the items from the case. "I thought this bag had a little heft to it." This was where Rooster had trust issues. He liked *his* guns, *his* bullets. Borrowing felt hazardous, even when it was a friendly handing them off. If it was an unknown quantity with a possible revenge mindset, it made Rooster even more squirrely. A soldier had to trust that his weaponry was functional.

Randy picked up one of the guns and worked the slide. "You think he wants us arrested? If we strap these on, we're going to need to Sharpie the consulate's phone number on our arms for easy access."

"Good toys?" Nutsbe asked over the speaker.

"Good enough." Rooster pulled out three covert ballistic vests. "He found a vest in my size in short order. I'd say he's got some pull. He has one here for Randy, and I'm assuming this little one with the boob space is for Meg Finley. Did you get the connection? Her brother is Special Agent Steve Finley. Someone might want to pull him into the loop. We don't need to be burning bridges."

"You're right if Meg stubs her pinky toe, and we had operators around and allowed it to happen, it could sour our relationship with the Bureau. Oh, and Randy would be the worst brother on the face of the Earth. We can't forget that part."

"Ain't happenin' on my watch, bro."

"As of right now," Nutsbe said, "Spencer has a request out to the CIA for permission to read Steve Finley into the program, at least up to the part where we have operators functioning in the area. We haven't heard back yet. It's their call who we include on the need-to-know list."

"Is Meg on that list?" Randy asked.

"That's an emphatic negative. Your assignment is eyes and ears. There should be no reason to get any civilians involved."

"Out of twenty should-be scientists, we know that three of that number are operators. Have you vetted the other seventeen?"

"In process, both in-house and at Langley."

"Looking at this equipment, I'd say Randy and I are missing a big chunk of the information pie." Rooster pulled out two mace cans and two knives with belt holsters. "I could take down an African village with the shit we've got here. We're missing blast cord and flashbang, but other than that..." He scraped his fingers through his short-cropped hair. "Seriously, Nutsbe, you can't be sending us into a trap we're not prepared to handle. I'm not big into shadowboxing. I want to know who or what I'm looking for. Why is Panther Force mobilized?"

"Need to know."

"Screw you," Rooster growled.

"Seriously. I haven't got any information to hand you. Titus is grabbing his go-bag over at the barracks. I'll give him your update and see what he's willing to give up."

"When are they wheels up?"

"It's still Friday here. They leave at twenty-two thirty hours, Zulu time. They expect to arrive in Dodoma at zero five hundred hours your time Sunday. It's a twenty-eight-hour flight to Dodoma if all the legs run on schedule. You should be waking up in Arusha when they get in-country. The team will be catching up on their sleep and setting up the new crib there in Dodoma. They'll interface with our CIA head of station and be ready for you when you come into the capital with Meg Finley's group. You'll need to kiss her goodbye at the airport. We want her to think you're heading to your next destination. We have tickets in your names for Rome. I'll text you the name of a restaurant where they make good pizza. We'll send one of our team to pick you up at baggage claim."

"Roger that."

AT ZERO FIVE HUNDRED HOURS, Meg Finley knocked on Rooster's door, as promised. She smelled like peppermint shampoo. Her hair was pulled back into a still-damp braid that hung down her back over a warm jacket. Her headscarf was poking out of a pocket. She smiled as she held three cups of coffee in her splayed fingers.

"Is it cold out? Thank you," Rooster said, relieving her of two of them.

"Yeah, a little bit. July is the best time to be in Tanzania—lows around seventy, highs around eighty. But that wind must have brought in some weird front. It's sixty-two."

Rooster lifted the cups. "Does it matter which is which?"

"The one in your right hand is mine. I already doctored it." She held out a cup to Randy. "This one's splash of milk, no sugar."

"Good woman." Randy put a hand on Rooster's shoulder as he reached around him to retrieve his cup.

Rooster watched Meg's gaze move from Randy's hand to the two suitcases perched side by side next to the bed. The new bag filled with Mossad goodies rested next to them. Meg brought her focus back to Rooster with a bit of a sigh and a tight-lipped smile. Rooster wished he could read her mind in that moment. Whatever she was thinking, she shook it off quickly. Reaching into her pocket, she pulled out packs of sugar, packs of Splenda, and four plastic containers of cream. "I didn't know how you took your joe."

"Black is fine." Rooster handed Meg her coffee.

"Meg, I need a favor." Randy took her by the hand and led her to the bed, where Rooster had quickly pulled the covers in place, and Randy had laid out the ballistic vest.

In a follow-up discussion with Nutsbe that morning, Randy and Rooster were told that the case they were working had to do with Momo Bourhan and not the scientists with the Key Initiative. That The Ghost was an adjunct to the group was interesting but not game-changing. The equipment was there as a courtesy, nothing more. "Enjoy your adventure, gentlemen," was their last directive from their commander, Titus Kane, before he boarded the plane.

Rooster and Randy both took in the information with a big old grain of salt. They got that they'd been excluded from the need-to-know loop. The CIA wasn't big on sharing. They decided that they were going to treat this as a covert personal security operation, the kind they'd go on when executives didn't want their wives fearful of where they traveled but also wanted them kept safe. In those cases, the operators usually posed as private tour guides, chauffeurs, or personal aides provided for their convenience. In this case, they'd go with "fellow tourist" as their cover. Randy and Rooster had been playing gigs like this so long that it should be as comfortable as an old shoe. But this was Meg's safety they were planning for, so the tension was there.

"A favor?" Meg asked as she pulled her cup away from her lips.

Randy held up the ballistic vest. "Well, we both need a favor, right, Honey?"

"That's right."

Randy focused back on Meg. "Sometimes, we deal with hostage situations. Girls. Women. Sometimes we're pulling them out of hot spots, and we need to get them to safety. Iniquus is trying out a new vest." He jostled the vest up and down. "We need input from a regular woman—well, I wouldn't call you regular." He smiled. "We need input from a woman without military training about how comfortable this is and if it's a problem for them to wear as an everyday thing."

"You sound like you two are up to something." She narrowed her eyes at Rooster as if trying to read him from across the room. She focused back on Randy. "Are you up to something?"

Randy didn't answer. Rooster thought that was a smart move.

Meg walked forward and fingered the poly-cotton outer shell. "This is soft."

"It should be thin enough to not show under your clothes."

"My clothes?" Her eyes flashed up. "You want me to *wear* this thing?" She looked over to where Rooster leaned against the wall and gestured toward him. "It might not show if you're built like a man. This thing isn't going to follow my curves, even if it does have this weird shelf thing in it. It's gonna look like I'm wearing some kind of brace. And surely, I won't be able to move freely in it, bend and twist. What a terrible way to endure a plane ride."

Rooster stood and held his arms out. "I'm wearing one now. Randy too. So far, it's okay. I've been inside and out, and the design keeps up with the temperature changes."

She wrinkled her brow. "You were out already today? So much for my weather report. Where did you go? It's five in the morning."

"I did my jog earlier to get it out of the way." He leaned back against the wall and crossed his arms over his chest.

"In the vest?" She moved forward to rap a knuckle on his chest.

"Yep."

"It doesn't show through your clothes. I don't think it

changes your silhouette." She moved toward the bed and lifted the vest from Randy's hands. "It's not as heavy as I thought it would be." She cocked her head to the side, looking at Rooster. "What's it supposed to protect me from?"

"You? Honey badgers, maybe." He smiled. "It's rated for stab protection and small arms fire."

"Handguns are illegal where we're going."

"Right, well, this is just to get some feedback on comfort. We're hoping you'll forget you have it on," he said. "It's a big ask. You're free to say no."

Meg's brow creased. "You just happened to be carrying my size of bulletproof vest in your bag with you? You didn't know I was going to call and invite you."

"Bullet *resistant*. There's no such thing as bulletproof. We have a friend in the area we came from who had some with him. He lent these to us to try. We'll return them later."

Meg squinted. "Fair enough." She carried the vest to the bathroom to put on.

Rooster turned to Randy. "That went better than I thought it would."

"Our vests are still in the bag. And you let her knock on your chest, you asshole."

Rooster reached for the briefcase. "All right, let's get them on. I don't want to be lying to Meg."

12

———

MEG

   The Road to Ngorongoro Crater, Tanzania

MEG SHIFTED IN HER SEAT. The vest that she'd agreed to wear wasn't as bad as she'd envisioned, but she still wondered how long she'd have to keep the damn thing on. If it had been Randy asking, she'd probably have worn it for an hour or so to be a good sport. But Rooster had asked. Okay, that was bad. She really had to find a way to shift her thoughts from Rooster. Right now, it was hard not to think about him since he was sitting right in front of her in the passenger van that was taking them from the Kilimanjaro airport to the Ngorongoro Crater Safari Hotel and Conference Center, where their safari vehicles would meet them for their excursion.

   Randy and Rooster weren't sitting together. Rooster didn't fit on the bench seats with the rest of the group. He had to sit next to the driver, where he had a little more legroom. Meg got to stare as much as she wanted to at his broad, muscular shoulders.

It seemed unfair that all the guys she met who had what she was looking for—the triumvirate of intelligence, looks, and personality—seemed to be taken or gay. Or, in this case, taken *and* gay. At what point had they all been scooped up? Seemed like she should have started looking earlier to find a good match. Like when she was three or four years old. "Sucks to be me," she muttered under her breath and took a swig of water.

The driver pulled into the hotel's side parking lot. An English breakfast waited for them on the lawn under a yellowwood tree. She checked her watch; everything was going well. They had arrived at 8:40—a mere ten minutes later than they were scheduled to begin. She glanced over at the string of Land SUVs with pop-up tops they'd be using later. That should give Rooster more headspace. Meg bet Rooster would like to get hold of a pop-top for everyday driving back in the states.

The group debussed, standing in loose groups, waiting for a directive. Rooster and Randy were having a tight-knit conversation. It was kind of cute how they talked to each other. They'd maneuver until their heads were side by side and talk softly into each other's ears. A discussion for them alone.

Meg decided to give them some space and moved with the others toward the buffet. They had a small window to take advantage of the breakfast and use flushing toilets before they took off for their first stop at the Maasai village.

A boy with a bag popped up by her side.

"Miss Dr. Finley?" he asked.

"That's me, but you can call me Meg." She sat down on the stairs and patted the place beside her. "What's your name?"

"I am Ahbou Sulenah. I was hoping I might come with you to the Maasai boma."

"Sure, we can take you with us to the boma." Meg searched

the area. "Where are your parents? Did they say it's okay if you go with us?"

"Oh, yes." He pointed to one of the waiters, who waved at them. "My uncle said I should come today and ask you for a ride."

"But how will you get back here to your uncle?"

"I will walk."

"By yourself? That's tens of kilometers. It would be dark before you got back." Distance on foot was a relative thing. Here in Africa, she knew that walking many miles a day was quite normal, especially for women looking for water. But she didn't like the idea of a boy this young walking alone. It piqued her protective instincts.

"I'll stay the night there. I have something I need to give them." He patted his bag.

"What have you got in there?" Meg looked over curiously. "Will you show me?"

Ahbou untied the sack and opened the flap. It was full of wires and lights. She saw several solar panels on spikes, like the ones lining American sidewalks.

"This looks like an interesting project. Want to tell me about it?"

"A lion killed a Maasai cow last night." Ahbou was very serious. "The rangers have already gone to the village and talked to the warriors about it. They are supposed to file a claim and be paid. But the warriors are very upset that the lion came so close to the boma. There are babies there. Little children."

"Will the warriors help the scientists tag the lion and move it to the Serengeti?"

"They are discussing this now. There are some warriors who wish to kill the lion so they can become men, as is the tradition.

And there are others who are afraid that they will no longer be allowed to graze their animals in the crater if they kill the lion."

"I see." Meg tapped the bag. "You think you might have a way to help them?"

"Yes, Miss Doctor Meg. You see, I grew up hating lions. They killed our livestock. When the warriors were gone doing their training and their rituals, it was my job in my family to sit outside at night and watch for lions. It was very hard for me to stay awake the next day at school."

"I can imagine that was true, and school is very important."

"Very important. I tried to solve this problem." He tapped the side of his head. "First, I tried fire. But that only helped the lions see better in the night. Then, I tried to trick the lions. I made scarecrows."

"What gave you that idea?"

"I read a story in a picture book. An African boy had learned a way to keep the birds from eating the family garden by using a blow-up plastic snake in their vegetables. Three and four times each day, he would move the snake to make the birds believe it was real. That was my mistake with the scarecrows. The first day, the lions came, they saw my scarecrow, and they left. I was very happy. But the second day they came, they realized the scarecrows did not move, and the lions killed one of our cows. We were a poor family. We did not have many cows, to begin with. This was a great loss. I am not yet old enough to be a warrior, but I was responsible for my mother and my sisters."

Meg looked at the boy. She'd guess he was nine, maybe ten years old. That was a lot of responsibility for a child. Though knowing there was an uncle involved was some comfort.

"I kept looking for a means to keep the lions away so I could go to sleep at night and go to school by day. One day, I talked about it with Billy—he was in our village from Canada doing volunteer work at my school. We did an Internet search and found a boy like me who lived in Kenya. A Maasai boy. He discovered that lions do not like blinking lights. Billy sent a message on Facebook to his friends and family, asking them to help us to save the lions and the cows. The friends sent solar garden lights for power and blinking Christmas tree lights."

"And that did the trick?" Meg asked.

"Yes. The lions didn't bother my family's cows anymore. And I could go to bed at night. I changed the lights a little to slow down the blinking and to make the bulbs farther apart, one from the other. But they work very well. That is what is in my pack. I wish to give this as a gift to the family who lost their cow and ask them to please not hunt the lion. It must be a very young, very hungry lion to come near the boma that way."

"You know a lot about lions, it seems."

"I read as much as I could about them so that I could go to sleep."

Meg sent him a sympathetic smile. "Do you need to stay the night with the Maasai to show them how this works? Or are you staying the night, so you aren't walking alone after dusk?"

"To not walk alone."

"We're planning to be with the Maasai for about an hour or so this morning. Would that give you enough time to set this up and teach them what they need to know? You can come with us on the safari, then we can bring you back to your uncle at the end of the day. We'll be eating dinner here around seven."

Ahbou nodded his head energetically. "Yes, that would please me, thank you."

Meg watched Ahbou's eyes grow round, and from the sudden shade that crossed her face, she knew Rooster had meandered over.

"Ahbou, this is my friend Rooster."

"Rooster, sir?" He lifted his hand to cover his broad smile. "*Rooster?*" He looked at Meg and stuck his hands into his armpits, flapping his elbows.

"Pretty funny, huh?" Meg asked and patted his leg. "Come and get something to eat before we go."

"Oh no, Miss Doctor Meg. The food is for the guests."

"And today, you are my guest. Come on, let's get you a plate fixed up."

Rooster put his hand on her back as they moved toward the table.

"You checking to see if I ditched the vest?" She looked over her shoulder to catch his eyes. "We haven't gotten our room assignments yet. Where would I stash it?"

"So far, so good?"

"Yes, so far, I'd say it's mostly forgettable. The weight over the day may be a bit of an issue. I wish I were wearing a bra with some padding. It chafes a bit. You might want to offer that suggestion to your damsels in distress."

"If they were in distress, I wouldn't be doing a very good job. I'm supposed to help them avoid any issues beyond maybe a broken nail."

"Seriously? That's the kind of women you secure?"

"I'd say it's a seventy-thirty mix. Seventy percent of the women are business executives who need to be in the right place at the right time."

"Bullet free."

Rooster nodded. "But we still have the thirty percent of our female clients who just need someone to carry their packages when they go shopping."

"And who says you don't lead a glamorous life?"

"Not me. Can you tell me the plan for the day? Nice t-shirt, by the way."

Meg looked down at her gray t-shirt with a picture of a test tube. An arrow pointed toward the pink liquid, and the line read, "If you're not part of the solution…" Another arrow pointing at the sparkling solids gathering in the bottom and continued, "You're part of the precipitate." She gave a little chuckle. "I love geeky t-shirts. My kind of humor." She tilted her head back so she could look Rooster in the eye. "First thing, we'll meet with the Maasai elders to listen to some of their concerns this morning. We won't be offering them any solutions. We just want to know what's happening right now in their community. The rains weren't nearly as heavy this year as they should have been. I want to know how this is affecting the pasturing of their herds. About how much competition there will be between their herds and the wild animals for grazing. Ahbou is the one who is bringing a solution. I'm incredibly impressed."

Ahbou, hearing his name, turned to look at her.

"Before I leave today, I want to make sure you have my e-mail. I want to stay in touch with you."

"Thank you," he said, plate in hand as the server plunked a spoonful of baked beans next to his eggs.

Meg focused back on Rooster. "After that, we'll head out farther into the crater to see the animals. It's a beautiful day for it." Meg's eye fell on a middle-aged man with a yarmulke approaching the group. "That must be Abraham Silverman. He flew right into Kilimanjaro. I should introduce myself to him."

"Can I ask you something first?" Rooster said, running his hand down her arm.

Her skin under his fingers warmed to his touch. "Is this about Randy?" she asked.

"Just a general question. We try to keep a thumb on the pulse of things. You've been here in Eastern Africa for a while. You've talked to the people. Do you feel safe here?"

Meg drew a long breath through her nostrils. "That's a relative term. I feel safe enough. How's that?"

"There was a recent acid attack on a pair of British teenagers in Zanzibar."

"Yes. The government is going after the men who did that, tooth and nail. The girls were in the old customs house back in Stone Town, just up from our hotel. I read in the paper just this morning that they've detained five men. The Zanzibari police are interrogating them."

"Did the paper say what they thought happened?"

"It's very likely they're low-level Al-Qaeda operators. You know, there was a time well before 9/11 when Osama Bin Laden was very well received on the island. The Zanzibari boats, the *dhows*, even had his picture on their sails. Al-Qaeda doesn't want Western tourism to grow in Zanzibar. But that is counter to everything the Tanzanian government is working toward for its people."

"And the radicals are making their distaste for westerners known?"

"Well, we *are* Satan's spawn, right? Beyond Al-Qaeda, there are traditionalists who are concerned with progress. 'Cultural infestation' is the best translation for the term they're using. They're scared because languages are dying out, cultures are dying out. Different tribes are growing too small to continue, so they're merging with other tribes and adapting their languages. It's very fluid right now. There are anthropologists and linguists who are scrambling to document everything before these groups are lost. We're talking a generation, maybe two, until they're *gone*. The speed of loss is too much for a lot of people. That's one of the keys we hope to develop with our project. A way to protect cultural diversity while also helping with national and international assimilation."

They moved toward the food table, and Rooster handed her one of the white china plates, and a napkin rolled around a fork. She sensed something under Rooster's questions that she couldn't put her finger on. Was he worried about her safety in the area?

"How would you describe the atmosphere you'll be working in?" he asked.

Meg smiled and nodded toward the bowls of fruit, and the server put one on her plate. Rooster was after something. She wished he'd just flat-out ask what he wanted instead of pussy-footing around. "Things are churning for sure. It's like being at the confluence of two rivers—modern and traditional. They both have to exist in the same space, but that doesn't mean they flow together smoothly. Yes, please," she said to the eggs. "All the water has to share the same channel. There's only so much space. There are obstacles that we can't see easily. It makes things roil."

"And where are you in that picture?"

"One sausage, thank you." She glanced sideways at Rooster before stepping down the line. "I choose to be on the rock in the center, looking up and down the scene, trying to figure out how to keep things moving along, avoiding the treacherous whitewater, to continue the analogy."

"Three, please," Rooster said to the muffins. "Some people like whitewater. They think it's adventurous."

Meg got the impression she was getting a warning of some kind. "It's all fun and games until you hit a whirlpool." She picked up a champagne glass filled with juice.

"Meaning?"

"Whitewater can be deadly."

13

—————

MEG

The Ngorongoro Crater, Tanzania

THERE WERE TWENTY-SIX IN ALL. Twenty-one tourists. Eighteen of them were scientists. Randy, Rooster, and Ahbou were along for the ride, and five of their group were the hired interpreters required by the government to go out with tourists to keep them safe. That was the official line, but really it was to keep the visitors from doing stupid shit like trying to cuddle a cheetah cub or start a brush fire. The last time she was out, there was some guy who wanted to ride an ostrich-like he'd read about in Swiss Family Robinson when he was growing up. His boyhood dream was snapped—well, his femur was anyway.

The safari trucks held six each, so they divided among five vehicles. Meg, Randy, Rooster, Ahbou, and Abraham Silverman would be traveling together. They stood beside their truck, waiting for their driver.

"You're the only woman here," Rooster noted.

"That's usually the case. Science is still a man's world. Women are taking on bigger roles, but it's slow-going getting girls interested in math and science. I read a recent study that says girls start doubting their genius by the age of six."

Randy bumped his hip against Meg. "Meghan never doubted that she's a genius."

Meg gave Randy the stink eye. "I was born a scientist. Before I come to any conclusions, I need to see empirical data. Having been presented with nothing that would bring me to another conclusion, I stand by my hypothesis that I am intellectually capable until a peer-reviewed paper proves otherwise." She looked up as the lilting voice of their ranger called her to attention.

"Welcome to Ngorongoro Crater. You can call me Robert. As we drive to the Maasai bomo, I will be giving you a little background on your hosts, since today you will be greeted as their honored guests. Normally, visitors are only welcomed at two designated Maasai cultural bomas one near us and the other on the road to Serengeti. I am a member of the Maasai Tribe, and I live in the boma we are to visit. I will be translating our language, Maa, into English, and back again. I hope you will be patient with me as I do so. The elders have invited you because they are interested in learning what is happening to the weather. We thank you for coming." He gestured toward their SUV, and everyone climbed in.

"For many thousands of years, the Maasai people have been herders," Robert said, putting the SUV into gear and lurching forward on the red dirt road. "They traveled about to find good lands for their livestock and also were chased away by warring people. About two hundred years ago, our numbers became substantial in this area. We have lived in harmony with the wildlife and with the environment. We have strict taboos on eating wild animals. We only eat *our* animals." Robert stopped to point out the left-hand side of the vehicle. "You look there in the trees. You see vervet monkeys. Troop of monkeys, yes?"

"Yes," Meg said.

"Vervet monkeys are so close to your hotel because they are naughty. It is important that while you are in Ngorongoro that you witness the wildlife, but you do not interact with them. It is dangerous for them to become habituated to humans. We want them to remain shy, so they do not become pests. It is especially important that you do not feed them anything."

The vervet troop squatted along two of the wide tree limbs. Their big, round, brown eyes were set in black masks. White and grey fur covered their bodies, but it looked like each head was topped with a little brown toupee. One of the mothers hugged her infant to her shoulder. Meg raised her camera and adjusted the lens to zoom in on his little pink face and pointy ears. After she snapped the picture, Robert put the SUV back into gear, and they bounced forward again.

"The Maasai people are strong physically and mentally. Our ancestors developed different rites of passage to make this always true. Our children come to adulthood through a series of tests that involve pain. These tests help develop us as a people to have shared experiences. It makes us hardy and able to get through times of deprivation. We must follow our ancestral ways in order to survive. But as I am here talking to you as a cultural interpreter and not as a herder, some of us understand that we must both hold dear to our way of life but also adapt."

"Will you tell us some of the more important rites of passage?" Abraham Silverman asked. Meg knew this was his first trip to Africa. She remembered her first time here, how she had soaked up the culture like a dry sponge. It was ever fascinating to her.

"There are similarities between the girl children and the boy children, and there are differences. When they are around four, the children have their bottom incisor removed."

Meg turned to Ahbou and put her hand on his chin.

He grinned and showed her he had a gaping hole in the center of his bottom teeth.

"Ahbou, are you from the Maasai tribe?"

"No, Miss Doctor Meg, but many, many Africans remove that tooth, so if they get sick with lockjaw or cholera, they can have nutrition go into their mouth."

Robert nodded. "It is thought that the tooth gouging became important at the turn of the twentieth century when western medical doctors told us that lancing the gum at the tooth line could cure convulsions and diseases of the stomach, like cholera. They began to do this in Sudan, and before mid-century, it became common practice here in Tanzania."

Meg's brow drew together. "But that's wrong."

"That is what the doctors now tell us, but for over a century, we have tried to protect our children from becoming ill by following this ritual. And now, though we are told it has no merit in protecting us from cholera and other diseases, it is a big part of our rites of passage to show no fear. The children are not to flinch or cry when the tooth is removed, or it will be shameful. The young boys are also tested to face pain with a calm face by hot coals on their arms and legs, and as they become older, the boys are tattooed on their stomachs and arms. The elders do not do this with the needle like they use in the cities, but by thousands of little cuts into the skin."

"Only the boys? The girls are not tested this way?" Abraham asked.

"Both boys and girls are tested, but some things are different. The next way they do this is with the ear piercing. They take a hot iron, and they burn the ear. When this heals, they cut a hole in the earlobe. They gradually grow this hole bigger. This is now a fashion with some people in the west. In Europe and in America, they put plugs in their ears to make the holes big. Here, they grow the holes by inserting leaves and balls that are sometimes made of mud and wood. Though sometimes tourists will give us their plastic film canisters if they still use film instead of digital cameras. The bigger the hole, the more beautiful. The Maasai people feel that the most perfect earlobes hang to the shoulder."

Meg reached up and touched the little gold balls in her earlobes, thinking that she would not be considered very beautiful and probably a wuss because her holes were so small.

"Another rite of passage is circumcision. This is the most important ritual in a Maasai child's life. It is called excision for the girls."

Meg's whole body tightened down.

"It is the father's duty to make sure his children undergo this rite of passage," Robert said as they jostled over the uneven surface. "This, of course, involves a great deal of pain. It tests the child's courage. Flinching is a shameful thing. It brings dishonor to the families. If the boys flinch or cry out, the family will pay cattle for the shame. If he does not, then he is showing his bravery, and his family will be given cows and goats as a reward."

"How old are the boys when this happens?" Meg was looking at the side of Ahbou's face. His expression was neutral, but he held his body very still, as Robert explained.

"They go to the ritual hut as they are entering pubescence with their age mates. After the ceremony, they will have time to heal. You will see some youngsters in their grey or black cloaks, showing that they are recovering and healing as this rite has been performed recently for several youngsters in our boma. After this process, they will become warriors. This is a civic requirement. It is like military service in Israel. Is that not right, Dr. Silverman?"

"That used to be right. When I turned eighteen, I was required to do military service for three years. But that is no longer the case. Israel has become more selective, and now it's considered a privilege to serve."

"Ah, well, it is an honor to be a Maasai warrior too. The young boys look forward to this special time in their life. Believe me, it goes too fast."

"What makes you say that, Robert?" Meg leaned forward. "What did you like best about it?"

"Oh, the attention of the girlfriends. You could have as many girlfriends as you wanted. And being together with our age mates. We did everything with each other. We began our training by going and living in the bush, which I liked very much. I like to be with the wild animals. I feel a deep kinship with them. I liked having long hair. Only warriors are allowed long hair." He chuckled as he patted his shaved head. "When I danced, I could make my braids sail up and then land on the top of my head. It made me very popular with the girls."

Meg sent him a smile.

"The bush has many lessons to teach. It is important to learn respect for others and how to contribute to the welfare of the whole community. We were all very sad when our warrior time was over, and we went through our ceremony to become elders. Thereafter we must take a wife and provide for a family."

"And the girlfriends?"

"We could not keep them. We must choose a wife among the circumcised women. The girls must be very strong to go through this rite. It is good for them to go through the process. It prepares them for the pain of childbirth. It shows they are ready to be women. This rite happens as the girl becomes the right age to marry. If they were to become pregnant before excision, they would be banished, and they would carry this stigma for their whole life. After they go through this rite of passage, our women feel they do not have to be afraid of anything."

Meg felt her stomach churning. And while these girls could and would sit stoically while an elder cut away the hood of her clitoris, Meg simply couldn't wipe the sour look from her face just hearing about it. Rooster handed her a bottle of water. Meg took it gratefully, hiding her reaction by tipping the bottle back and drinking.

"When the girls heal, they will be ready to give birth to our next warriors. A few months after the rite, the young woman's husband will come to take her to live with his family." Robert pulled up under a tree and put the SUV in park. "Come, let me introduce you to the elders. They are gathering to welcome you."

Randy and Rooster stood beside Meg as she adjusted her clothes. "Randy, for heaven's sake. You owe me so big over this vest thing."

Randy gave her one of his grins, the kind he used when he wanted to be endearing. "I'll buy the drinks tonight."

"Least you could do," she grumped. Meg knew she was venting her feelings about the horrible plight of the Maasai girls —her view of it, at least—not her discomfort in the vest. The vest was mostly forgettable. She cast her gaze over to Horace Brindle. He was the Key Initiative's sociologist, and the *rites* of the girls versus the *rights* of girls was a big question that he was supposed to grapple with. Still. The pictures she'd conjured on the ride here were sticky and clung to her imagination, turning her stomach and making her wish she hadn't eaten so much of the English breakfast back at the hotel.

Randy scuffed his toe into the red dirt. "That's messed up,

man. I don't think I could sit through it if they wanted to circumcise me without flinching. My family would have to deal with the dishonor and pay a bunch of goats. I'm telling you, I'd scream like a girl."

"The girls aren't allowed to scream," Meg replied.

"Okay. I'd be squealing like a pig." Randy raised his brow. "That better?"

Meg canted her head. "You're not circumcised?"

"Not something that happens in El Salvador. The idea is kind of odd to me."

"But Rooster is from America. I imagine he's been circumcised." Meg wondered if it was weird for someone who was uncircumcised to be with a man who was. Then the pink rose in her cheeks as she realized she was imagining Rooster's dick.

Randy turned to catch Rooster's eye. "I thought they only did that to babies in the hospital with anesthesia and shit." He looked back at Meg. "Isn't that what happened with Kelly's baby?"

"Yes, and you know, in my duty as an aunt, at first I was going to try to talk her out of it, but there's a lot of science that says circumcision can be healthier for boys—reducing AIDS transmission, phimosis, and cancer, stuff like that. But there are no positives to excising a girl."

"Phimosis?" Rooster asked.

Meg held up a fist and wrapped her other hand around it to demonstrate. "That's when the foreskin becomes tight over the penis's head and becomes difficult to retract."

"Okay." Randy pushed her hands down. "I'm done with this conversation. I am not talking about retracting foreskin with my sister." He pointed toward their group. "That guy's waving us over."

"Hey, Randy." Rooster bumped into Randy as they moved to join the others. "If you need to piss, you might want to do it in private. These Maasai warriors see you've still got everything intact. They might insist on making a man of you."

"Asshole."

Rooster clapped his hands on Randy's shoulder, pushing him along in front. "I hear you, baby boy."

14

———

Meg

Ngorongoro Crater, Tanzania

Meg's stomach growled loudly. Ahbou covered his wide smile with his hand, but his eyes were laughing outright at the noise as they walked back to the SUV to head to the spot where they were to lunch. A group of warriors was to meet them there with a special treat.

Ahbou had been introduced to the boma by Robert. The two had both English and Kiswahili languages in common. Meg thought it was a good thing that Ahbou's words were spoken by a Maasai elder to his fellow elders. It gave them importance. The group was intrigued by the blinking lights and their success in Ahbou's village. Meg had been straining to hear them talk as she sat at a distance with the women. That the Key Initiative was populated by men would be an asset in this male-run world. But there was hope that the women could be empowered along the way, especially through education. Baby steps.

"Where did you learn English, Ahbou?" Rooster was standing next to the SUV, holding their door open for them.

"My mother was very clever with languages. She collected them like other women collect necklaces. She thought that English was going to be the most important language, so that is the language she taught us as babies."

Rooster shut their door after she and Ahbou climbed in, and leaned his arms on the window, listening.

"Was that a problem with her village?" Meg asked. "Teaching her children English as their first language?" The great mosaic of African languages, while wonderful, also caused confusion in terms of complex business dealings and modernization.

"When my mother married my father, she left her village. We lived in my father's village. They did not know she was teaching us English. They thought she was speaking to her children in her native language."

"But where did she hear English?" Meg pressed. "How did she learn? Did she go to school?"

"No school for girls, no. When she was little, there was a man who came from the Peace Corps in America to help them build a well and teach them to farm. He stayed for two years, and then he went home. He taught her English and how to read and left her with three books. The Bible. The Dictionary. And a book by Mr. Rudyard Kipling."

"Rikki-Tikki-Tavi?" Rooster said with a grin. "One of my favorite stories when I was your age."

"Yes, this is my favorite story too," Ahbou said. "I have always wished for a mongoose to protect me from the snakes here. The snakes are very deadly."

"You speak very well," Rooster said. "It's good to be able to communicate with lots of languages. Do you like to speak in English, or should we speak in Kiswahili?"

"English, please. When I was old enough to go to school with the boys from my father's village, they began to teach us English. But I spoke already, so I got to read the English textbooks and improve. I like to practice with English speakers too. If I go to university, I will need to be a very good speaker."

"Where is your mother now?" Meg reached around and tugged her ballistic vest down. "You told me your father had died."

"Yes, she died too. She and my sisters. They had cholera. This is why I study hard to become an engineer. I want everyone to have clean, safe water. I want to make it so good water is possible, no matter where the people live."

"That's very admirable. Your mother would be proud, I'm sure." Meg wanted to hug Ahbou, but she knew his stoicism was part of his culture, and to treat him as if he were to be pitied was the wrong thing to do. She worked hard to swallow her emotions. "So now you live with your uncle? Or do you have other family?"

"My uncle is my only family. I visit him. But I live at the school, in the dormitory."

"I'm glad you get this time with him. And I'm glad to have been here while you are on holiday." Meg's stomach rumbled again, and Ahbou lifted his hand to hide his grin. "Aren't you hungry, Ahbou?"

"We eat twice a day. Once when the sun comes up and once when the sun goes down. It is the tourists who must eat so many times a day."

Meg grinned. "Like the babies who must eat often?"

Now Ahbou was laughing. "Yes, like the babies."

A warrior climbed on top of their roof, and Robert started the car and drove. At the boma, each vehicle had picked up one Maasai warrior who rode on the roofs of the SUVs. Having a warrior along for the ride was a win-win. It gave their families money, and there was no better way of staying safe. These men could read the ground, the sway of the trees, and lethal spears were wielded by those who had been raised to face down lions.

They were considered men here. By American standards, the warriors were just entering their teenage years. An age when many US kids would be hard-pressed to get their rooms clean and take the trash out, Meg mused. Of course, here, the village relied on their abilities to safeguard the herds that were their family's wealth. They were revered by the village and given special honors for their courage.

They drove past a herd of zebras grazing next to a majestic giraffe. It was all so postcard perfect. Rooster and Randy were snapping pictures as Robert fed them information. "Just ahead, we have prepared a special demonstration before your lunch. There will be English-style food served, but first, we show you an example of Maasai foods."

An SUV angled across the field and drove toward them. Robert brought his vehicle to a stop. "Here is Inga Koskinen. She is a field biologist with the Serengeti Wildlife Project. She has been documenting the comings and goings of the lion population and helps the Maasai take evasive action so that the lions do not kill our herds." He leaned his head out the window and gave her a wave.

"*Jambo!* Robert. I'm tracking two lions—Tamu and Furaha. Their mother was killed about two weeks ago, and I'm worried about them. They were just beginning to hunt. I hear there was a killing last night near your village. Have you spoken to your elders?"

"They are working with our warriors—they are saying to not

track the lion and kill him. But there is agitation among the warriors. They want the same opportunity to prove their bravery as their fathers and grandfathers had. The elders are advocating that the papers be filed, and the family paid for the lost cow."

"We don't want any of the warriors to be arrested. I think it might have been one of the lions I'm trying to find. They're probably very hungry. If they killed a cow, though, they'll need to be relocated to the wildlife preserve."

"The kill happened very close. The mothers are frightened for their children."

"Understandably so. I would appreciate the Maasais' help in locating these lions. I want to make sure everyone is safe."

Robert turned and gestured back. "Ahbou has brought us an invention he says works in his village to keep the lions away."

Inga looked into the car at young Ahbou and got a bemused look on her face, then she saw Meg sitting beside him. "Meg, good to see you. I heard the Initiative was getting underway. Let us know how we can help."

"Thanks, Inga. I'll do that."

"I don't mean to hold you all up." She turned her attention to Robert. "You were a warrior. You know how they think and how they will act. You also know how imperative it is for your boma to follow the new laws. You'll do everything in your power to stop the warriors from hurting these lions, won't you?"

Robert's body grew tense. "I will continue to talk to them. I will call you if we find the lion."

"Thank you." And with a wave, she drove off.

The picnic area was just ahead. Meg could see that the SUVs were forming a protective circle around a trailer.

Robert stopped and turned to speak to their little group. "The Maasai people are known for our Olympic levels of stamina and conditioning. We can run for miles on end without stopping to eat or drink. We get our good health from our diet. We eat very little. Some tea in the morning. If it is the rainy season, then we may drink some milk or a yogurt-like drink that is fermented and lumpy. Though we also eat a little fat, honey, and tree bark, the Maasai diet is almost one hundred percent protein, which comes from milk, blood, and meat.

"We get our salt from the blood we drink. Otherwise, salt is prohibited. Other foods that are prohibited are chicken, fish, and any wild game. For the warriors, though, their sole source of nutrition comes from their livestock. They eat meat as a group in a quiet place away from women. There are many taboos about food. For example, men must not eat meat that has been in contact with a woman, or has been handled by an uncircumcised boy after it has been cooked." He looked directly at Meg. "If you please, as there are Maasai here for the demonstration, and male cooks here from the hotel, if you would allow me to serve you and Ahbou, it will allow these men to be able to eat, as well."

"Um, yeah. Sure." Meg replied.

Meg could just barely hear Rooster when he leaned over and whispered into Randy's ear, "You should sit next to Meg and Ahbou and let Robert serve you too. You don't want to taint a man's meat."

Randy's elbow slammed into Rooster's ribs.

Robert continued. "First, we will show you how the Maasai traditionally butcher their goats. We will then demonstrate how to make honey beer, and you will eat the catered foods which are more comfortable for westerners. I believe today you have beef kababs with rice and vegetables. And chocolate cookies. We will leave before the goat is ready to eat, and the warriors will have it tonight for their supper."

Meg's stomach gave an all-out plea for food that made the whole group chuckle. "Meg will want a snack first, of course.

Rooster, the Maasai warriors would like to give you the honor of killing the goat." And with that, they all climbed from the truck.

"Hear that?" Rooster said. "I think they've guessed your secret, baby boy. They need a real man to do a warrior's job." Rooster stretched to his full height and flexed his muscles.

Randy gave him a shove.

They moved inside the circle of SUVs. The warriors stood beside a bed of leaves. Robert gestured for Meg to sit on a fallen log and Ahbou to sit next to her, then handed Meg a napkin with four chocolate cookies wrapped inside.

She watched Abraham looking into the trees and shadows as he wandered toward the others. She could tell he'd done a stint in the Israeli military. He, Randy, and Rooster all had that same vigilance thing going on. The scientists all sat on the other side of the circle, and Randy was shooed in that direction, though he had tried to stay near her. She and Ahbou were clearly segregated from the group. She handed two of the cookies to Ahbou.

Robert and Rooster moved toward the goat. Robert was pointing and using his hands to help explain what it was that Rooster was expected to do. The little white goat was munching contentedly on leaves, held in place by a slim rope held by one of the Maasai. *This kind of sucks.* Meg had no idea this demonstration would be taking place. It certainly wasn't anything she'd agreed to. She understood it was an honor to witness, but one she would gladly have foregone.

Rooster nodded and then looked her way. She read worry on his face and thought it was directed at her. Like he was asking her to turn her back and not watch. Yes, that was the distinct impression that he gave her, *don't watch.*

"Ahbou, is it bad for a woman to be here while the goat is being killed?"

"I don't know, Miss Doctor Meg. Women cooked the meat in my village, and the children served it to the men."

She looked back at Rooster. He still had his eyes on her, only turning away when they pressed the rope into his hands.

Rooster reached down and caught the goat in his arms, turning his back to block the sight. She'd expected them to hand Rooster a knife. Instead, he went down into a squat, laying the kicking goat in the leaves and leaning forward with one knee on its shoulder and the other on its hips. The goat struggled but couldn't squirm his way out from under the weight that Rooster brought down on it. He caught the goat under the chin with one hand and held its muzzle with the other. He was suffocating the goat as it thrashed under him.

The warriors were smiling and nodding at Rooster's technique. It went on and on. Finally, the goat stopped moving, and Meg thought, thank god, its suffering was over. Then from some inner will to survive, it thrashed again, desperate to get free. Bile gathered at the back of her tongue. Now she realized why Rooster hadn't wanted her to see that. It wasn't a quick plunge of the knife into its heart or the flash of a blade across the carotid that would have bled out almost immediately. This was a scene of misery. But thankfully, it was finally over.

Meg looked at the ground between her legs. *That definitely sucked.* She realized she was gripping the cookies, crushing them in her fist.

Robert stood a little ways apart from the warriors, speaking to the men gathered on the other side of the circle. "Come forward, and you can see why we do this. It is our tradition to suffocate the goat because it keeps all of the blood in the vital parts of the body. Blood is not wasted by making the goat bleed to death. Blood is an important part of our diet."

One of the warriors sliced the goat open. "You see here? The blood is coagulating in the chest cavity and is easy to retrieve. This is the time the warriors like to eat the blood. It is still warm from the body. The warriors invite you to try it."

A few of the scientists moved forward and scooped up some of the jelly-like blood globs and sucked them into their mouths. Others demurred. Robert sent Meg and Ahbou a look that told them they weren't invited. *Thank goodness.* Meg was the kind of person who was all-in when she traveled. If they ate it, she ate it. If they slept there, she slept there. If they jumped off a cliff, well, she wasn't suicidal. She'd check it out and see if she thought it was doable for her, and then she'd jump off the cliff. Granted, some of those experiences were awesome, and some not so much.

One of the Maasai reached into the carcass and pulled out the kidneys, offering one to Robert and one to Rooster. Meg assumed that these were choice parts offered to Robert as the elder and Rooster as the warrior who made the kill. Rooster reached around to draw Randy forward. Meg couldn't tell if it was to include Randy in the honor or if he was still giving Randy shit. Randy reached out his hand to accept the kidney, then popped it in his mouth.

"The fresh kidney tastes sweet," Robert explained to the others. "Much better than when it is cooked." He poured a little water on his hands and then wiped them with a cloth before he helped Randy and Rooster wash up too. "The warriors will put the meat onto skewers and put them over the coals in the fire they made on the other side of our circle."

A man moved into the ring. A big blue plastic bucket with a lid tightly attached dragged at his hand.

"This is honey beer." Robert grinned. "In just a moment, I will show you how it is made. But first I would like you to taste it. Be careful, though. Honey beer is very strong."

There was a visible shift in the warriors' moods. They had been happy enough before, but now they were all smiles. Meg stood up to stretch her legs. The log was making her butt numb.

As Robert set up to dispense the beer, Rooster came to stand next to her. "I can see it in your eyes. You're upset with me."

"I'm upset, yes." She thought she'd done a better job of hiding her emotions. "Not with you." Meg turned her head and tried to swallow, but her throat had closed up, and her mouth was filled with saliva. She reached into her pocket for her bottle of water and shoved her crumb-filled napkin into the other one to free her hands to get the top off. She took a swig, hoping to clear a path. "I get that the warriors plan to eat the goat. This is how they survive. In the wild, I watch animals kill animals all the time. I don't know why watching this affected me like it did. I know you were trying to make it as quick and as painless as possible. It's probably very hypocritical of me. I eat meat. I just don't want to see the death process." She chuckled before taking another swig. "I'd make a terrible farm girl."

Rooster considered her for a moment. He seemed to be choosing his words carefully. "I have the feeling you're not so much upset about the goat, but that the way it died made you remember something you would have preferred to leave in the past."

Meg thought back to the three things Rooster had told her about herself that Randy wouldn't have mentioned. Rooster had been correct on all three. He really did seem to have the knack for reading her like she was words on a typewritten page.

Rooster was close enough that Meg could smell the clean scent of his laundry detergent. She stared at one of his buttons, not wanting to acknowledge that he was right again. She had the sudden urge to curl into him and lay her head on his chest. She wanted nothing more than to cower there until the memories passed. When Rooster held down that goat, and it had struggled, that was a scene she had seen through stair rails when she was little. Her father had trapped her mom, struggling in her white nightgown. Her mom had fought and fought against his hands until she stopped. Limp, he dragged her by the foot to the other room.

Rooster slid his hand down Meg's arm and held her hand in his. "I'm sorry you remembered."

Meg tipped her head back to see his face, and she found concern and kindness in his eyes.

He reached up to catch a strand of her hair that blew across her face in the breeze, pushing it back behind her ear. Meg's gaze drifted to Rooster's mouth. She wondered what it would be like to kiss his full lips. They looked warm and soft.

"Honey," Randy called, and like a light switch snapping on, Meg came back to her senses. What the hell was she thinking? Even if he weren't in a relationship with Randy, as a woman, she was definitely not Rooster's type.

15

———

Ngorongoro Crater, Tanzania

MEG TOOK another sip from her cup. It didn't taste like beer at all. It tasted sweet and fermented, like a fruit drink. She moved the beer around her mouth, trying to decide what it tasted like. Watered-down orange juice, maybe? But it was delicious. She took another drink as she watched Robert demonstrate how it was made.

"This will be ready in three- or four days' time," Robert said. "I have started the processes by warming some water. Then I take this." He held up a section of root. "This is aloe vera root. It is farmed here in Tanzania. We dip each end into ash and put it in the water. Now we add hot embers from the fire. Most important is the honey." Robert called out some words in Maa. A warrior came over with a paddle that was covered in honey, with bees dancing angrily in the golden goo. He put the whole thing down in the water. A few bees escaped before Robert clapped the top onto the bucket.

Robert caught Meg's eye. "Do you like this?"

"I do. It's refreshing and fizzy."

"It's strong, though, so be careful. It is stronger than most wines. If you drink too much, you will be singing and dancing." Robert lifted his elbow and flicked a bee from his skin.

The warriors were refilling their cups from the first bucket. They were laughing and singing together, preening each other like Meg had with her girlfriends back in high school. Fixing each other's hair.

Meg leaned over to tap Ahbou's shoulder. "I bet your wife will make honey beer. Have you thought about what she will look like?"

"Oh, yes. Her gums will be black. She will have very white teeth, and her legs will be slightly bowed."

"That sounds lovely. And what kind of person will she be?"

"I would like her to be a teacher. To know a lot of things from books. And she will smile with her eyes and talk softly."

Meg had her eye on Robert. He had moved to the side and looked at his arm. She thought he'd probably been stung. She wondered if the kitchen trailer had any ice for him and started to go and check. But she second-guessed herself. If the Maasai men could sit there and be circumcised without flinching, going over and mothering Robert over a bee sting might be dishonorable for him. She wasn't even sure she was allowed on that side of the camp.

As she watched closer, Robert didn't look good. He touched his lips. Ran his hand down his throat. His face looked like it might be swelling. He slapped a fist into his chest.

Meg stood up and stared right at the back of Rooster's head.

She must have been sending out palpable thought rays because Rooster, Randy, and Abraham all started toward her.

Meg kept watch on Robert as he wobbled around the back of the food trailer. "Rooster, can you go check on Robert? A bee stung him, I'm pretty sure. I think he's having an allergic reaction."

Rooster slid away, blending with the shadows, doing a good job to preserve Robert's privacy if Meg were mistaken. After a moment, Randy's phone rang. He pulled it from his pocket. "You're on speaker."

"I need the Kiswahili word for Epinephrin."

Meg shook her head. She had nothing. "Ahbou, do you know the word for Epinephrine?"

Ahbou looked at Meg and blinked. Meg explained. "It's a medication that comes in a shot. People who have bad allergies carry it with them. Do you know the word?" She drew an arc with her arm as if she were administering the shot into her thigh.

"I have seen this. I can explain the word," he said and leaned over the phone to speak Kiswahili words that Meg had never needed to know and so had no fluency in.

Meg understood Robert's "no." She heard how labored Robert's breathing had become. She turned to Abraham. "Look in the other SUVs see if they have anything that would help. Ice pack. Decongestant. Anything."

She grabbed Ahbou's arm and moved toward their SUV to do the same. "Can you tell me what he said?"

"That he has swollen from bee stings before, but this time it is swelling his heart in his chest. He can't breathe."

She pulled out the first aid kit and clawed through the contents. *Nothing*. She pulled Ahbou into the SUV and drove behind the canteen, parking it where they could load Robert up.

Randy was checking Robert's pulse. Abraham came around the corner, shaking his head. "There's nothing."

"Let's move," Rooster said. He, Randy, and Abraham worked like they were a trained team as they lifted Robert and trundled him over to the SUV.

Meg jumped into the driver's seat. She drew Ahbou along with her. She felt responsible for his whereabouts and didn't want him getting lost in the shuffle. And she might need him to translate. Meg scrolled through her contacts and got the hotel on the phone. "This is Meg Finley. This is an emergency, is there a doctor on staff?" She thought that of the scientists on their task force, Dr. Clemmons, the other American who was a physician, would have been the most helpful. But he was stuck back in the US with visa issues.

"No, miss. No doctor."

"Can you direct me to the nearest clinic if I give you GPS coordinates?"

"No, miss. No doctor."

Okay, this wasn't helpful. She said a quick goodbye. They had Robert in. Randy held him up in a half-sitting position in the center row. Rooster and Abraham squeezed into the back.

"I don't want to just start driving. We need a destination, or I might just end up backtracking. I need a second." She pulled up a Google search and put in *Ngorongoro Clinic* and found only one. When she pulled up the GPS coordinates and put them into her map, it said she was fifty-two kilometers away as the bird flies. Shit, that was far. The wheezing behind her head sounded dangerously labored. Meg shoved the SUV into gear. Pushing the phone toward Ahbou, she shifted to second. "Hold this out and make sure that red arrow stays on the green line. Randy, how are we doing?"

"The sooner, the better, Meg."

When they had loaded Robert in the car, he had all the signs she knew to look for—his dark skin seemed overly pale, his face and lips were swollen, his eyes mere slits. She could imagine how tightly his windpipe was being squeezed by the swelling. Her foot came down on the clutch. She jerked them in quick succession from second to third to fourth gear, then she kept her foot pressed heavily on the gas pedal. Meg was accustomed to driving in the wilds of Africa, but she berated herself for unseating her passengers as she plowed ahead, hitting the rocks and bumps at near-reckless speeds. Meg's hands were shaking. She was sweating profusely. The bulletproof vest was hot as hades, and she longed to have the luxury of time so she could rip it off. "Ahbou, do you know of any herbs or anything that is available at the villages that helps people when they swell from bee stings?" She turned her head toward him for a split second. "Put your seatbelt on this minute."

Ahbou reached for the belt as he was told. "If they swell a little, there are pastes that the grandmothers make by chewing herbs and then mixing it with clay. They put this on the sting. But when people swell like Mr. Robert, there is nothing to do but sing."

The SUV bounced hard, and Meg set her teeth. "Sorry. Sorry." She glanced down at the phone to make sure they were on track. She was on the line, but they didn't seem to be making any progress. "Have you ever heard of a tourist getting hurt or sick out in the crater? If they are badly hurt, is there someone who comes to help?"

"The park ranger is there to help." He sat quietly for a moment, then added. "My uncle told me that one time they called the helicopter to come."

"A helicopter? Yes. Great. Who sent the helicopter? Is there a military base near here?"

"Not soldiers. The doctor helicopter."

"From…?"

"From the hospital in Arusha."

"Rooster?" Meg called.

"On it."

"Meg, he's got no airway," Randy called. "Stop. Stop."

Meg brought the SUV to an abrupt halt. She was out of her seat and popping open the door to where Robert lay. He looked inhuman as she picked up his limbs by the pants legs the way she'd been trained in her survival courses. They hauled him out of the vehicle and had him on the ground. Meg started mouth to mouth, trying to force her breath through even the slightest of passageways down into the man's lungs.

Randy was checking his carotid, and she guessed he didn't find a heartbeat because he started CPR.

"Fifteen minutes," Rooster said as he joined the scene.

They worked as a team. Ahbou watched the time. Every three minutes, they switched positions. She or Abraham did the breaths. Randy or Rooster did the compressions. Their battle-hardened chest and arm muscles bulged with the effort of forcing Robert's chest to descend the two-inch minimum that could force his heart to pump. When Ahbou called time, and the teams switched places, those who were catching their own breaths put their back to the scene. It was imperative that they kept a keen eye out for the predators who could smell the sick and dying in the wind and might be coming in to feast. This was dangerous for all of them. Buzzards circled above to direct the predators to the right spot. The birds needed the hunters to open the carcasses so they could pick the bones clean. A hungry hyena or cheetah would see Robert as a feast and also see that he had a comparatively weak and ineffectual pack around him. "Ahbou, get into the SUV and roll up the windows. Keep watching the time for us, and when you get to the three-minute mark, I want you to blare the horn for a count of five. Leave the window down a few centimeters so I can talk to you," Meg ordered as she took her place on the other side of Abraham, ready to switch when Ahbou signaled.

Randy was singing a song that kept the pace and set the tone. It sounded hopeful. But Meg's hopes dwindled with each switch.

"Time," Ahbou called from behind the closed door. Then he blared the horn that Meg hoped would keep the predators at a distance.

In Meg's mind, if she had three minutes on and three minutes off, she should only have three turns before she heard the rotors on the helicopter. This was her fourth cycle. All she heard was Randy singing. It was a fast-paced beat that had worked its way into her pulse, making her blood run furiously through her veins. Randy wasn't giving up. She shouldn't either. They'd keep working on Robert. But God, he looked awful. She blew as hard as she could, and she felt most of her breath slipping out between where her lips locked around his. The seal she'd tried to create was failing under the pressure of her breath. Her lungs hurt from the effort. Robert's lips were blue. And there was nothing.

No signs of life.

"I hear them," Ahbou screamed from inside the car. He popped the door open.

Meg turned her head to suck in another mouthful of air but used it for Ahbou instead of Robert. "Get back in that car and stay there," she yelled with an authority she'd never heard come out of her mouth before.

The wind picked up around them. Debris sprayed every-where. Randy had ducked his head down, he was no longer singing, but she could feel the movement as he kept pushing down that vital two inches. One hundred and twenty times per minute. Two times per second. He was a robot.

She had her mouth back on Robert's, but the air she was sucking in to transfer was filled with pebbles and sticks. She coughed it back up. Rooster pulled his shirt off, leaning over her, using his body and the fabric to encapsulate her head and Robert's in a makeshift tent, protecting them as she sucked in air through her t-shirt she'd pulled over her mouth, then lifted her chin to clear the cloth and sealed her mouth over Robert's swollen lips. It was slower. But it was something.

The copter set down at a short distance, and the wind died down a bit as the rotors ground to a stop. Rooster switched places with Randy. Randy lay on his back, sucking air, exhausted from his exertion. Meg didn't sense Abraham nearby. She assumed he was helping the rescue workers somehow. She longed for a break but kept powering through, forcing air down Robert's windpipe.

Rooster sat back, clearing her view as a syringe plunged into Robert's thigh. She felt a hand on her shoulder, and Meg scrambled out of the way. She sat on her heels as she watched the medic try to force an intubation tube through Robert's nostril. Another medic ran an IV.

The medical team worked with precision and mastery. When they didn't get the results that they wanted, they rummaged through their bags and pulled out a surgical kit. They would perform an emergency trach right there in the red dirt of the crater.

Meg moved to the SUV. "Ahbou, don't blare the horn anymore. The medic needs to cut open Robert's neck, and we don't want his hands to jump."

Ahbou looked over to where the doctors were working. The surgery was fast. The tube already inserted, a ventilator in place, and one of the men was bagging Robert with an attached oxygen tank. On the count of three, they rolled Robert onto a backboard, strapped him down with spider restraints, and carried him to the helicopter. From the time they set down until the time they were loaded for take-off, it was probably another two cycles on the watch. But Meg felt she'd aged a decade.

16

MEG

Room 508

MEG HAD SHOWERED and taken her time drying and curling her hair, putting on her mascara and perfume, and choosing her dress. She wanted to feel the opposite she had out in the crater, among the dusty gusts of the helicopter's take off. She was biding her time before she made the call to check on Robert. She was afraid of what she'd hear on the other end of the line.

She sat on the side of her queen-sized poster bed draped in filmy mosquito netting. Her room could easily have been in a movie. Dark wood, white walls, deeply saturated jewel-toned cushions. Her window was open to a tiny balcony, and the floor-to-ceiling lace curtains murmured in the breeze.

She picked up the phone with a shaking hand. Even if Robert hadn't made it, they had tried. They did everything they could. She tried to console herself. The medic on scene had reached into his pocket and thrust a card at her before they rushed off.

She looked at it lying next to the phone, pushed her hair back, and released her breath in a rush. She dialed nine for an outside line, followed by the numbers listed for Dr. Kabourou's cellphone. It was funny to her how she ran into cell tower issues at home in Maryland, but here in Tanzania, there were few places the cellphones didn't work.

Almost every Maasai tribal member that she knew had their own phone.

Dr. Kabourou answered on the second ring.

"*Jambo!*" she said, encircling her throat with slender fingers. "I'm Dr. Meg Finley. You gave me your card this afternoon when you took our guide to the hospital. He called himself Robert. I'm sorry, I don't know his real name. But I was hoping…" Meg blinked away the tears that warped her vision. She had little hope, actually.

"Yes. Yes. The guide had disrepair from the field tracheotomy. He was taken to surgery. He is in recovery now."

Meg was stunned. Robert's condition when he left was, she thought, not survivable.

"We don't yet know how much brain damage he sustained. You may call again tomorrow."

"Thank you, I will." Meg's elation was dashed by the possibility that Robert would be left brain damaged. What kind of life would he have if they saved his body but not his brain?

Dr. Kabourou must have sensed her angst because he added, "I will tell you that when we checked his oxygen levels on the helicopter, they were much better than we expected. Your team did everything possible. Call tomorrow, maybe around lunch. I will check his charts for you myself."

"Thank you," Meg repeated and hung up the phone.

She looked around the room. Her hand skated over her rose-colored bedspread. She wondered who had slept there before her.

Were they happy? Were they in love? Did someone love them in return? She wondered if Robert had a wife and family and if they knew what had happened. Maybe she could send word somehow. She made a mental note.

On the dresser lay the vest she'd had on all day. It was saturated with her sweat. It was going to stink. But Meg didn't know how to clean it. She'd just take it to Randy and let him deal with it. She wasn't sure which room Rooster and Randy would have chosen. They'd each been handed their own key when they came in to talk to the hostess.

She headed to the closest one first, stopped at the door, and gave a light rap.

Randy swung the door open. He was still damp from his shower and had a white towel knotted around his waist. He stepped back and let her in. "Where's Rooster?" she asked as she took in the empty bathroom, moving toward the chairs.

"The others came in from their day. We figured they saw us hightail it out of there, but no one saw Robert go down but us. He's telling the guides what happened and making sure word gets to Robert's family."

"Oh, good. That was next on my list of things to do. So now all I have to check off is drinking."

"Sounds good to me. Let me pull my clothes on and text Rooster to meet us in the bar. You look nice, by the way. What do you call that color, plum? It looks good on you." Randy pulled a pair of trousers and a button-down shirt from the closet.

"Thanks." Meg adjusted the spaghetti straps of her full-length dress. She loved the feel of silk blowing against her legs in an evening breeze. "They unpacked my clothes and ironed them for me. I'm impressed by the service."

He moved to the other side of the dressing screen and pulled off his towel, flipping it over the top. "A huge step up from where I just came from."

"I called the hospital about Robert. Tell Rooster when you text that he's alive, but they don't know about the long-term effects yet."

Randy came out, tucking his shirt in his pants, then doing up the top button and buckling his belt. "Wilco."

"Come on. Let's go have that well-deserved drink. You said you'd buy." She pointed to the vest in her hand to remind him why.

ROOSTER WAS HEADING down the hall in their direction. Meg raised her hand from their bar table to wave him over. He was dressed in a pair of trousers that showed off his slender waist. His blue silk shirt displayed the expanse of his chest and shoulders. Meg got a flash of him hunkered against her, bare-chested, using his shirt to filter the debris kicked up from the helicopter, blocking the battering winds and allowing her to continue with the resuscitation. It hadn't registered at that moment but had obviously made its way into her subconscious. She tipped back her glass of hibiscus wine. Yup, she was undressing Rooster in her mind, and she was well aware how wrong that was and on how many levels.

She showed her empty glass to the bartender, then turned back to Randy to respond to the jibe he'd made before she'd caught sight of his boyfriend. "Randy, you are so full of crap." Maybe she should watch how much she drank tonight. She probably needed to have control of her tongue and her expressions with Rooster's powers of observation. How horrible would it be if he knew what was *still* playing in her mind?

"You calling me a liar?"

"I'm telling you you're full of crap."

"Yeah? I'll tell you what, I challenge you to a game of bull's-eye/bullshit." He tipped his head toward the dartboard at the back of the room.

"You're on." Meg stood and headed toward the board, pulled the darts off, and moved to a closer table where Randy carried his beer.

Rooster strode over. He laid his hand on Meg's back as he pulled out a chair for her.

She looked up at him with a smile. "Hey there, where's your shadow?" Meg asked a little too brightly as Rooster's warmth spread across her bare skin. "Did Ahbou go home with his uncle?"

"With you and Randy over here cussing up a storm, I'm not going to subject the little guy to your locker room behavior."

The bartender brought Meg another glass of wine. "And you, sir?"

"I'll have the same as Randy." Rooster pointed at Randy's beer. "You good? Can I get you another?" He put his hand on Randy's shoulder.

"Thanks, Honey."

Rooster lifted two fingers.

"Ahbou?" Meg redirected the conversation.

"The cook is giving him dinner in the kitchen. He's going to hang out there until his uncle is done for the day."

"He's still working? But he was here at breakfast."

"He's covering for a friend who's sick. What's this game you've got going on?"

"Randy's getting ready to bare his soul. The game goes like this—there are a questioner and a player. The questioner can ask any personal question they want. The player then tries to get out of answering by hitting a bull's-eye. If they get one, their turn is ended, and they're no longer in the hot seat. The danger is that the longer you play, or the drunker you get, the more personal the questions become. Truth is a requirement. The questioner can't go on forever. They only get three questions, and then, if there are more than two people playing, the questioner and player shift one to the right. Okay?"

"All right," Rooster said, reaching for the darts Meg held out to him. "Normally, I'd say ladies first. But having just learned that the questions get more private as we play, seems like a good strategy to request that I go first."

"Fine by me," Meg said. "But you have to stand farther back than the line, Rooster. If you stand where a normal-sized person would, you could just reach out and place the dart on the board."

"Are you calling me a freak?"

"Is that my first question? I thought you wanted to play first."

"Funny." Rooster didn't even line himself up, he just threw the dart, and it landed in the green circle just outside of the bull's-eye. "So close."

"An inch is as good as a mile." Meg leaned her hips back into the table. "First question—how'd you know about me?"

Rooster canted his head. "More specific?"

"How did you know I took ballet but wanted to climb trees?"

Rooster smiled. "You point your toes when you lift your foot. You stand in third position when you stop walking—"

Meg raised a questioning brow.

"My sister, Mary Margaret, took dance most of her life, and I got dragged along when I wished I was climbing trees instead. As to the tree part, you want to be out in nature, and you have an adventurous spirit. That's something you were born with."

Rooster was grinning when he threw a haphazard dart at the board. "Next question?"

"My horse?" She sat down in her seat.

"When you sit, you put the balls of your feet on the rungs of your stool like a stirrup. Heels down. Mary Margaret and I rode as kids. I saw firsthand how the girls at the stable were in love with their horses. That one was part observation, part guess."

"Here's the one I really want to know, how'd you know my father was left-handed?"

Rooster looked over at Randy.

Randy tilted his head. Meg guessed Randy was wondering too. Rooster lined his body up and took a few practice jabs with his arm. On the last extension, the dart flew toward the red center.

Meg held her breath. She really wanted to know the answer. Especially since this time, Rooster obviously didn't want to tell her.

Randy lifted off his stool and walked toward the board. "Guess I'm the referee on this one." He pulled the dart from the very top of the tiny center bullseye on the line between the red and green. "I'd say it's a miss." He set his jaw and looked at Rooster square on.

Meg was intimidated by the power behind Randy's glare and his slow walk back toward Rooster. Rooster didn't rise to the bait Randy was laying out. Meg wasn't clear what that was about. But she found herself holding her breath.

Rooster raised his eyebrows, a question, nothing else.

Meg was still confused. And she still wanted her answer. She waited.

Rooster sniffed and turned away from Randy, moving around the table to sit on her right-hand side. He laid his hands flat on the table, fingers splayed. "When I walked out to greet you at the airport, I was watching you and Randy."

This doesn't have to do with baseball, Meg thought. He had observed something other than how she caught the puzzle ball that Randy tossed her.

"When I approached, you noticed that I was tall, but when you went to hug me, and I lifted my left hand, you squinted and ducked your head. Your dad used to hit you in the face and head with his left hand. Randy and you are close to the same size, and you know and trust him. You didn't know or trust me yet. I'm guessing you were about ten when your father left your life."

Meg blinked. She had been exactly ten when Paul left. He'd gotten drunk on her birthday, beaten her mom and all three kids, then passed out. It was the last straw. Her mom called the cops, and he'd been hauled off to jail and convicted in short order.

Men who abuse kids don't fare well in prison. He died when one of his ribs was broken and perforated his lung. Jim Finley came into the picture about a year later. He'd married her mom and adopted all three kids. Old memories didn't lie so deep that they couldn't be dredged up by the simple fact that Rooster was damned tall, he was an unknown quantity, and she still protected the right side of her face.

"You handled me somehow, to make me feel safe, didn't you?" It wasn't exactly an accusation, but some part of her was a little ticked off to think about all that shit again. And Rooster had brought it up by his sheer size. It was the second time today she was swimming in those memories. Of course, she *had* asked. And the rules were the rules. You were honor-bound to tell the truth. She didn't want to think of herself as damaged goods. She didn't want Rooster to think she was either.

"I manipulated the circumstances, not you."

Meg tried to blink away the unexpected surge of anger. "What did you do?"

"I kept my distance, and when we walked together, I offered you my left arm to hold. That way, I wouldn't do anything that would surprise you. I didn't want you triggered."

Well, that was reasonable. And gentlemanly. Meg swallowed. "Thank you."

"Fuck, Meg. Why didn't you ever tell me about you and your family?"

"I guess we both have secrets about our lives, huh, Randy? Things that we're just now letting each other know about?" Randy looked like he was thoroughly confused. Meg hated that this little walk down nightmare lane was marring their brief time together. So what if Randy hadn't told her he was gay? He had every right to explore his relationships in private. "Let's change the subject. Let's focus on Randy." She forced herself to smile, even though she knew Rooster could tell she was trying to end that conversation.

"I'm up." Randy moved to the dartboard.

"I know just about everything I care to know about Randy," Rooster said as he sent her a wink. He was playacting too, Meg knew. He was probably worried about how much he'd upset her, how many bad memories had been dredged up. "Why don't you ask the question?"

"All right, good. I want to know about your call sign. Why do they call you Randy?" Meg had always assumed she knew what the call sign was about. But if he'd been hiding his sexuality from his teammates, then it wouldn't be the British term for horny.

"He didn't tell you?" Rooster asked.

"All he said was that for security's sake, once he became a Ranger, to please only call him Randy in public."

Randy threw his dart and missed. "Randy is an acronym, not a word."

"That's not enough." Meg protested.

Randy popped his eyebrows a few times and grinned.

"Fine. What's the first letter of your call sign stand for?"

He threw and missed.

"R is for? What? Come on, Randy."

"Ricochet," he said.

"—ing." Rooster added. "Ricochet*ing*."

Randy squinted his eyes at Rooster and shook his head.

Oh, she'd found a hot spot. "Okay, I get another one. What's the second letter stand for? The way you throw darts, I'll get the whole truth before the night is through."

Randy hit a bull's-eye.

Meg got up for her turn.

"I'm coming for you, Meg." Randy sent her a wicked grin. "I've got a good one too."

Meg wrinkled her nose at him, then turned her shoulder to the board, threw the dart, jumping up and down cheering when she saw she'd made a bull's-eye.

Rooster held out his hand for the darts.

"Okay, Rooster, an easy one—what's your call sign?" Meg asked.

Rooster looked over at her, puzzled.

"What? You don't want to share? Something embarrassing?" Meg sing-songed.

Rooster stared at her. Meg could see his mind working something through. He sat down heavily, propped his elbows on the table, and dropped his head into his hands. His whole body started shaking.

Meg thought that somehow she'd brought him to tears. She'd crossed some line. She scooted her chair closer to him and put her hands on his shoulder, leaning her cheek onto his arm. She sent Randy a searching look. Maybe something happened when he was in the military that was painful. Maybe he didn't use a call sign at Iniquus.

Randy was watching the scene with his brow knit together.

Why didn't Randy come and console Rooster? Meg turned until her forehead rested on Rooster's biceps. "I'm sorry… Did I say something to upset you?" she whispered.

Rooster put his hands over his face and sat up, then leaned back with a groan. He scrubbed his palms over his cheeks. His face was red.

Meg could see tears still clinging to his eyelashes and frowned her apology, rubbing a soothing hand up and down his arm.

Rooster pointed to Randy. "Randy's my partner."

"I know, he told me." She sent him a gentle smile. "That's great. I'm glad for you both."

Meg was thoroughly confused when Rooster grinned at Randy, his chest and shoulders shaking. Was he *laughing*?

Randy looked back at him. Then a light seemed to go on. "What? Wait. *Woah.* No, no, no. Rooster and I aren't *partners*. We're partners. We work for the same company. You know that. I date women. You know that too. You've seen pictures." He stopped and looked at Rooster. "You thought Rooster and I were a *couple*?"

Meg was so uncomfortable. She took a deep breath in and opened her mouth to say something, but the only thing that came out was an exhale.

"How'd you know she thought that, Honey? Were you egging her on?"

Rooster slapped his hand on the table and doubled over; he was laughing so hard.

Randy's brow was furrowed. "If I went for a man, you think *Honey's* my type?"

Rooster grabbed his stomach, trying to stay upright.

Meg wanted an exit strategy. She stood up, trying to find an excuse when she spotted the women's room sign. She took a step in that direction when Rooster gently reached out his right hand to still her.

He worked to sober his amusement. "Meg, come sit down." When she didn't comply, he said, "My call name is 'Honey.' And you heard it as a pet name. You were absolutely right to get the wrong idea. But I'm not gay." His eyes still glittered with amusement. But also gentleness. And a warmth that Meg wasn't expecting to see there.

"*Honey* is your call name? But why?" She let him pull her back to her chair and sat down, working to realign her thoughts with this new revelation.

"From the honey badger. You're an animal migration specialist. You'll understand."

"They're terrifying. They'll take on lions. But they're little. The males are about thirty pounds. And you're…" She waved her hand over the length of his body. "Not."

"They're small compared to the foes they go after. It's a matter of scale. I might seem big to you, but my enemies are bigger."

"Rooster's last name is Honig, which means honey in German." Randy pointed his finger at Rooster. "This is a game of truth."

Rooster picked up the darts and stood up again. "You tell your truth. I'll tell mine."

"You know, you two fight like an old married couple. You can understand why I'd get confused. The waiter's coming over. Can you get me a glass of water while I go to the ladies'?"

As she walked away, Meg heard Randy say, "Go on and throw the darts, honey badger. I've got a few questions of my own."

MEG LOOKED at her reflection in the mirror. She pinched her cheeks and adjusted her dress before brushing her hair back and trying to scrunch a little body into it. *Primping, huh? What are you thinking, girl?* She'd had two days of stuffing her interest away because she'd misunderstood the situation. She stopped with her hand in her hair. Meg was definitely better at reading animals than people. People confused her.

Okay, she'd let herself off the hook about her conclusions about Rooster, what with Randy calling him honey and all. But she'd felt that pull—the one that said this is going somewhere good—before he'd even spoken to her in the airport. Humans are animals, after all. And sexuality follows a standard sequence of behaviors in all primates. When she'd watched him walking toward her, she must have given him the opening cue with a flick of her hair and a flash of her neck. Yeah, her inner "I need to get laid, and you look like just the one to do it" must have shown up in her subconscious behavior.

The more she scanned through their interactions, the more Meg realized they'd been doing a mating dance all along. She'd just convinced herself that he was being attentive because of her association with Randy. She pulled her lip gloss from her bag. "Girlfriend, this is probably going to end badly," she muttered under her breath as she leaned in to swipe a little color onto her lips.

She went to give her hair one last fluff when her mind went to the last guy who'd made an overt play for her, Momo

Bouhran. Only he hadn't been interested in her in the conventional way. His poorly masked plays had felt more predatory than intimate. He'd given her the willies. Standing by the side of Lac Assal, she'd felt endangered the whole time. Even her interpreter had seemed ill at ease. Rooster and Randy might know Momo, but they certainly weren't friends. She knew that for sure. They were probably trying not to scare her by letting her know he was dangerous. The situation was over; after all, no need to warn her off.

To be honest, she'd been scared a lot lately. Scared by her findings and their ramifications, scared by the atmosphere that she felt spreading as an undercurrent through the world. Meg decided that she'd be asking the guys what they knew about Momo with her next round of questions.

She didn't think she'd even need darts to get that information. Rooster would be honest with her if she asked him directly. *Rooster.* She sighed. She'd only have the climb up Kilimanjaro tomorrow, then the guys would be leaving the next morning. That's damned depressing, Meg thought as she pushed back through the bathroom door. She'd better take advantage of what little time they had.

Randy stood outside the bathroom, waiting for her. "You good?"

"Yup."

"I'm beat from the last few days. I'm going up to my room and ordering room service. What do you want to do?" he asked.

"Is Rooster going up?"

Randy sent a glance toward their table. "Nope."

"I think I'll hang out with him for a while then."

"Have fun." He kissed her cheek and headed off.

When Meg walked back into the room, Rooster smiled at her.

She slid into the chair next to him. "What did I miss? Randy was asking you a question when I left the room."

Rooster considered her for a long moment. "He was asking me what I thought about you."

"Good things, I hope," Meg said.

"He wanted to know how I felt about you."

"Ah, that was a different question, wasn't it?" Meg's face heated.

"I don't want to make you uncomfortable. But I do want you to know how much I've enjoyed getting to know you. I think you have a big heart and a sharp mind, and the most beautiful smile I've ever seen."

Meg looked into the warm depths of Rooster's brown eyes. She found sincerity there. And concern.

"I'm wondering if you can shift gears from thinking about me as a gay man." He offered a lopsided grin. "If you'd *want* to shift gears, that is to say." He tipped his head.

Did she *want* to? Um. *Yeah.* She rested her hands on his thighs, balancing her weight as she leaned in to kiss him softly. She pulled back, hovering near his mouth, as a smile played at her lips. A hum of harmony moved through her. It was like the feeling she got when she finally unlocked her front door after a long trip, walked into her place, and thought, *it's so nice to be home.*

She heard the waiter clear his throat. That kiss, while okay in America, was not okay here. "Muslim country," she whispered. "How about we finish this conversation upstairs?"

Rooster reached into his pocket as he stood. He lay the colorful Tanzanian shillings on the table. "*Asante.*" He thanked the waiter in Kiswahili and held out his hand to Meg.

17

———

MEG

The Lounge

MEG SLID her hand into Rooster's. As they moved toward the elevator, Rooster scanned the room. His gaze settled into the darker shadows, then swept along. She knew every glance was full of thought. Where's the exit? Where's cover? Where are the dangers? She had to think that way, too, when she was in the bush. Which animal might be stalking her? What would she do if she were attacked?

Because of the time she spent with Randy, she was used to a soldier's level of awareness. Randy said that after you'd been in a hot spot for a long enough time, it was hard to ratchet down the vigilance. Randy was no longer code red whenever he was out in public, but code orange was probably his sticking place. Then Meg remembered the guys' odd behavior in Zanzibar when Rooster watched the elevator stops, and Randy was racing up the stairs. There had been a sense of danger to that moment that they had never explained to her. Now she wondered if Rooster's code orange vigilance was grounded in habit or concern.

Those thoughts vanished when Rooster pulled at her hand to tuck her under his arm. In primates, this was a claiming signal. It told all the other chimpanzees to back off. That thought sent a thrill through Meg as they moved toward the elevator, giving her whole body a tremble.

"Are you cold?" Rooster asked, rubbing her arm and pulling her tighter to him.

"I must have walked through a draft." *That was lame*. Meg wished she was the kind of girl who was seductive and mysterious, the kind of girl who always seemed to win the hearts of the heroes in the movies. But she had always felt more geek than goddess divine.

Studying animal behaviors, Meg knew that females made the choices for mating. But males were picky too. They could and would fight amongst themselves, sometimes battling to the death for a particular mate. But that mate had to be desirable. Meg didn't have the first clue how to make herself desirable. She'd not put a lot of thought into it because it never really mattered to her before. It mattered to her now. A lot. She wasn't sure she could pull this off. Now, here was her body betraying just how much she wanted Rooster to want her.

The elevator doors slid open, and they walked in. Rooster stood next to the panel and let his hand hover; he was waiting for her to tell him where to go—his room or hers. Beginnings were always awkward. She would feel more comfortable in her own territory. Meg reached into the evening bag that hung from a slender gold strap on her shoulder and pulled out her hotel card. "Room 508," she said, handing it to him.

With just the two of them in the elevator, Rooster tugged on her hand until she was standing in front of him, back to front, then wrapped his arms around her and pulled her tight. Her body felt perfectly supported as she molded herself against him. She leaned her head onto his chest and willed herself not to moan as his thumb glided up and down her stomach.

The door dinged, and they moved to her room, her nerves sizzling with excitement and a little panic. She had to decide where she was going to let this go. Time was an enemy; Rooster would be leaving the day after tomorrow. Randy was in her head. He'd taken off to give them some space. They were all adults. He probably knew what they'd be doing, and that was…just weird. And frankly, she didn't do one or even two-night stands. Given her travel schedule, she'd turned into more of a "friends with benefits" kind of girl. True relationships were off the table. Deep feelings weren't a consideration. And then suddenly, Rooster.

Rooster swiped them in. Meg was still trying to figure out how this should best play out. She decided to follow Randy's lead and order room service. She could use the time to have a nice intimate conversation and work forward from there. Give herself a little time to go from Rooster's off-limits status to seemingly ready and available. She stood next to her bed and let her purse drop onto the nightstand. She laid her hand on the menu, resting beside her phone. Turning, she looked up at Rooster, who had leaned a shoulder into the wall and was obviously waiting for her to set the pace.

Her eyes slipped down his length. *Oh my.* As her gaze found his again, she said, "I'm hungry. Aren't you?" Her voice came out in a low, breathy tone that made it clear that her libido had taken the reins, and food wasn't in the picture.

Rooster sent her the most lascivious smile she'd ever seen. "Starving," he said, pushing off the wall and stalking toward her.

That got her blood flowing.

He reached into his pocket and pitched a condom onto her bed. She followed the arc with her gaze. Okay. He had a destination. She was on board with that.

She turned her head to look up at him and stopped breathing as his hands slipped under her arms and down her body until they rested on her hips. He pulled her against him, holding her there possessively as he leaned down to kiss her. Soft. Warm. Yes, that's how she thought it would be. He was a gentleman. And Meg felt like challenging that.

She had liked the predatory quality of his smile just then. It made her feel… As Meg searched for a word, she lifted onto her toes and crushed herself against him. Their lips met, and her hands came up to the sides of his head to hold him in place. *Wanton.* Yes, that was the word she read in books and scoffed at. Nobody *actually* felt that way, did they? It was a made-up word that writers used to describe fictional feelings. But oh god, this felt real. This was…surreal. Wonderful. This was amazing. She felt her toes curl in her high-heeled sandals.

Rooster pulled away and held her gaze as he squatted down and ran his thumb up the back of her calf, up her thigh, dragging the silk of her dress with his hand. The sharp bite and the slick of fabric lit up her nervous system. The dress was whisked over her head, up into the air, and she saw it land neatly over the nightstand. He tangled his fingers into her hair as he leaned her backward to deepen the kiss, letting his tongue slick over her lips and into her mouth.

Rooster lifted her up until they were face to face, his arms wrapped around her back, holding her tightly in place. She found herself laughing as he spun them around. His eyes were darkly intense, his gaze locked on hers for a long moment like he was drinking her in, filling a space with her. Somehow entangling her. She was buzzing. High on the hormones that flooded her body. Giddy. Meg didn't understand what was happening. Her mouth dropped open as she panted.

A slow smile spread across his face, then he closed his eyes to kiss her again as he let her slide back down to the ground. As her weight came to rest on her own two feet, Meg kicked off her heels. He had lifted her breasts and was running his thumbs over the satin covering them. Their weight swelled, growing heavy. Her system was all fired up, ready to go. She reached around to unclasp her bra. This was no time for sultry teases; this was a time for action.

She needed him then.

Right then.

No room for bashful first-time-with-this-guy jitters. Meg let her bra drop and reached for his shirt buttons. Her fingers shook as she worked to open the first, the second.

Rooster seemed to feel the same imperative she did. He quickly had his cuffs undone and yanked the shirt over his head. Meg stepped back to admire his chiseled abs, the goody trail he revealed as he pushed his pants and boxers to his ankles. His dick bounced up against his stomach, then pointed straight toward her.

"Fuck," she heard the word blow across her lips with her exhale.

"Yes, ma'am." Rooster lifted her up and laid her on the bed, reaching out to draw her lace panties down her legs. Slowly. Much too slowly. It was a torment. She pulled the bedspread into her fists and squeezed, trying to expel some of this energy. He was making her angry with frustration. She wanted him on top of her, not teasing her. He lifted her ankle and kissed her instep. She kicked at him. She didn't want to play. She had serious needs.

He chuckled as he brought his mouth back to her ankle. He ran his tongue up the length of her leg, then went back to the starting point to place warm kisses along the cooling line where the moisture was evaporating. Meg's whole body trembled, and a moan replaced her growl of displeasure. That stalled him again.

She reached demanding arms to him, but he shook his head.

He pushed her legs farther apart, running his hands over her inner thighs, then rested his weight on his forearms between her legs.

What? He looked like he was settling in. That's not what she wanted. "Stop teasing me, Rooster. I'm ready. Already."

"Shhh," he whispered. He stroked her thighs and kissed them until her muscles were taut. He stroked the pad of his thumb gently, reverently, over her swollen clit. The desperation she'd been feeling lost its bright edge as the sensations morphed into something warmer. Something much more connected than the bawdy tumble she'd envisioned since he stepped off the plane in Zanzibar.

Rooster moved to his knees. The bed dipped under his weight. He lifted her leg and nuzzled the back of her knee. He made his way with slow kisses up her thigh. He stroked his hands over her body. He moved farther onto the bed until he could hold her in his arms.

He lay a string of kisses across her brow, down the side of her face. Onto her lips. "The first time I thought about making love to you, I hadn't even met you yet."

Meg ran her fingers through his dark-brown hair cut military tight and so soft to her touch. She held his head to her neck as he nuzzled her. "Oh? How is that?"

He pushed onto his elbow, his fingers played with her earlobe as his eyes moved around her face, from eyes, to nose, to cheekbones, to lips. He shifted himself and gave her a lingering kiss. "Randy showed me a picture of you laughing." His lips were so close to hers that when he spoke, she could feel them forming the words that made her feel precious. His hand moved down her throat over her shoulders. He cupped her breast, his thumb and finger rolling and teasing at her nipple. "I can pull that picture up at will. It was the easiest, most open, most joyful picture I've ever seen." His hand moved down her body, over her hip to her thigh.

He pulled her knee across him, then rolled until he was lying between her legs. He held his weight up with his elbows as he hovered there. "I have another picture of you in my head. We had just walked out of the Zanzibar hotel, and you were standing like a jewel in front of the sun setting over the Indian Ocean. I want to paint that picture, but I could never do you justice." He pushed back onto his heels, leaving Meg longing for his warmth and weight. "And now I have this picture. It's the most beautiful of all. The look in your eyes is the sexiest thing." He stopped to give her a wicked smile. "It's also impatient." He moved down and nipped at her nipple, slicking over the moment of pain with a soothing lick that made her moan. "You've been tormenting me since you slid your hand in mine at the airport." He nuzzled her breast. "I won't let you rush me. I plan to enjoy every inch of your body."

Meg blinked. Men didn't say things like that to her. "Okay," she said. She'd tell herself she was a moron tomorrow. It was the best she could do in the moment.

Rooster chuckled. "Good, then we agree."

His hands, his tongue, his lips moved over her.

All of her.

There wasn't an inch that was left unattended. By the time he'd worked his tongue back to her pussy, there wasn't an ounce of bashful left in her. Her thighs clamped around his head as he gave her crazy, rollercoaster sensations. Her orgasm built to a point where the intensity started to frighten her. Then she was crashing down, and Rooster gathered her tightly in his arms. His warmth and strength making her feel safe and cared for. She was drunk on sex. Slurring, limp, disoriented.

She reached down to hold his dick. Stroked her hand over the velvety length until she sobered a little. He pressed the condom packet into her hand. She rolled it into place and swung her leg over his hips, guiding his penis inside her, then she collapsed on his chest. She needed another moment to recover.

18

———

ROOSTER
   Room 508

ROOSTER LIE on his back with Meg's hair brushing over his chest. He clamped his hands around her hips, stilling her gyrations. He pushed his weight onto his elbows to lift his shoulders off the pillow, turning left then right, trying to hone in on the sounds he was hearing. A *pop-pop-pop* had drifted through her open window. It happened twice before he could wrangle his attention away from the sensation of Meg riding him toward another orgasm. He could feel her muscles wrapping his dick, quivering faster and faster. It was driving him nuts. He was holding off his own explosion until she was there with him. He wanted to crash over the cliff with her.

But that was gunfire.

Meg looked down at him with bewilderment. She pushed on her legs to free herself and slide up his dick.

Rooster held her tighter. His mind raced. The way the hotel

was built to replicate the rolling hills and rocks of the crater's edge made echoes that masked their origin. How far away were they? "Do they use rifles to keep predators off the hotel property?"

Her responding *"What?"* was peppered with another set of shots. Her face shifted instantly, a worry line ran between her brows. "No," she whispered. "That's why we have to sign paper-work about not going into the crater after the sun starts to set and not going outside on the first level after dark. It's tourist board policy that this is the animals' home, and we're just visiting."

A *rat-a-tat-tat* was partially hidden behind screams. That wasn't fear. That was pain. Someone had been shot. He needed to get to Randy, get them suited up, get Meg safe.

Meg froze in place, eyes wide, gripping Rooster's wrists.

His mind went through a quick calculation as he eased her off him and rolled from the mattress to squat beside the bed in one smooth movement. He gestured for Meg to follow suit. But she sat back on her heels, staring at the door as if she expected rifle-wielding men to burst their way in at any moment.

Assessment: they were on the top floor. He had a gun with one extended magazine, one in the chamber. Seventeen bullets. He had his knife. And he had two flights of stairs to get her down to get to Randy's room. Since he had a known position, and Rooster and Meg did not, Rooster knew Randy would sit tight and wait for their communication. First things first. He grabbed his clothes and slung them on as he sent his gaze around the room, searching for options. "Where's your vest?"

"In Randy's room." Her voice warbled. "I gave it back to him."

Rooster froze for a nanosecond, taking in the picture. Meg was kneeling on the bed with her hands clasped together, pressed to her mouth. Her creamy white skin glowed in the soft gold of the lamplight. Her copper hair swept over her shoulders. The pink of her nipples and the beautiful curves of her hips. The look of complete trust in her eyes. Another shot. Another scream. Rooster yanked his phone out—no bars. Were they savvy enough to jam them? He lifted the hotel phone's receiver—no dial tone. Dead. His eyes fell on the wispy dress that he had just pulled off Meg, her satin bra. He took Meg's hands in his and looked into her eyes until she could focus on him. This was a tactic that lost time on the front end but saved time in the long run. He needed her to stay steady and not panic. Panic was deadly.

He used a firm voice, modulated so anyone in the rooms next door couldn't hear. "You need to get dressed in hiking gear." He nodded his head and waited for her to follow suit. "Put on layers. A sports bra. Three or four t-shirts. A hoodie. A weather-proof jacket. Liner socks and wool socks like you're going on a long hike, but I want you to put on two or three liner socks, yes?" It was a list. A long list. But a list gave someone something to focus on, something to tick off. If he just said, "Get dressed," she'd probably pull on what he'd just taken off her, and she'd be fleeing the bad guy like some heroine in a damned film, teetering in strappy heels and getting tangled in flowing fabric. This wasn't Hollywood. This was the real deal. She needed to be ready for fight or flight. And he hoped like hell it was only flight.

Meg looked at him like he'd lost his mind.

"Hiking boots." He pointed a commanding finger. "Do it now." Rooster drew his belt out of the loops of his pants as he moved to the window and lifted the drapery just enough that he could get a look at the grounds. Meg's room faced the front of the hotel. Three canvas-covered trucks sat outside in the circular drive, with a Jeep behind them. He could see into one. A driver sat with his hands on the steering wheel. Men with AK-47s were positioned strategically, so they were working the angles. They knew what they were doing. *Fuck.*

When he looked back at her, Meg was sloppily dressed. She was perched on the bed, trying to tie her boots, but her hands were shaking too hard. "They're shooting in the hotel?"

Rooster came over to her and knelt, taking the boot in his hands but focusing on her eyes. "I need you to center yourself. I'll get your boots on. You check your breathing. Do you know how to use a gun?"

"A dart gun for tagging animals, yes."

"A pistol?" He lifted her other foot, rearranged her sock so the heel was in the back, and pushed her into the second boot.

"I've never tried. They're not allowed in Tanzania."

"Could you use one? Could you look at someone and pull the trigger? Be honest." Rooster yanked on the laces to tighten her boot. Meg sat very still while he tied. Rooster looked up to catch her eye. He raised his brow to remind her that he'd asked a question.

"No, I don't think I could. Rooster, there are no authorities here. No cops. No soldiers. There's no one to call. No one is coming to help us. How many of them are there out there?"

"A lot. At least a dozen. We need to keep ourselves together and think smart. I want you to look at this." He pulled his belt around. "The belt can act like a whip. Also, here, look at how the buckle works." He flipped it to the back. "Here's your signal mirror." He lifted the release latch. "This is your high lumen flashlight. Small but mighty, yes?"

"Yes," she breathed out.

"This releases the knife. It's not long enough to be a weapon unless you really know what you're doing, but you can cut through rope or zip ties. You can use it to strike a fire. This is your fire-starting rod. In here, there is a shim for opening padlocks and a handcuff key. And under here, that's your button compass. A nice little survival kit." He started to work it through her belt loops, He had a 38-inch waist, and he'd guess that she was about a 26. He'd just have to force it through her loops twice.

"Why are you giving that to me? Do you think we'll be separated?" Panic edged into her voice.

He had to get her off that mindset. "Our priority is survival. I have no idea why the gunmen are here. If they came to rob the hotel, they'll come in, take what they want and go."

"You don't think that's why they're here. I know you don't." Her bottom lip quivered, making her words lose their shape.

"Focus. Our priority is survival." He held her chin still and tried to use his eyes to give her stability—a piece of tradecraft that he'd used throughout his career, pulling victims out of deadly situations. "If you get out into the crater, we don't know who to trust. I would say to run for the Maasai. Their warriors are strong and brave. But these men have rifles, and their warriors only have their spears. It might be dangerous for the tribe for us to run in that direction. You're going to have to think things through."

"Why would they be chasing me to the Maasai boma? You won't be with me? Rifles? They're soldiers?" She made a move toward the window.

Rooster held her back. "We're going to stay away from the windows. They aren't dressed like soldiers. I don't know why they're here. Now take the water bottles from the fridge and zip them into your jacket pockets. Do you have anything here like candy? Nuts?"

"Protein bars. I have protein bars."

"Good. Put those in your hoodie pocket under your jacket."

Meg leaned over her suitcase and pulled out a box. Rooster

took four out. One went into his pocket. He unwrapped another two and ate them down quickly. "You need to eat at least one."

She was shaking her head as he unwrapped the bar.

"Don't think about the food. Think about my words and just chew mechanically." Rooster did a weapons check, making sure he was locked and loaded. Randy had the ammo boxes. The goal was Randy's room. Maybe on the way, he could relieve one of these guys of their rifles and a few mags. But with Meg on his heels, he didn't want to lead her anywhere near the destructive power of those rifles.

Meg licked her tongue around her teeth, getting the last bits and swallowing.

"Now you're going to use the bathroom and get a glass of water."

"This is ridiculous." She moved toward the bathroom and left the door open a crack as she shoved her pants around her ankles and sat to pee. "You have me eating and drinking. Shouldn't we be running?"

"We don't know where to run. We'll need energy to keep going. If your bladder is full, you're going to pee down your leg, and it will slow you down. Don't flush the toilet."

Meg was working to get the belt back into place as she emerged from the bathroom.

"We have a moment to get ourselves situated. We need to be tactical." He stood at the toilet and yanked down his zipper. "Meg, you were outstanding when Robert had his medical crisis. You were outstanding when I had to kill the goat. Bad things happened, and you worked your way through them. You did what needed to be done. That's what we're going to do now. Instead of thinking, 'I feel scared,' you're going to tell yourself that what you're feeling is *power*. Your brain and your body are built for survival. Animal instincts. You know all about those."

He came out of the bathroom and gave his hands a quick wash and dry. "Say that to me." He gathered her into his arms, gripping her chin and tilting her head up until they were eye to eye.

"My brain and my body are built for survival."

"Good. Now, this is the time for your lizard brain to rule—the oldest part of your brain, the one that remembers how to survive. Let your survival instincts do what needs to be done. *Whatever* it is that needs to be done. No matter what. That's what you'll do. That's what you'll keep doing. You will never give up. Say it."

"I will never give up."

"Okay, let's see if we can't get to Randy. He doesn't know where we are, but I'm assuming he knows we're together. That makes his room the rallying point. We can get your vest back on you."

"You knew they were coming? Is that why I had the vest?"

"No," Rooster said as he took another quick look out the front window then slid back to her door to review the fire escape map.

The stairs were four doors down to the right, ten down to the left. There were thirty rooms per level. Four levels of rooms made a hundred and twenty rooms. They were at the top. There might be some way to get to the roof, but once on the roof, there would be little cover and fewer options. That would be a last resort move unless he could find something to use to get Meg down—a rope, some power cord.

The hotel said that since it was July, one of the most temperate months of the year, the place was booked solid. A hundred and twenty rooms, everyone confined to the hotel by the mandate of darkness in the crater, nowhere else to go for restaurants or entertainment, so that meant approximately two hundred guests, and at this time of night with the bar and the restaurant open, he'd guess a minimum of twenty staff. If they were rounding people up, that would take time. Time was their friend.

He'd seen minimal security cameras. One per floor, one per elevator, several in each of the common areas, reception, the restaurants. He hadn't seen any security guards. But they had to stream those videos somewhere. Maybe they had a guardroom. Maybe they were in place for management to keep an eye on things. Either way, if the gunmen had access, he and Meg could be tracked.

"Meg, do you have any shaving cream?"

"Uh, yes." She hustled over to her bag and dug through it until she pulled out a can and brought it to Rooster.

"You're going to do what I say to do when I say to do it, without question. I need to leave you for just a second. When I get back, you're going to put your hand on my back, and you're going to leave it there. Where I go, you go. That way, I can keep tabs on you without having to turn my head to look. You will always make sure that you're lined up behind me, so I'm shielding you."

She nodded her head, eyes stretched wide, unblinking.

"If I run, you run. If I crouch, you crouch. We work as one unit. Okay?"

Again, she bobbled her head. The air split with the sound of screams as gunfire erupted.

"Meg." He planted his hands on either side of her head. "I swear to you, you're going to make it through this." He bent down to kiss her forehead, and she leaned in. It was an intense moment. One that gripped his heart hard. Now he needed to find a way to keep his promise. But from the sound of things, the tangos' mission was ramping up. Getting caught in the confines of this room was a death trap. They needed to get out and get options. Now.

19

ROOSTER

Fifth Floor, The Ngorongoro Crater Safari Hotel and Conference Center

THE FIRST CAMERA was going to be at the far end of the hall. He put the shaving cream can in his waistband and pulled the gun from his kidney holster. He felt Meg tense up. "I'll be right back." Rooster turned the knob and slid the door open a sliver. He took in the area directly in front of the door. Let his senses expand. No footfalls, no heavy breathing. He edged the door wider, taking in an ever-increasing arc of the hall until he could get his head out the door to scan.

Rooster stalked forward in a crouch. His gun was pressed between his palms. His trigger finger lay ready on the side of the guard, his elbows tucked tight. His gun held barrel down, ready to punch out like a rattlesnake, get the tango in his sights, and pull the trigger three times in the blink of an eye. He pressed his shoulder to the wall and moved toward the stairwell. When he got there, Rooster pulled out the can of shaving cream and shot a stream at the camera lens. It was a gamble that favored their escape.

True, those cameras, if he could get to the control room, might serve to help him locate the bad guys, do a headcount. But if these men had working comms, it meant that someone could be feeding the tangos their escape route. The goal was to get this camera out of commission, then head to the other end of the hall toward the back of the hotel and make their way down the two flights to Randy's room on the end. If the tangos were tracking, they'd probably assume they were headed for the first stairwell and the fastest exit.

Rooster moved back to Meg's door. "Come on. Hand on my back. Moving." He felt Meg's hand contract then splay flat across his scapula. He took that as a "Roger. Wilco."

The elevator dinged to a stop. Rooster looked left then right. They were in the center of the hall, an equidistant run to either stairwell. He didn't want their backs to those elevator doors until he knew what was on the other side. He pushed Meg into the slight indentation of a door frame and put a hand on the top of her head so she would slide down to a crouch. He stepped forward, pressing his back to the wall as the doors slid wide.

A muzzle stretched out as someone did a slow sweep, first to the right. Rooster shoved his gun into its holster and pulled his knife in one smooth, practiced move. If he could, he needed to take the bad guys out, silently. He didn't need to advertise his position or his skills. As the muzzle traced to the left in his direction, Rooster grabbed hold of the end and yanked it violently. The strap around the man's shoulder pulled him into a run to catch his balance. As the tango came into reach, Rooster sliced through the man's carotid artery, then followed the arc to divide the strap and free the rifle. Rooster let his body fall to the carpet with the man, rolled to his back, and lifted the gun between his knees to spray bullets into the elevator. Three men fell to the ground, unmoving. Rooster curved his back and rolled to standing, lunging forward to trap the door open, but before he could get his hand in place, the doors slid shut. The elevator descended.

He jabbed his finger into the call button, tapping violently, but to no avail. Someone was about to find the dead soldiers. Someone would know there was an opposition force. He cussed under his breath, banging a fist into the metal doors.

He turned to Meg. She had both hands clamped over her mouth. Her face was white with shock. She was making guttural gasping noises, her eyes focused on the wall beside them. Rooster turned his head to see the size of the arterial spurt.

Blood dripped down the wall like fresh paint.

He grabbed her wrist and pulled her to standing. "We've got to move." He pressed the release button on the rifle, and the spent magazine dropped out. Rooster pulled two magazines from the dead tango's vest. He hammered the first one into place, ready for action. The second one, he slid into his pocket.

"He could have been a good guy," Meg pointed. "He could have been coming here to protect us."

"Not likely. He had his face covered with his shemagh."

Meg was shaking violently.

"Don't look down. Don't look at him." He grabbed her wrist. "Come on, we've got to move."

He stepped around the prone body, then pushed back against the wall, slinking to the far stairwell, cautious at each door he had to cross. As they reached the exit, Rooster pushed Meg to the side and cracked it open, cussing under his breath at the loud *kuchaw* as the release latch echoed in the stairwell. Once he was sure the space was empty, he reached his hand around, stretching his arm as far as it would go, and sprayed a stream of foam at the camera lens. Only then did he pull Meg forward.

"Two floors." He tucked her tightly behind him, then worked his way to the next camera, sliding along the shadow on the wall where it was least likely his presence would be picked up by the lens that pointed toward the handrail where most people chose to walk. He sprayed the lens. "This is pretty good stuff. It's got a long-range." He was looking for any bright spot to feed to Meg. Her hand still trembled on his back—one more flight.

Down they went, when suddenly from below came a *kuchaw* as someone depressed the bar to open the door. It held at an inch wide, then slowly pressed open. Meg turned as if to run back up the stairs. Rooster reached his left hand back and grabbed at her pants' leg as she moved. His right hand held the rifle snug against his shoulder. "Stop," he hissed. "Randy?"

The door swung open, and Randy slid through. "Shit, man. What the fuck?" Randy was holding a rifle and had another one slung on his back.

Rooster nodded toward the weapon. "I see you made contact. I took out four. You?"

"Two. Looks like I have some catching up to do." Randy had his bullet-resistant vest in place. Another one hung from his left shoulder. "Here, Meg. I brought you a present." He glanced at Rooster. "Sorry, man, but your door was locked. I was trying to break in when my pair jumped off the elevator. I took them out, but the doors closed. It was heading up. The car had maybe four still on."

"Yeah, I found them and put them to sleep. But I didn't get the elevator stopped. The doors shut, and it went down. That doesn't make sense. They weren't letting their people off at each level if they moved from the third to the fifth."

"Roger that. An older couple pressed the up button on the

elevator. They were in their nightclothes, so I'm sure they thought up was a safe direction. I called to them to take the stairs, but the elevator opened, and two-stepped off to nix them."

"They got the couple?"

"Affirmative. Here." Randy pulled two pistol mags from his pocket and handed them over to Rooster. "I see you picked up a rifle and ammo. That's good 'cause now they know they have competition," Randy said. "They'll go hunting."

"My thoughts exactly." Rooster adjusted the Velcro straps on Meg's vest, so it was held tight against her body.

"Can I have a gun, please?" she asked. Her voice almost back to normal. The initial shock was wearing off. Rooster thought that Randy was probably a calming force for her. Rooster eyed her, then pulled the gun and holster from his back. He turned Meg around and tucked it into her waistband, then spun her back in place. He took her hand, pushed it around her back under her windbreaker. "Pull it out."

She did.

He put it back away. "Leave it there. I'll do the shooting. I don't want your finger on a trigger if a noise makes you startle. You'll take off the back of my scalp. But you know you have it. Okay?"

"Yes, okay."

Randy had positioned himself next to the railing and moved his eyes from top to bottom, checking for anyone who might be stalking them. "Where were you headed?"

"To get you," Rooster said, blocking Meg in the corner with the bulk of his body.

"Then where?"

"Out."

"You want to head to the first level or go out a window up here?"

"The back drops off pretty far. Too far to rig sheets. They've got the front well covered. I'm sure they've got a scope on all the exits—doors and windows. We could try to get into cover somewhere, fridge or something, but they were unloading boxes from the trucks out front."

Randy nodded. "I saw that too. I'm thinking inside is going to get real unhealthy real soon. I say move while there's still chaos."

"Right. Down we go." Rooster went first. Then Meg. Randy was last man in the stack. He walked back to back with Meg as he covered behind and above them.

The group advanced cautiously down the stairs. As they came to the landing, Rooster shot the last of the shaving cream onto the camera and set the empty can in the corner. There were two directions to choose from.

Heads, you win. Tails, you die.

Rooster pulled up a mental image of the hotel's layout. "This must lead to one of the lounges. I don't know where this other staircase might lead. We're too far toward the center of the hotel for it to go outside. No signs saying an alarm will sound. What do you think?" Rooster asked under his breath, making sure his voice didn't echo up the stairwell.

"Kitchen? Laundry? That's the route I think we need to take."

"Roger that." Rooster turned to Meg. Her eyes were dilated almost black with adrenaline. He kissed her forehead. "Ready for this?"

20

———

ROOSTER

The Back Stairwell

ROOSTER PUSHED through the door while Meg and Randy hung back. He fired his rifle as his brain sorted the people in front of him. Three tangos with shemaghs covering their heads and lower faces stood in front of him. Two pointed their muzzles at a group kneeling on the ground, their hands behind their necks. One covered the back door. As Rooster's bullets found their targets, the hostiles fell. Ahbou raced forward, grabbing Rooster around the leg and squeezing tight. Rooster dropped his left hand both to soothe the boy and to make sure he wasn't tangling under his feet in case Rooster had to move fast.

Rooster scanned the room, his eyes on the back door. One of the tangos moved, and Rooster squeezed off another round that punched a hole between the hostile's brows. He hoped that the bad guys in the other parts of the hotel would think the gunfire came from their side of the battle. As silence fell, Randy swung his gun through the door, assessed, and pulled Meg in behind him. "That makes seven. Shit. I've got catching up to do."

"You see The Ghost?" Rooster asked.

"I was just wondering the same thing. Here's the question. Do we trust the Mossad? Can we trust *him*? There's bound to be bad blood from the Rex Deus side of things. I wonder if he was told we're from Iniquus, or if they mentioned the Panthers happen to be en route, and that you're assigned to that unit."

"I bet he wouldn't mind a little payback. But right now, I'm more concerned about what he knows about Djibouti."

"What's his skin in this game?" Randy asked.

"None that I know of, besides his own. Ahbou, son, I need some blood circulation in that leg. You can hang on, but stop squeezing so tight."

The hostages remained in place, kneeling with their hands on their heads.

"You can all relax," Rooster said with a lift of his chin.

No one moved. They stared at Ahbou.

Rooster tapped Ahbou's shoulder, and he translated the message. The people fell to the floor, some coming up on all fours to pant for air.

"Ahbou, does anyone know what's happening here?"

"I was with my uncle." He stopped to point. "The men came into the hotel. Everyone was running. We hid behind the waiter's cart. They took the guests from the restaurants and bars. They are making them sit on the floor in the main reception room."

The uncle rose to his feet.

"Did you see how many men are at the door?" Rooster asked in Kiswahili.

"They had many soldiers there, bringing in the boxes. Once they finished unloading, they closed the doors and put chains and locks on so no one could leave."

"Okay. Did you count the number of men? Do you know how many there are?"

There was a brief discussion amongst the workers. The uncle focused back on Rooster. "We don't know. Many. Three trucks filled with men and boxes."

"What's in the boxes?" he asked.

Everyone shook their head.

"Any idea who they are? Where they came from? What they want?"

They had another conversation. Rooster steadied his impatience. Better to get intel then to go off half-cocked.

"We believe these are Somalians. They have a few men who speak Kiswahili, and one—the tall one in charge—is ordering the guests around in English."

"Ahbou, I want you to translate this." He waited for Ahbou's nod. "Are there any servants' passages out of here? Any private routes where you bring in the food and supplies?" Rooster hated wasting time with translations, but specificity was key, this was no place for misinterpretations, and Ahbou was fluent. "Any way out that the soldiers may not know about?"

After a brief discussion, Ahbou said, "Uncle thinks that we should hide in the wine cellar. That's where we were heading when these bad men came to us."

"Okay, that's not going to work. We need to get out of the hotel."

"There is no way out the front of the crater wall that is not guarded by the soldiers. And out the back of the hotel, we will not be safe from the night animals."

"We're going to have to take our chances. Do you know a way?"

Ahbou consulted with his uncle. "Yes, we know a way."

21

ROOSTER

The Kitchen

ROOSTER GLIDED behind Ahbou's uncle as he led them to the back of the room. Ahbou had moved back with Meg and was holding her hand. "You keep tight hold of Miss Doctor Meg, so she doesn't trip," Rooster said, hoping to make the boy brave by giving him responsibility.

The uncle pointed at the door that led down to a basement area. A single bulb hung from above, lighting up the unpainted wooden stairwell. "Stay put," he said to the man.

Rooster slid through the door and aimed his rifle up the center opening, where the stairs twisted to the upper levels. He scanned down over the railing. He saw no signs of movement and no cameras. He gestured for them to follow. The uncle, Meg, and Ahbou silently shuffled forward, followed by the rest. Rooster put his finger to his lips, then started slowly down the stairway. There were five male hotel workers, three females, along with Ahbou and Meg. It was a big group to herd. It made things riskier with so many, slow-moving, with lots of personalities, languages, and cultural barriers.

Rooster paused on the landing and looked up to make sure they were all together. Randy was slicking the door back into place silently. The sound of voices drifted down the stairs toward them. Rooster caught Randy's eye, then moved his gaze from Randy up to the light bulb and back to Randy again.

Randy nodded.

Rooster put his finger to his lips again, and they began their descent. When they crowded in front of the door at the bottom of the steps, Rooster once again made the sign for quiet, then pointed their attention up to what Randy was doing so there would be no gasps of surprise.

Randy licked his fingers, reached up, and turned the light-bulb with a hissing sound as his spit evaporated with the heat. They were plunged into darkness. Rooster knew that would ramp up their terror, but they needed every advantage they could get.

Rooster pulled the door open, his eye to the crack, casting his gaze around the room. Clear. He opened the door and stood to the side. The uncle held it only partially open as they slipped one after the other through the crack and to the opposite wall, where they hunkered in the shadows. Rooster's gun was pressed into his shoulder, at the ready.

Back in formation with Rooster in the front and Randy bringing up the rear, the uncle pointed toward a garage door.

"Anything smaller? A regular door?"

"Not here. This is for food delivery. The trucks drive in, and we cart the food off. There is an elevator to bring them to the kitchen just over there near the bay door."

Rooster squatted and spit onto his fingers, using their wetness to draw a map onto the cement floor. "Where are we right now? Where is the front of the hotel? Where is the road the trucks drive down?"

The uncle spat on his fingers and drew as well.

"Okay, so if we exit here, we're on the left rear of the hotel, right near the crater, correct?" Rooster asked.

"That's correct."

"If we go out here," Rooster put his finger where the dock was drawn, "is it possible to get over the rocks into the crater?"

"It is very steep. Too steep, I think. But there are ledges. We could hide there, at least. There is no safe place to run outside of the hotel. The only escape would be to get to the hotel hospitality vans and perhaps drive to the ranger station."

"Does anyone have the keys?" Randy asked.

The uncle nodded. "The keys are left in the vans. The doors are all unlocked. There is no reason to protect them here. It is too far from anything."

Shots fired above, and screams erupted. *Not far enough, apparently*. The group hunkered into tighter balls in the modest protection of the shadows. "How do we get to the vans from here?"

The uncle traced a route along the crater to a distant area. Too far. Too many in their escape group. Too many bad guys with weapons. "Ahbou, son, I need you to say this, so everyone is very clear." He waited for Ahbou's nod. "I'm going to push the door up just a crack. One at a time, we will lie down and roll out under the door. Roll to the edge of the dock and drop down into the shadow. I'll go first. Once everyone is out, Randy will shut the door behind him, and we will move to the crater and hide in the boulders. When things look safer—when we have a clear route—we'll get to the vans and drive away."

Ahbou translated after each sentence. Rooster looked each of the people in the eye to make sure they understood and that they could and would follow directions. He got an affirmative nod from each. "Ahbou, you're with Miss Doctor Meg."

Rooster was in his crouch walk with his rifle to his shoulder as they moved to the bay. He squatted and grabbed hold of the rope tied to the handle, and as slowly, and as quietly as he could, he edged the door up two feet. It groaned and complained as the trolleys moved over the tracks. Rooster lay flat on his belly and assessed. Sensing no movement, he squirmed under the door. "Okay, here we go, Randy. As soon as I jump down, start sending folks out one at a time. Start with Ahbou, then Meg."

Rooster froze in place as the crunch of footsteps rounded the corner. A silhouette appeared, a rifle to his shoulder, a high lumen flashlight attached to the top. Rooster was on his stomach with his hands in pushup position and his face up when the beam caught him in the eye.

"Don't move," a voice ordered in Somali.

Rooster tucked his head down and whispered. "Back. Back. Back. Back. Back." He extended his arm, pushing his rifle through the opening.

He heard quiet scuffling from inside the door. He knew Randy would be on his stomach covering him. If need be, Randy would take the guy out. But if he did, that would pull other eyes on them. They might get pinned down in a gun battle. Rooster kept moving, hoping like hell this guy didn't have a twitchy trigger finger. "I'm going to get down and put my hands in the air," Rooster replied in Somali. He swung his legs over the dock and jumped down. He splayed the fingers of his left hand and lifted it slowly into the air as his right hand snagged on his shirt, exposing his stomach to show he had no weapons. Turning slowly, Rooster lifted his shirttail to confirm he had nothing there either, glad that he'd handed his pistol off to Meg.

The hostile had moved up quickly. When Rooster turned

forward again, the blinding light shone inches from his face. "Hey, friend, how about not shining that right in my eyes?" Rooster brought his elbow across his face and lowered his head as if to protect himself from the glare.

"I'll do what I want," came the reply from the man Rooster couldn't see behind the glare.

Rooster needed the tango to talk, so he had an idea of distance and height. "But that's burning my eyes."

The Somali moved his gun closer to poke Rooster in the chest. "Put your hands on your head. Turn around," he ordered.

Rooster dropped his hand to the barrel and jerked it violently forward as he got his other hand on the weapon and drove the stock back to hit the bad guy across his eyes and the bridge of his nose. He rotated around the much shorter man to get the length of the rifle across his neck, one hand curled protectively over the trigger guard, keeping the tango from firing a warning shot. Bending his knees and jerking the rifle back to his chest, Rooster stood.

The man dangled six inches off the ground, kicking his feet, grappling with the rifle, trying to find an airway. Rooster backed slowly around the dock, being mindful that this guy might have a buddy who would be checking up on him.

By the time Rooster made his way to the other side of the loading dock.

Up against the wall, the man hung, unconscious.

Rooster dropped the bad guy to the ground, grabbed his head and shoulder, and yanked in opposition until Rooster heard the crack of the hostile's neck bones, finishing the job. He snatched up the Somali's rifle and patted him over, looking for an extra mag, but found none.

Rooster turned off the flashlight, plunging himself back into the dark of night. Hunkering down, he closed his eyes for the count of thirty to retrieve some of his night vision. Then, ducking low, Rooster hustled along the dock and ran along the exterior wall to check for others who might be making a guard circuit.

As he edged toward the corner, he heard the crunch of boots against gravel. Rooster slung the gun to his back and jerked his knife from his pocket, pulling the blade free with two hands instead of flicking it open, so there was no click echoing into the night as the blade locked in place.

The light of the bad guy's flashlight swung around the corner. Rooster was a statue. The tango moved hesitantly forward. His voice sounded very young as he whisper-called, "Rashid?" He stepped forward. "Rashi—"

Rooster's knife swung over his head and slid behind the man's clavicle into his heart. The target dropped instantly. Rooster used the tango's collar to pull his body closer to the wall. He pulled off the man's rifle and patted him down for an extra magazine, but there was none.

This told Rooster that they hadn't expected anyone to escape the hotel.

They probably put their least trained men on perimeter and gave them the minimum in supplies.

Their escape might just be possible.

Rooster chanced one last glance around the corner.

The coast was clear. Now was the time to move. And move fast.

22

———

Meg

The Loading Dock

Someone had caught Rooster as he was scooting out under the door. Rooster was still out there. Somewhere. With no gun. Meg was too afraid to breathe. A few words had filtered through the crack. Some sounds made her think there was a struggle—no gunshots. Randy was on his belly, focused hard on the action. He had pushed a rifle back from under the door, and Meg took possession of it. It was hers. Her responsibility. She forced herself to inhale. Then exhale. After a few times priming her lungs, they took off working on their own again.

She desperately wanted to keep everyone safe. Meg looked the rifle over. It wasn't like this was a completely foreign object, she thought as she pulled the strap over her head and arm. She'd had dart guns in her hands enough times. There were almost always rifles in the cab of her vehicles when she was out in the bush, just in case. See? She had some familiarity, she encouraged herself. She assumed that targeting with a dart gun and a gun that shot bullets would be the same. She *hoped* it would be the same. No. What she hoped was that this was all just going to be over, and she'd never had to decide whether they were the same or not.

There were decisions to be made, though. Rooster wanted her to decide. That's why he'd been making her parrot back those phrases when they were up in her bathroom. *My brain and my body are built for survival. I will never give up.* And she wouldn't. She would fight for her own sake and for the sake of those with her. The strangers as well as the people she cared deeply for—Randy and Rooster... Ahbou looked up at her with wide eyes, and she laid a hand on his shoulder. And Ahbou. She wouldn't let anything stop her from helping Ahbou.

God, Rooster, what the hell's going on out there?

She gestured for everyone to move up against the walls to try to protect them should bullets start to fly. She made sure that Ahbou was under his uncle's wing. For such a young boy, he was stoic in the face of danger. Meg wished she was too. She adjusted the strap over her neck and moved farther into the room, so they were covered from both sides. The gun was growing heavy in her hands. She trembled with exertion and fear. Tears slid down her cheek. And snot. She sniffed. *Screw your damned courage to the sticking place, Meg.*

Every second felt hours long.

There was a scramble at the door, and Rooster was back with them. Meg held her position. She noticed, though, that the first thing Rooster did as he stood up was scan the room until he found her. He stared into her eyes, assessing. He nodded. Whatever he saw, he approved of. Snot or no snot. "It looks clear. We're going to try this again."

Just then, there was a loud bang. A group of men poured

through a door to the right of the stairwell. Before Meg could get her rifle turned in the right direction, Randy aimed and fired. The men scattered and ran. As they bolted away, Rooster chased them down, but they got through the metal door and got it locked off before he could stop them.

"They know where we are. We have to move. Go. Go. Go."

Randy slung the door open and jumped from the dock. As people came out, he was catching them and setting them down. Pointing. "Run."

A Jeep careened around the corner. They were lit up by the headlights. Shots rang out as the vehicle closed in on them, and people fell to the ground. Meg wasn't sure if they were hit or diving for cover. Rooster took the rifle and had her in his arms, pulling her off the dock. He tried to throw her back up so she could escape back inside, but she was clinging to him too tightly. She wasn't about to separate herself from him.

The elevator doors opened, and four men were stacked up, and all of them had their guns trained on the escaping group.

23

———

ROOSTER
Ngorongoro Fucking Hotel

FISH IN A BARREL.

Nothing to do but lower the rifles to the ground, raise his hands, and pray like hell they forgot to pat them down. The man in the back was yelling at Randy. Randy shook his head to say he didn't understand. Randy's language skills were from the Middle East; he hadn't worked many African assignments. He spoke some Kiswahili, but the Somalians were speaking with a heavy accent.

Brave little Ahbou translated. "He says, Mr. Randy, that you are to give him your protection vest."

Randy removed it, and the man immediately pulled it into place, grinning. Taking a cue from his comrade, one of the tangos in the front moved toward Meg. He touched the vest, and she recoiled.

"Take off your vest, Meg, and hand it to him. Keep your back to the wall."

Meg followed Rooster's instructions, handing off the vest. The man putting it on immediately realized that it had been molded for breasts. His comrades jeered at him. The guy ripped it back off and threw it into the Jeep.

Rooster caught Meg's eye, then turned his back to her and stepped backward until she was compressed between him and the wall, hidden behind his bulk. He ducked his head. Under his breath, he muttered, "Randy and I had the rifles. We're clearly the soldiers and will be subject to extra attention. You need to keep your distance from us. Don't let them know I'm protecting you. You need to decide how safe you feel with a gun in your waistband. At this point, it might help, and it might make you a target. It's a coin toss. Your call."

"What should I do with it?"

"Put it back under my shirt. There's an off chance they won't do a pat-down. If they find it on me, I've already got their attention, so it won't change my dynamic."

He felt her body shifting behind his. The cool air on his skin as she lifted his shirt, the push and tug as she secured the automatic back into place. "Good. Now make sure that you don't associate with me. Don't look at Randy or me. You can be mama bird for Ahbou. Focus on him and his uncle. The uncle may know a way out. He'll protect himself and then Ahbou. You want to be glued to that group." He felt a pat-pat on his back as she agreed to the plan. He inched away from her, still keeping her hidden but making it less obvious.

One of the Somalis prodded Rooster's chest with his muzzle. If it weren't for all the civilians in the area, this guy would be such an easy takedown. But if Rooster grabbed at the guy, and the others started shooting, the ricochet alone would be lethal.

He spoke, and Rooster understood him to say, "You are hiding people out here?"

"No. Sorry. What you see is what you get." Rooster's words must not have had meaning to the guy, who was speaking Kiswahili as a second language, just like Rooster.

Ahbou's uncle said something, and the tango nodded.

Each of the men was put one at a time against the wall and searched. Rooster lost his gun and knife. As the women were moved to the wall, Rooster noticed the hostiles hadn't patted down any of the females. That was interesting. He'd have to process that.

The good thing was that so far, Meg kept her belt, food, and water. That was something.

Randy kept his belt, and Rooster knew he would have something hidden in it, even if it was just a razor blade. As the tangos finished up their searches, the hostages were made to lace their fingers together, place them on their heads, and walk in single file. Rooster and Randy each had their own guard shoving them along with the barrel of their guns.

These guys were probably going to parade them in like heroes. They'd want immediate acknowledgment for their fine soldiering. That meant they were going to be taken to the leader. That meeting would give Rooster some much-needed intel.

They took the stairs, maneuvered through the door, and were marched into the main lobby. And there, like a circus ringleader, was Momo Bourhan. Meg gasped, and Rooster maneuvered her behind his back. Ahbou craned his head up to look at him, and Rooster cut his eyes to the left, then nodded at him. Ahbou silently shifted back into Rooster's shadow to stand with Meg. Smart kid. As the tangos were excitedly telling their story of the capture, Rooster reconned the room. The Ghost was on the floor leaning against a pillar, his face purple and swollen.

He had made a sling out of his belt, trapping his arm against his chest.

Rooster's eyes swiveled to the boxes piled throughout the room. Wires ran from one to the other. The two men who guarded the front door looked like they might have suicide vests on underneath their windbreakers. They had the unfixed focus of those who had been given potent drugs to relieve anxiety—a common practice used by handlers to overcome a human's fear of dying.

If these were suicide bombers, they had some time. Momo wasn't about to be caught in an explosion. He had future plans. Personal plans that moved him up the terror echelon. Rooster needed to get over to The Ghost and gather intel.

Momo raised his hand to shut down the babbling tango. He said in Kiswahili and then in English. "Take a seat."

"Hand," Rooster said. Immediately, he felt Meg's hand on his back. Rooster hoped she remembered what that meant. Where he went, she needed to be his shadow. Indistinguishable. It was a difficult dance to both be there to protect her and distance himself, so all options were available. When Rooster took his first stride, Ahbou's uncle came up just beside and slightly behind, helping to shield Meg and Ahbou. Making it seem like they were just all moving as a group.

Good man.

Rooster maneuvered to sit next to The Ghost. Randy moved to his other side, where he sat squarely, shoulder to shoulder with him, making a wall to hide Meg and Ahbou. Out of sight, out of mind. Maybe Meg and Ahbou wouldn't be in the headcount, and they could make a getaway. He trusted Meg had the cunning to do it. She knew the plan to hide in the boulders. He just needed to find the right time, the right diversion, and the right route.

Rooster pulled his knees up and wrapped his arms around them, hunching his shoulders and lowering his head to cover the movement of his mouth and keep his words from traveling farther than The Ghost's ear. "What've you got?"

"Besides a fucking fractured skull and a broken arm? It's hard to get a good headcount with them coming and going with their faces covered. At least two dozen. They were saying they have men down. That you?"

"We got eleven. Obviously not enough."

One of the gunmen paced the room, pointing his gun to scare people into submission. They ducked their heads, trying not to make eye contact as he passed them.

There were blood smears across the floor where people had been dragged away. Rooster focused on The Ghost, then over to the blood, then raised his brow. The Ghost flashed four fingers and mouthed, "Tourists."

The tango turned as he reached the far wall and paced past them again. Rooster had his eye on the doors. Chains ran through the door handles, holding them shut with an old-fashioned padlock. If people wanted out, they'd have to throw a piece of furniture through one of the windows. Rooster picked out a sturdy table and the window he would choose. That plan was so far down the alphabet that it didn't even have a letter. He needed to get options for a more feasible Plan A and Plan B. And he needed to decide what to do with this Rex Deus operative. Rooster wasn't convinced that The Ghost wouldn't feed them to the wolves to make his own escape.

"The boxes are explosives. They've run wires," The Ghost confirmed. "Momo has a detonator. That's what he's flicking like a Bic in his hand. He's making people piss themselves with fear. If a few made a run for it, with all of these rooms? Most could probably get away. I'd even advocate we overpower them—you, me, and your partner. Though frankly, at this point, I'm of little use. I think that detonator is the real deal. And I think the two Somalis near the door might be looking forward to their virgin reward party at the end of the day."

"Noted." Rooster also noted how slurred The Ghost's speech was and how his pupils were radically different sizes. Shit. The Mossad and the CIA would think they had each other's backs. No man left behind. Escaping with someone with brain trauma was going to be a hell of a risk multiplier.

There was a commotion in the hall as two gunmen brought another pocket of guests out of the elevator. Their fingers were laced and sitting on their heads. From the direction they were coming from, they wouldn't be able to see the other captives in the lobby. One man panicked and ran toward the front door. The guards who stood on either side didn't flinch. The hostages on the floor threw their hands over their heads and flung themselves to the ground, anticipating an explosion. There was a bang of rifle fire that echoed off the walls and cathedral ceiling that made Rooster's head ring. He could hear nothing as the man spread his arms wide as if flying then fell flat onto his face. The shuffle and bumps behind his back made Rooster think that Meg had pulled Ahbou mostly into her lap and draped herself over him.

Momo nodded to the new tangos, who jabbed the muzzles of their guns into the people's backs, herding them over to sit with the hostages on the other side of the lobby. In Somali, Momo called for a man standing by the computer to come and check the dead man.

The hostile ran forward, bringing some papers fluttering in his hand. He looked from the face to the first page, from the face to the second page, from the face to the third page, then shook his head. "This is nobody."

Rooster thought that the woman who had crumpled to the floor, reaching toward him and sobbing, probably thought the guy was *somebody*.

"Be careful with your shots," Momo continued in Somali. "Not everyone is equally expendable." He turned to the man with the list. "You've identified those of interest?"

"A few more registrants to research," he said and moved back to the computer.

"What are they doing over at the computer?" he asked The Ghost.

"Near as I can tell, culling names of hotel guests."

"They're looking for specific people? This isn't just a hit on tourists?"

"I don't know. I caught a look at the first page and saw at least one of the scientists from today. I can't tell whether I'm hoping they're looking for me as Abraham Silverman, a member of the Key Initiative, and they're pulling me out of here to Stage 2, or if it's better to stay and get blown to bits, quick and easy." He sniffed and wiped his wrist under his nose to catch a trickle of blood.

"How'd they get you?"

"I happened to be talking to the concierge about the possibility of a massage when they burst through the door. They patted me down and took my weapons."

"They did a thorough job."

He gave a wheezing chuckle under his breath. "Yeah, you could say that. They wanted to know why I had so many guns on my body. I said I was afraid of lions. That's when the head-banging began."

"He's got a three-page list. Do you think he's looking for Israelis? The scientists? Some other demographic?"

A gunman turned his rifle on them. They focused on the ground.

After he passed by, The Ghost whispered, "I'd be guessing. Could be any of the above. But yeah. I'm starting to think that my little Tanzanian safari adventure under the name Abraham Silverman was probably the worst decision of my life."

24

———

MEG

The Lobby

MOMO CAME FORWARD, front and center. He waggled his hand in the air, and the man at the computer scampered over and thrust the pages he had used earlier to identify the dead man into Momo's waiting hand.

"Dr. Meghan Finley, stand up, please."

Meg felt her breath catch in her throat. If she hid behind Randy and Rooster, they'd still find her, and then they might be even angrier with the guys. She stood but pushed Ahbou onto the floor. "Hello, Momo." She tried to sound professional and to make him remember that they had spent a day together. He knew her as a person. Wouldn't that make it harder to kill her? She was sure she had read that somewhere.

"Meg, come. Have you enjoyed your stay in the crater?" He gestured her forward with a curl of his fingers.

"I've actually found it a rather difficult day." There was a warble in her voice, but she was still intelligible. Who wouldn't have a warble in their voice under these circumstances? At least there were no guns trained on her.

"I'm afraid that's going to continue for a while. You are the only female on your team, yes?"

"Yes, the only female."

"Sit over there." Momo pointed to the reception desk.

Meg, by sheer will and concentration, got her legs to move forward, then sat where indicated, cross-legged.

Momo turned to the rest of the hostages. "The rest of you women, you will stand slowly and walk to the dining room. You will be much more comfortable sitting in chairs rather than the cold floors."

The women bustled to comply. The gunmen trained their rifles on them and kept a vigilant eye, lest someone else try to bolt. Meg was sure that wouldn't happen after the very real, very horrible display that had just taken place. One of the terrorists at the front door followed along behind them. His clothes bulged strangely, and Meg wondered if he was wearing a tactical vest under his shirt.

The lobby's reception area was large. Very large. But even so, there must have been about two hundred people sardined into the space. Meg wondered if her place by the desk was a good thing or a bad thing. If it was a good thing, she needed to find a way to make that good fortune extend to Rooster, Randy, and Ahbou. If it was bad, she needed to make sure to keep her distance. Just like Rooster had wanted to do for her. As the women filed out, the men dotted the floor. Probably a little over a hundred, she'd guess with the practiced eye she'd gained estimating herd sizes.

"I will now call a list of names. When I say your name, you will come and sit with Meg." Momo gestured her way. He began to read. One after the other, her colleagues stood. Alphabetical order, she noticed.

As they stood, Momo consulted the sheet then looked them in the face.

He'd nod, and they'd come over and sit beside her.

Each gave her a searching look, trying to gather information. Was this a good thing? Was this bad? She had no clue, other than Momo had locked onto the Key Initiative.

"Abraham Silverman," Momo called.

Rooster stood and got Abraham to his feet. Abraham wove his way unsteadily forward. He looked like he was about to pass out.

Momo considered him. "You are Silverman?"

"Yes," Abraham breathed out.

Momo called out something that Meg didn't understand. He must be speaking Somali. Meg longed to look at Rooster. To catch his expression, so she'd know what to think. But she forced her attention to Momo. She would not connect herself to Rooster in any way unless she thought it would help him.

The man who responded was talking animatedly with his hands. He must have been explaining why Abraham had been beaten.

Momo turned his eyes on Abraham and raised a brow. "You had multiple guns on your person?" he asked in English.

"I'm afraid of wildlife." He shrugged and lost his balance.

Momo put a hand on his shoulder to steady him and scrutinized his face. He glanced down to the paper in his hand. He shook his head as he caught Abraham's squinted gaze. "You introduced yourself to everyone as Abraham Silverman. But that is not correct." Momo turned to Meg. "Is this Dr. Abraham Silverman?"

Meg was wide-eyed, her brow in her hairline. What should

she do? Claim him? Disavow him? What would keep him safe? Her safe? She decided to go with the truth. "Dr. Silverman introduced himself to me when we met earlier this morning. We have only had electronic correspondence."

"This is not your picture," Momo told Abraham. "Who are you?"

"Abraham Silverman. But not *Dr.* Abraham Silverman." Abraham showed his hand, then slowly reached into his back pocket and pulled out his wallet. He flipped it open and handed it to Momo. "He told me I could use his name and go on this safari, and he'd straighten everything out once he got on site. A free holiday, if you will."

"This license says Abraham Silverman. You two happen to have the same names?"

"Imagine that." Abraham attempted a smile, but only one side of his face was working. "We have a lot of fun with it."

"You are having fun, then?"

"I was. I'm not having fun now."

Momo lifted his chin toward one of his men and handed off the wallet, giving an order in Somali. He turned back to Abraham. "It says you're an Israeli."

"I am an Israeli. Abraham and Silverman are common names there, like John Smith in America." Abraham's words slurred as he strung them together in a wet jumble. "Sometimes Abraham and I use this to our advantage, buying a single membership and both using it. It takes a little coordination. But it's not hard. We've done this for decades. I just happened to be using his safari pass while he's at his father's funeral. If you're looking for scientists, I'm no use to you."

"I believe you will be of use to me." Momo pointed. "Sit over there."

Abraham took a halting step then went down hard, landing

on his broken arm. He screamed in agony. Meg went over and helped him up, supported his weight, and brought him next to the base of the desk so he could lean against it for support.

When she next looked up, Momo was looming over Rooster and Randy. "Identification?"

Both men leaned to their sides to access their wallets in their back pockets and handed them over. "Rooster Honig. Eduardo Lopez. Both American citizens, yes?"

"Yes," they said in unison.

"What do you do for your livings?"

"We're industry consultants here to help get the Key Initiative going."

"I see, so you are part of this group?" He pointed back at her, and Meg dipped her head. "Meg," he yelled.

She popped her head up.

"I called two names, and they did not raise their hands. Lemmings and Clemson. Show me who they are."

Meg pushed to standing. She needed to feel a little more in control. "They aren't here. They had visa issues. I don't expect them to join us until Monday."

Momo gestured toward Rooster and Randy. "And these men are connected to you?"

To her? She sent up a quick prayer for choosing the right response. Rooster obviously wanted them to be associated with the scientists, but was that to help save her at their own detriment? Or was that because Rooster thought that that was their best chance of getting out of this alive? She decided to trust Rooster knew what he was doing. "They are industry consultants here to help the Key Initiative get going." She parroted. Meg could feel the sweat in her armpits soaking through the many layers of clothes Rooster had instructed her to put on. She felt overly warm and confined in the layers, and the heat and constriction were making her claustrophobic and angry.

Momo turned back to Rooster. "How do you speak Kiswahili?"

"I've worked in Eastern Africa for years."

Meg noticed that when Rooster spoke, he affected a slightly deeper tone and a rather defined Southern drawl. She wondered why.

"And you speak other languages?"

"A bit of Arabic. And English, of course."

"And you?" Momo pointed at Randy. "You speak Kiswahili? What languages do you speak?"

"A very little bit of Kiswahili. I'm learning that and Arabic. I'm fluent in English and Spanish."

Momo stared at them hard. He nodded his head toward the scientists. Randy and Rooster rose, side by side, shoulder to shoulder, then broke apart, so they were tightly staggered. They moved to the far side, away from her. But when they sat, she saw Ahbou's slender leg disappear behind their backs. And her heart stuttered. She was going to keep that little boy safe. That goal became enormous inside of her, taking up space and depth, like a tree setting its roots in the ground. She had a purpose, and it helped her. Made her feel powerful. Now to turn that purpose into a good outcome.

The man that Momo had spoken to returned with a laundry cart and a roll of trash bags that would fit the small bathroom bins. Momo tipped his head toward Meg's group. "One at a time, you will put all of your personal effects in your bags. Wallets, jewelry."

Another man came up with a Polaroid camera.

Meg wondered where they got one. Hadn't they stopped making film for those about a decade ago?

Her mind had been whirring a thousand miles a second. Filtering information. She wondered why it had suddenly settled on that song—and now the lyrics were playing in her brain.

That stopped the second the guy with the camera pointed to her then indicated she should stand. He took her picture and gathered her gold stud earrings and a ring her mom had given her for her eighteenth birthday. Did this mean they were being held for ransom, and this was proof of identity?

Momo had moved with one of the gunmen to the other hostages. One by one, he looked at their IDs, asked them their job, and collected their items. Each in a separate bag. Each bag tossed into the laundry hamper. No other person was added to the Key Initiative's group. The man rolled the basket down the hall. Meg imagined he was heading to a door that wasn't padlocked shut.

Momo finished his task and then said, "Please, if you will follow me."

They rose and moved in the direction the cart had gone.

Meg tried to help Abraham, but Rooster stepped in and took hold of him.

They walked down the hall and turned right. Down another hall to a door marked "Exit." Meg tried to angle herself along the way, so she drifted toward Randy to help hide Ahbou. There were plenty of places that they could have stowed Ahbou along the way—under a tablecloth, into an open door. Randy seemed determined, though, to keep him hidden and keep him with them.

Meg's mind went to the men with the lumpy shirts. To the boxes and wires. To Momo, flicking the object in his hand. Then to Abraham passing some information to Rooster in what she assumed was Arabic. And though it was probably as clear as glass to everyone else, she just then realized that they were going to explode the hotel with all those people inside. And the only survivors would be the Key Initiative scientists.

That's why Randy and Rooster wanted to be attached to her group, and that's why they were bringing Ahbou along.

Meg's blood iced. Her teeth chattered against each other. The moist fabric of her clothes wicked what had been unbearable heat from her skin and left her shivering. Ahbou's uncle, the last of Ahbou's family, was about to die.

And Ahbou would be left with no one.

But me. He'll have me.

Now, she just needed to stay alive and see that through.

25

———

ROOSTER

The Front Drive

THERE WEREN'T a lot of options. Not any good ones anyway. They had been divided up into groups of seven. Each placed beside a truck. Each truck had a driver and someone sitting shotgun. Literally. Rooster made sure to be positioned with Meg and Randy. He had half-carried half-dragged The Ghost over with them. They needed to keep tabs on this guy. He held secrets that Momo might find overly interesting, like that Rooster and Randy were the ones that had been negotiating the hostage release back in Djibouti. And they were the ones to blow up his crew and take the Bowens.

Yeah, that just might be an extra ticket to the torture chamber and a long-ass death. If Randy and Rooster had different moral compasses, it might just be a reason to drop The Ghost down and hold his airways closed like the Maasai goat.

The Ghost should count his blessings they held tight to their code.

There were three other scientists huddling together who were assigned to this truck. They had been around in the crater, but Rooster hadn't had a conversation with them. Had no idea who they were. He hoped their specialties were ones that could help them when they escaped.

None of the scientists, apart from Meg, looked like they could lift their body weight or run any kind of distance.

Rooster would leave options open, but it looked like their escape crew would be Meg, Randy, and him, and they'd send back help.

Escape looked like their only option. He had no idea if The Ghost had a check-in time that might have passed, something that might give the Mossad a clue that things were amiss. Doubtful. Black-ops kept their distance. Worked alone. And would be disavowed if taken. Rooster looked down at The Ghost leaning against the boulder. This guy was shit out of luck from his end of things. They were too. Panther Force wouldn't even be wheels down for another six hours or so. The terrorists had taken his watch, so now he was guessing. Even if somehow his unit had an immediate heads up, they'd still need to arrange to get to the crater, or wherever it was, they were headed in these trucks.

Their guard was about as big as Rooster's right leg. But he was the one with the rifle. The hostile pulled each of the scientists by the arm, separating them out, so they couldn't speak to each other. Made sense. The problem was Ahbou.

As soon as Meg was dragged to the side, Ahbou was spotted. The man demanded to know why this boy wasn't in the lobby. "The boy goes over there." He pointed to the front door.

"This is my son," Meg said, tucking him under her arm.

"No. This is an African boy." The hostile reached for Ahbou's arm.

Meg snatched Ahbou back and tucked him behind her back. The ferocity in Meg's face would make anyone who's ever seen a wild animal protect their young believe that this child could only have come from her body. "I was married to an African man."

The hostile flicked his finger toward the group. "He is here?"

"He is dead."

Momo called out, pointing his finger. One of the scientists that was supposed to load onto their truck was trying to use Meg's altercation as a distraction for escape. He had climbed up on the rock and was just starting to make his way down the other side. Rifle fire was trained in his direction.

Rooster grabbed Meg and Ahbou, pushing them to the side of the rock, the only place around them that had any cover. He pressed them to the ground and draped himself over them.

A scream rang out and fell away as the runner tumbled into the crater.

"*Fuck*!" That was Randy swearing.

Rooster swung his body around the rock, expecting to see The Ghost had been hit, but Randy was gripping his thigh. Rooster was instantly at his side, jerking off Randy's belt and pulling the end through the buckle when Meg showed up at his side.

"Fuck!" Randy yelled through gritted teeth.

"Hang in there, Randy. We've got this," Rooster said.

As Rooster pulled the belt tight, Meg slid her fingers into the wound. She looked up at the sky and blinked with concentration as she felt around. She pulled her hand up, clasping a severed piece of Randy's femoral artery between her index and middle fingers. Clamping it down with her left hand, she twisted her right hand and quickly tied it off with a figure-eight knot.

"I'm fucking going down with a ricochet. Isn't that an ironic slap in the face?" Randy gasped out.

"You're not going down. You're going to fight your way through this—mind over body, brother. Your femoral was blown, but you only bled hard for a second or so. Meg's handling it. You're going to *fight*. That's an order, Sergeant."

"Yes, sir," he slurred as he passed out.

Even with Rooster cinching down tight on the belt, blood continued to seep from Randy's leg. Meg wore his blood in her hair, on her face, and up her bare arms. Somewhere in this, she had pushed her sleeves out of the way. She reached back in, digging around. Meg pulled another piece of artery out of the hole and yanked it into a knot. Better, but still bleeding.

"Meg, this belt isn't doing it for a tourniquet. I need you to give me three of your liner socks, lash them together."

Meg fell back on her ass and was tugging off her boot and wool sock.

"Ahbou, son, give me your shirt." Ahbou pulled off his shirt immediately and handed it to Rooster, who packed the wound. "Okay, now, run to that tree and get me a stick at least as big around as three of your fingers."

AFTER ROOSTER RIGGED the makeshift dressings and tied down the tourniquet, he slowly released the belt. It looked like it was holding. Randy wasn't bleeding any more.

Meg was tying her boot back in place. Her hands dripped blood. She was beseeching St. Jude for miraculous intercession under her breath.

Rooster pulled Randy into rescue position, on his side with

his good leg bent to hold him in place. He gently raised Randy's chin to tilt his head back. Two fingers at his carotid told Rooster that there was still a resolute heartbeat, even if it was faint. The back of his hand under Randy's nostrils told him that he was breathing. Even if they'd gotten the bleeding to stop, the pool of blood under his leg meant that he needed fast action to keep him from brain damage. If a helicopter was en route, he'd have a better chance.

Rooster ducked his head, shaking it back and forth with grief. He placed a hand on Meg's shoulder. She bent her head against his shoulder, rolled into his arms. "He's stabilized as much as possible. It's best if they think he died. I have a plan."

A wail swelled from Meg's throat, raising the hair on his scalp. He wondered if she hadn't heard and understood him or if she was one hell of an actress. He stood and half-lifted, half-dragged Meg back to where the gunman was.

He kept his head down near Meg's to give her comfort, but also so he could look around for options.

They were slim and few.

He drew a bottle of water out of her pocket and used it to wash off her hands and face. She might need that water later for survival, but her mental health was as important as her physical health.

Maybe more so.

Rooster moved to the far side of the group, over to the tree where Ahbou had collected the tension stick.

Ahbou was his shadow.

Momo had a soldier focused on them.

Another gunman looked over the rock to make sure the scientist had died.

When the guard was distracted, Rooster pulled Ahbou onto his back. He leaned his head back to talk to him quietly in

English. "Ahbou, how do you like trees? This tree here—it will hold your weight, and it has enough leaf cover that you can get right up next to the trunk and hide there until this is over, yeah? I bet you can climb like a monkey. You could hide in the tree for as long as it takes. Right?"

Rooster could feel Ahbou nodding.

"When they take the trucks out of here, you are *not* to go back to the hotel. Where can you go instead of to the hotel? Where are the closest people with phones?"

"To walk? The Maasai boma. To drive? The clinic."

"But no one will be here to drive."

"I can drive," Ahbou said. "I have driven there before when my uncle hit his head. I push the chair back and drive standing up."

"Ahbou, Randy's alive and needs help as soon as you can get it for him. You can do that for Meg and me, can't you? Help Randy? Get him a doctor?"

"Yes. I can *do* it." There was conviction in his tone.

Rooster knew that Ahbou had been the head of his household as a very young child. Responsibility was something Ahbou shouldered with familiarity. Rooster believed him when he said he could do it. Believed that more than *could*, he actually *would* do it. And he also believed that having a mission gave someone a forward-thinking brain—a survival mindset.

"Good, now up you go, quiet as a cheetah stalking his dinner."

Without any assistance, Ahbou scrambled up onto Rooster's shoulders. With remarkable balance, he bent his knees and sprang up to a limb. Rooster peeked up just long enough to see Ahbou swing his legs like a gymnast on the uneven bars to get the momentum to catapult himself onto the limb and clamber up until he disappeared. Rooster edged over to the remaining hostages. Meg sat on a rock, staring at her knees.

Momo moved back toward Meg. "Your scientist made a stupid move. Rash and deadly. His decision cost not one but two lives. We cannot afford such stupidity." He raised his voice to a pitch that could be heard by all. "The next person who tries to escape will be beaten without mercy and then killed. And he will die knowing that it will cost the fingers of all of your fellow scientists. Weigh that in with your stupidity."

"Where is your son?" the gunman asked Meg.

Meg looked around at the scientists, then back between her knees.

The gunman prodded her with his rifle. "I ask you, where is your son?"

"My son?" She cocked her head to the side. "I don't have a son."

"The African boy."

Meg shook her head then turned to Momo with a *What should I do? I'm so confused* look.

Momo turned to his guard. "Meg Finley is not a married woman. She has no children. Why are you asking about a boy?"

Meg turned innocent eyes on the guy. Meg deserved an Oscar for her performance. It was so good, in fact, that Rooster saw the young hostile second-guess himself. Whatever it was that went through his head, it made him self-doubt.

That might be a key to help them make their escape.

26

———

MEG

The Truck—Ngorongoro (maybe?) Tanzania

A**BRAHAM** S**ILVERMAN**, or whoever he was, was passed out with his head in Meg's lap. Rooster seemed to know him. That was odd. Small world or not, the kind of people that Rooster would brush up against lived in the dark underbelly of things. Meg wanted to know whether Abraham was trustworthy, but there were others in the truck, and she didn't feel free to talk about it. Besides, Rooster had distanced himself from her. If she spoke, it would be for everyone's ears.

They had two guards in the cab and two in the back with them. They had put Rooster in the far back.

Smart move.

If he was sitting where Meg was, Rooster could grab them at the same time and shove them out the opening in the canvas and make his escape.

She looked down at her fingers and wondered if Momo's

threat was real or a psychological shackle. Making a life or death decision for one's self was different than for the whole group. Meg thought back to her studies of World War II concentration camps and how the Nazis reined in the masses by that threat.

Humans were, after all, animals.

Animals with a biological predisposition to save their community; however, that community was defined in the moment.

As if reading her thoughts, Jared Dolan, the scientist next to her, said, "That was a pretty horrifying threat the leader made about our fingers. I wonder if someone from one of the other trucks attempts an escape if they'd punish everyone, even if we weren't around. I'm rather attached to my fingers, don't you know." He tried to chuckle as if he were making light, but it came out as a rasp.

"Do you think they're planning to do that anyway?" another scientist, Johnathan Marley, asked. "Isn't that what they do? They ask for payment for the release of a prisoner or some such thing, and when there isn't compliance, then they chop off a finger and send it in a box to prove they're serious?"

"No, that's not what they do," Rooster said.

When Rooster spoke, the guards got nervous. They were non-English, non-Kiswahili speakers. They had mostly communicated with glares and gun pointing.

Meg could feel them stirring in their seats, their fingers moving to their triggers. If the one near her swung his rifle in Rooster's direction, Meg thought she could probably grab hold of the barrel and use it to shove the guy back. If she had enough power behind the move, it might just force him out the back hatch. Of course, with Abraham in her lap, that would make things difficult. But that was her plan—for this guy anyway. She didn't have a plan for the guy on the other side of the truck.

"How do you know that?" Jared queried. "It's what they do in the movies. They make stuff up, sure. But it has to be based on something."

"You're a scientist," Rooster said. "What's your specialty?"

"I'm an agronomist. I work in soil reclamation."

"Okay, good. Then you're aware of what happens when an organism dies. It decays. Apply what you know to this situation," Rooster said. "Say they decided to cut off someone's thumb."

Meg felt the anxiety in the truck rise. Not just the soldiers this time.

"The tissues would start an immediate decaying process, yeah? Where are you from?"

"Nova Scotia," Jared murmured. "Canada."

"All right. Some observations and conclusions—first, we seem to be headed farther into the bush, not closer to civilization. No electricity means no ice or refrigeration. They would have to get to the nearest post office, and that post office would need to mail the package. The package would need to go through customs. Then it would need to be delivered. Let's say that takes a minimum of five days. Do you think that your thumb would be a distinguishable part of you to your family? I mean, even if you were to receive a freshly sliced-off thumb and were asked to definitively say this was or was not the thumb of a loved one, could you? No. Unless there's something remarkable about your thumb, it would be a stupid way to make a point. Let that go."

Now Meg felt the collective brains mulling over the argument. Agreeing with the assessment and easing up.

"Okay, then," Johnathan said. "What will they do?"

"Most likely, they'll make a video of you crying and looking in the lens of a camera, begging your family earnestly to do whatever it takes to save you."

Rooster was very blasé about the information. Making her

cry wasn't going to be hard. In fact, Meg had been working over-time, trying to keep her emotions in check. But Rooster? Except for tears of laughter, like he'd shed when he realized she'd thought he was Randy's lover, she couldn't imagine anyone wringing a tear from him.

Randy. Was he still alive? She'd seen Rooster standing under the tree and Ahbou climbing to his shoulders and jumping up out of sight. He, at least, was probably safe. As their truck was being loaded, Rooster had said he and Ahbou had made a plan to care for Randy—and he reminded her to stay the hell away from him. "Distance yourself physically and emotionally." Physically was hard but doable. Emotionally?

Uhm, no.

That wasn't going to happen.

What actually happened was she had been sitting in a bar with this intelligent, funny, kind man who also happened to be handsome as hell. She had put her hands on his thighs, leaned in, and kissed him. And somehow, her fate had been sealed. Her heart belonged to a near-stranger.

Now *that* was a revelation.

About a half-hour down the road, an explosion lit up the sky, and the sound waves blasted the night. Meg shut down completely. Hundreds of people had probably just lost their lives. She, Rooster, Ahbou, and Randy could very well have been amongst them. Randy…had he survived it? Was he alive? Could she have done more for him? Guilt was an acid that burned through her veins. Horror seeped through her pores. She shook so hard she could barely stay upright. She could feel Rooster sending her strength. It was the only thing holding her together.

THEY BOUNCED over the ground through the bush. They hadn't been following any roads for what seemed like an eternity. Meg's stomach was growling. The adrenaline must be working its way out of her system. She was suddenly thankful for Rooster taking the extra minutes to get her prepared. The extra socks that she pulled off her right foot very well could have saved Randy's life. *Please, God.* And now she had a food supply. She wasn't sure how long it would have to last. She selfishly didn't want to share with the others in the truck. And if she pulled the protein bars out here, the guard might just take them from her. She'd wait.

She could see the other two Key scientists had fallen asleep. Rooster had his head resting in his hands. He was the only one who was restrained. They'd tied his hands together with rope. She'd slip him some food as soon as she was close enough.

Her stomach rumbled again. Maybe she could sneak a bite. She reached under her windbreaker into the kangaroo pocket on her hoodie. She'd stuffed it to the max, getting the bars in. This had kept them in place during their ordeal.

Ordeal?

That word didn't have enough octane. She needed a better word. But she couldn't land on one.

Terror? She had a feeling, though, that even though this night had been the worst thing that she'd experienced in her life, that she shouldn't call it terror— even that was overused and had lost the scale she was looking for.

But there wasn't really a step above terror. And she felt like she was balanced on one of the first rungs on that ladder.

Meg shoved the power bar deeper into her pocket. She'd lost her appetite. She'd also lost her will to dam her tears. She let them flow silently down her cheeks as they traveled farther and farther into the wilderness.

Meg came awake with a jolt as the rear gate of their truck banged open, and the canvas was pushed aside. She must have cried herself to sleep because it was dawn.

The sky was just beginning to lighten with the new day.

Abraham lay still in her lap. His mouth was open and hung slightly to the side. His lids weren't tightly closed.

Her body convulsed, and she almost pushed him off her lap. She thought he'd died there last night, and she had been cradling the head of a corpse. But then his tongue protruded, and he licked his lips and groaned. Still alive.

The guards came and lifted Abraham under the arms, and they got him mostly upright as they dragged him away. The door to the truck shut. The flap descended, and they were back in the dark.

"Is everyone okay?" Meg asked.

"Other than being in desperate need of some water and a tree to piss on, I'm fine," Jared said.

"I'm about the same," Johnathan replied, then leaned toward her. "Was Abraham still alive?"

"How about you, Meg?" Rooster asked. His quiet words came to her as if telegraphed so that no one else would hear the vibrations disturbing the atmosphere.

Maybe she imagined it. She sent him a thumbs up then answered Johnathan, "Yes, but he obviously needs medical attention."

"Do you think this is our destination? Why do you think we stopped?" Jared asked.

No one answered, but for her, it set off wild speculation as to what came next. Rooster had said they'd be making videos. She thought she was pretty much all cried out after last night. *Maybe if I drank some water, I could cry some more.*

Irreverent thoughts were often her go-to way of dealing with stress.

But this time, it backfired. Was there water to be drunk here? They were pretty far from anywhere, and you couldn't just drink any found water. Cholera and other waterborne diseases were a major problem in East Africa. She had a bottle and a half in her coat pocket—no one had taken that from her yet. How long could she make that last? Could she get some of it to Rooster? Would he take it from her?

Maybe those kinds of thoughts were irrelevant right now. Maybe she should be thinking about the video instead. What would she do if they asked her to say something horrible, like renouncing her reason for being in Africa, or renouncing America, for that matter? Would she? This was a question she'd never asked herself before. Was she willing to be hurt or killed for words said or not said? Would she say whatever needed to be said and know that what was in her heart was the truth, not the words? Meg guessed that depended on who would see the video. If the recording of her saying bad things about America was used to inspire terrorists who would jump on a bus with a suicide vest and kill dozens of innocent people, then she'd be complicit.

Maybe they'd just make the recordings and send them to the Gateway Foundation or her university. Proof of life, isn't that what they called it? If that was the case, they'd reach out to her family. Her mom and step-dad, her sister Kelly, and Steve. *Steve*! Steve was with the FBI. The FBI operated around the world on American hostage rescues. Surely, they would race to save any American, but maybe having a special agent's sister in the mix might add a little extra boost to their rockets. And there was Rooster. She knew so little about him, other than that he had a sister named Mary Margaret. If Mary Margaret got a recording, she'd definitely contact Iniquus. Iniquus had operators in Africa and the Middle East. They could probably get on-site quickly. How quickly? It would no doubt take days for them to mobilize. Yeah, this situation would go on for days and days.

The gunmen came to get her next. As she slid over the lip of the tailgate, she forced herself not to look back at Rooster. She could feel him burrowing inside her mind. Reminding her that she'd made promises to him. "That's what you'll do. That's what you'll keep doing. You will *never give up*."

I didn't get a chance to hand him some food.

The gunman grabbed the sleeve of her jacket and tugged her toward the building. A whisper of fear coated her. She blocked the images of what might be waiting for her as the only female in the group. She thought for a nanosecond that she might be safe. She was an uncircumcised female, and there were taboos barring the men in many African cultures from any sexual contact with uncircumcised women. And then she entered the building and thought, *Fuck*. And that's the word that hammered in her brain with a consistent beat as she walked down the cement hall lined with cells.

This must be an abandoned prison.

Old. Dank. Rusted. Filthy. They turned the corner. *Dark. Smelly. Leaking. Horrible*. On this corridor, there were four cells —two on the left and two on the right. The one on the left side at the end stood open. The man said in broken Kiswahili, "Momo says as his guest of honor you get the most beautiful room. Two windows." He waved her in. It was the last place she wanted to go.

"I need to use the bathroom," she stalled. As the only woman, would she be segregated from the group? Alone? Wasn't there something she'd read about what happens to people when they are isolated—put in solitary confinement? Panic was a palpable thing. It engulfed her.

Across the hall, she spotted a lump of clothes in the corner. That cell had a single window, and there wasn't much light outside at this time of the morning. After focusing, she realized it was Abraham, dumped in a pile in the corner. "Can I help him get more comfortable? He's badly hurt. His arm is broken."

The guard wagged a finger at her.

"The bathroom then?"

He pointed at a plastic bucket inside her cell. She spun around and saw that each of the four cells had a matching bucket, much like the one they'd drunk honey beer from just yesterday. Could that really be just yesterday? So much had happened in such a short time. The bees and Robert, the truth behind Rooster's call name, the wonderful follow-up in her bed that was interrupted by all hell breaking loose, and now here she was. Wherever "here" was.

"Some water? To drink?" She tried again.

"After everyone is put away."

She eyed the door to her cell. She'd be locked in there. The windows were too high to see out. Too small to crawl through, even if they didn't have bars. She'd be a prisoner. She had been a prisoner all night, sure. But this seemed radically different some-how. She just stared into the cell. And blinked.

Suddenly, the guard took his rifle in two hands, and, using it as a shield, he thrust it out at her, pushing her into the cell. The door shrieked against its hinges as he swung it closed with a final bang before she could catch her balance and contrive some other means of avoiding this fate. She moved back over to the wall made of bars and wrapped her hands around them as she watched the guard leave. What was she going to do now?

27

ROOSTER

Who the Hell Knows, Tanzania (?)

"MEG, ARE YOU ALL RIGHT?" Rooster sat with his back against the bars in the cell beside Meg's, thank God. Three walls made of cement blocks, one wall of rusty bars. He reached out his hand as far as it would go toward her cell and felt her fingers interlace with his.

"Abraham isn't moving," she said.

"He may be playing possum. Let's hope so." There seemed to only be natural light in this place. He was glad that Meg got the cell with two windows. That would help her morale. His cell was dark and mostly empty. They gave him a waste bucket—that was something—at least he didn't have to piss in the corner and lay in the puddle. Bonus.

Meg was pushing a power bar into his hand.

At first, he thought he should refuse. He'd eaten the one in his pocket surreptitiously last night in the dark. But the truth was, they had missed lunch yesterday because of Robert and had missed dinner because of this crap. He'd had three power bars—that gave him about four hundred calories in the last twenty hours when normally he ate ten times that amount.

He'd be more help to her if he was functional, and he wasn't sure the guards wouldn't eventually take the bars from her and eat them themselves.

Get while the getting was good.

"Thank you." Rooster quietly tore away the wrapper, shoving the wrapping into his pocket, then ate the bar down in two bites. Rooster reached out for Meg again. He had to stay wary, though. He didn't want to get caught holding her hand. He'd weighed the comfort he thought he might bring her versus aligning them in the eyes of the captors and decided this was worth the risk. Psychological studies, after all, had proven that holding a woman's hand—or better, hugging her—brought their stress levels down and increased their ability to cope. He'd seen that play out on the different missions he'd run. When women were touching someone, they cared about, be it a child or an adult, be it a man or another woman, they always were better off than if they were isolated from others.

"I have a pact to make with you," Meg said as soon as her hand was back in his. "You won't sugarcoat things for me, and be perfectly honest. And I'll do the same for you."

"Okay. First test of the pact. You didn't answer my question. Are you all right? Did they hurt you?"

Meg probably understood what he was asking. She'd been taken out of his view for almost a half-hour, but he wasn't going to say it out loud. He didn't want to plant any seeds in her mind if she hadn't already landed on that possibility.

"No one touched me. I've been in here wringing my hands and feeling selfish."

"How's that?"

"I'm so glad you're here with me. I should wish you weren't —that you got away, that you stayed behind to help Randy. But I'm going to tell you the truth. I'm so grateful you're here. I feel like I have a chance."

"You don't just have a chance, Meg. You *will* get out of this. You *will* get home. You *will* go on with your life."

"Okay." She didn't sound convinced. "My emotions are pretty raw right now. I'm not very comfortable doing emotions in normal life. I prefer being in the rational part of my mind. Is it okay for us to talk? Can I ask you some questions?"

"Let's just keep the volume as low as possible. These guys don't speak English, but Momo does."

"Have you seen Momo since we left the hotel?"

"No, but that doesn't mean he's not here," Rooster said, sending a glance over to The Ghost.

"How long do you think it will take before people start looking for us?"

That answer depended entirely on Ahbou and if he survived the blast or not. If Ahbou survived and got help, he would tell someone that their group had been kidnapped and the direction that they'd taken out of there. If he didn't survive, then it was Momo's timetable that would dictate when the world at large became aware that there were blast survivors. There was also the off chance that Momo didn't mean to tell anyone he had the scientists and that he had some evil-overlord plan where he needed scientific information. That might make sense when it came to people like Meg, who could help him interpret satellite images, but Rooster couldn't imagine what Momo needed with an agronomist.

"Don't expect anything to happen fast," Rooster answered. "This is going to be a long haul. Momo will make contact, and then the real work begins. I know you can't imagine that this is true, but slow and steady wins the race. If they're negotiating our release, time is one of the things that's used as a tool. I know that's not what you want to hear. But we only speak in truths, you and me. It would be good to know why they picked this group to bring out here, though."

"Explain the slow and steady wins the race bit."

"The terrorists are amped up right now, and they will be for a while. It will take time for the hostiles to calm down and get rational. We call it a 'cooling-off period.' Once the hostiles calm down enough to clarify their motives, the rescue team will move ahead. Gather intel. Formulate a rescue. You don't want authorities rushing in to bang their guns and end up saying we got ten of the twenty hostages home. You want *all* of the hostages to go home. That means even if the rescuers were hot on our trail, they'd lay out there in the field, figuring things out. Counting people, tracking guard duty, coming up with the most effective plan possible to get us out safely. And that takes days, in and of itself. But that's only if the negotiations fail."

"If negotiations fail. What could make them fail?"

Rooster was glad to hear her voice wasn't emotional but pragmatic. She was gathering data and obtaining a clearer picture of their circumstances. "Too many to name. And not someplace I want your mind to wander. It's best for everyone, safest for everyone that there is a negotiated outcome. Going in guns blazing is the stuff of movies. Flying bullets and panic are a lethal combination. Like I said, slow and steady wins the race."

"That sounds like a motto."

"It is. I have it tattooed on my right butt cheek."

"You don't either. I've seen your right butt cheek, I'll remind you."

"I don't need reminding. It's at the front of my mind. And I plan to finish what Momo interrupted in the not-too-distant future."

They sat quietly after that. Rooster brushed his thumb over Meg's hand, thinking how badly he wanted her in his arms.

"Meg, there are going to be times, probably several times a day, when panic is going to move in. When you feel that happening, you have to put those feelings into a box. Panic burns energy saps your ability to think and cope. Science, okay? Stay in that analytical part of your brain. When you panic, you excrete hormones. Adrenaline gets your heart racing. It burns glucose. Your body shoots out glycogen from its reservoirs. Without enough protein in your diet, your body is eating its muscle first, leaving the fat stores for later survival. Less muscle means less strength. Less strength can make a difference in the end. From a scientific point of view, what is the best way to be prepared for an opportunity?"

It wasn't how he'd normally speak to Meg because he respected her mind. But this was his piece of the pie—the thing he knew best. One of the things he knew was that under stress and shock, a brain needed to come to conclusions on its own—it would give her a sense of ownership. She would embrace the ideas. And he needed her to do just that.

"To remain calm and thoughtful," Meg replied.

"Exactly. Panic is contagious. You know that from your studies of animal migration. When one animal senses a threat and responds by running, does each animal have to distinguish the same threat?"

"No, they all start stampeding in the direction set by the animal who made the observation."

"When there is a stampede when you're in the field, do you feel obliged to run with them, or can you sit back and observe?"

"Observe," she said.

"And why's that?"

"I'm not in that herd. They are a different species than I am."

"If an elephant herd is stampeding, the zebras would keep on munching grass?"

"No, they'd run too."

"Why don't you run with them?"

"Because that wouldn't save me, that would just endanger me. I would make other choices—climb a tree, get in the vehicle."

"Exactly my point. The people here are part of your herd. They are your group. We are being held by another group. The kidnappers know they are being hunted. Do you think their adrenaline is high too?"

"I hadn't thought about that, but yes. I mean, we know at least eleven of the kidnappers died last night. They probably feel less frightened than I do since they have guns and I'm in a cage. But I get what you're saying. They're affected by adrenaline too. And that would have the same cognitive and physiological effects on them."

"As we stay here, most of the scientists will be panicking. They'll be crying and moaning, screaming, combative. The kidnappers will be panicking—yelling, trying to intimidate, banging objects, brandishing weapons, just like animals would brandish their teeth or claws. Randy told me the story of when you came face to face with a lion. You're here to tell the tale, while others in a similar situation are not. How did you survive it?"

"I know lion behavior. That lion was scared for her cubs who had crossed my path. I positioned myself to not be a threat to her children."

"You stayed in your scientific brain. You analyzed the situation, adjusted as was required, and lived. That is exactly what you have to do now. You need to separate yourself from any group. You are not in the scientist herd. Nor are you aligned with the kidnappers. You are a thinking machine. A computer that analyses, predicts, and generates possible outcomes, and you pick the best one. For *you*."

"I'm aligned with you." She was a brick wall, cemented into place.

Rooster couldn't help but smile, both at the ferocity of her conviction but also that it was how she felt. It was certainly how he felt about her. *Nonetheless.* "No, you're not. No matter what happens to me, you will remain a scientific observer."

"So I'm not aligned with you, but you're aligned with me? I know you are. I know you wouldn't find a way out and leave me here. That's inconceivable."

"I'm aligned with you. You're not aligned with me."

"This is a stupid conversation. And not fair." She snatched her hand away, and it felt like a punishment.

"Be that as it may, it's still the truth."

"What if I don't agree to that?

"Then you'll end up losing, and the kidnappers will win."

Meg sat silently with that thought. After a long moment, she moved her hand back to his. "I have to ask. Do you say that because you think things are going to go badly for you?"

"I'm a nobody. They'll keep their high-priced players on the board."

"You think this is about ransoms, then?"

"If it's about ransom, I have a shot. If it's about terror, it's a longer shot."

"Why?"

"I'm working on a theory. I'll share it with you once I have a little more information. But the quick and dirty answer is, I'm big, strong, and trained. That intimidates his gunmen. I'm not good for their morale. I'm betting I'm the only one handcuffed to the bars. They did that because they know I'm looking for a way out of this."

Meg's hand moved up his wrist as far as her fingers could stretch.

"It's my other hand, Meg. If you have my belt on, I can get out of the handcuffs, no problem. The locks on the cells, they're the first real obstacle."

"I have the belt. What's the second issue?"

"Where do we escape to? My last mission, they didn't even bother to tie the victims to anything. They had no food, no water, no direction of travel. Even if they were fit and trained survivalists, there were no resources in that area. It would be like clinging to a piece of wood in the middle of the ocean. All you can do is hang on and hope for the best. From what I can tell, we're nowhere near civilization. There may well be natural resources. But there are also dangers, as you know. But see, when I escape, I'll have you to figure out how to make it to civilization. You'll tell the lions I'm a good guy."

"That's your aim—escape, not wait?"

"Watch and wait and look for opportunities. In the army, we're taught how to get through this. Goals are imperative. The first one, we already tried together. Escape."

"We failed."

"I think we got Ahbou out alive. I think he's one of our assets. But right, the first moments of an abduction are the crucial moments. It's important to take advantage of the chaos. Remember, our captors are humans with human reactions. Adrenaline hits them the way it hits us. Tunnel vision. Shaking hands. Problems thinking and processing. The more grounded you can stay, the better. Those who've been in battle have learned to deal with that level of chaos. It looked to me like these guys were well-trained but not battle-hardened. That's information that might serve us well along the way."

"They taught us at the university that if there was a live shooter to run, barricade, and fight back, in that order. We tried the running, and you did the fighting. I'm thinking about the barricade. What if we'd just locked ourselves in the room?"

"They were counting heads and looking for all of the scientists in the Key Initiative. You were on the top of their list. And had they overlooked you, had you hidden or barricaded, you would have been killed in the explosion."

"Instead, I'm here."

"Instead, you have a chance."

28

———

MEG

Prison

MOMO HAD ARRIVED. Meg knew it because she heard a warning yell, and then all the gunmen ran through the prison, checking that everything was as it should be. A guard was now standing at attention at the end of her hall. Meg could just make him out if she pressed her cheek against the bars. His sudden appearance meant she could no longer hold Rooster's hand. As soon as she pulled her arm back through the bars, fear crept over her. She had thought she was starting to settle into this new reality and feel that though this would be a long road, she could walk it. Now she doubted her chances.

Meg huddled in the far corner until the guard left. There was a commotion down the hall. One of the scientists was yelling, "But where are you taking me? What do you want?" He continued to call out his questions as he was taken farther and farther away, and Meg could no longer make out his words.

The guard who had taken up a position at the end of the hall was gone. She checked Abraham's cell. He hadn't moved. She scrambled back to the corner she shared with Rooster.

"Is it okay for us to whisper to each other?"

"I haven't heard any guards' boots. I think they might be on perimeter. Can you see anything out your window?"

"Let me try." She hadn't even tried to look yet. That thought shocked her. She had looked up at the windows, seen that they were higher than her head, and that had been that. She had a lot to learn about surviving. There were bars on her window, and she could grasp them easily. She didn't even need to stand on her toes. She certainly had the upper body strength, she hit the gym regularly, and she was a rock climber. She pulled herself into a chin up and looked around, then dropped back to the floor. She went to the other window and did the same.

"We're at the eastern corner at the front of the building. From the north side, I can see that there's another building just behind this one, sticking out a bit. I saw three guards on this building. Two in the front, one to the north. Momo and another guard are walking with Jared to the other building."

"Good report, soldier. Do you know where we are? Any idea at all?"

"We drove northwest on a road for a long time. That had to be B144. Do you have any idea how long we did that?"

"Around three hours or so."

"I'm reaching out my hand for you." She waited to talk again until their fingers were laced.

"Three hours, and then we were out in the bush for a few more hours," he prompted.

"I'd say we're somewhere near the Safari Club or the Conservancy. If we can find the river and follow it downstream, the club is in the elbow crook. The conservancy would be harder to find. Though there are Maasai in the area. They might help us. Or they might track us for pay. They wouldn't necessarily pick our side. Not to suggest they'd be part of an act of kidnapping or terror, just that they might get handed a bogus story. And they're not only some of the bravest people around, but they are also some of the best trackers. We'd be an easy find."

"All right. Good. I'm switching our conversation back to earlier when we were talking about army training and our first objective, escape. Here's the next step—resist. Going back to the movies, you see guys who are getting the hell beaten out of them, and they keep repeating their name, rank, and serial number. That's a prime way to get killed. Without medical help, small things become big things quickly. Infections are a big risk, for example."

Meg sent her gaze toward Abraham, still in his pile in the corner. She wondered again if he was dead. No flies, she told herself. He'd be covered with flies within minutes of dying. She shook her head to clear those thoughts.

"Don't take your cues from anything you've seen on TV or read in books," Rooster was saying.

Meg wondered if she'd missed anything important when she was distracted.

"Think like a scientist. You can play dumb. You can obfuscate. If they want you to do some work, do it. Slowly. But do it. Just try damned hard not to piss off the guy with the gun."

"Okay."

"I need to let go of your hand for a minute. I'm losing circulation with the cuffs, and I've gone numb."

Meg pulled her hand back with a frown. She heard the clang of metal against metal. She imagined he was trying to massage circulation back into his fingers.

Then he began, "There was this guy," Rooster said, "who

was held prisoner in Vietnam for almost eight years. He stayed alive because he kept his strong faith in a good outcome. He believed with every cell in his body that the experience was a gift that was there to serve him."

"That's some pretty good self-hypnosis he had going there. Eight *years*?" Meg pulled her knees to her chest and wrapped her arms around them.

"Did Randy ever tell you about his teammate that was captured?"

"We were supposed to meet up last year in New York. But he called at the last minute to tell me Lynx was kidnapped. I met her when she first joined the team, and I really liked her. I know he worked to find her night and day. His communication with me became one-word answers to my questions. Was he okay? Yes. Any news? No." Meg rested her cheek on her knee. She was bone tired. And for the first time in her life, she knew what that term really meant. She was so exhausted that the marrow in her bones was begging for rest.

"I was worried about him. It was like an obsession. He was going to get her back, one way or another. For a while, I thought it was because he had a thing for her, but he told me that she was their intelligence officer or some such thing. 'Puzzler,' I think he called her, and then he said his girlfriend had broken up with him because he didn't have time for her. He hoped I was more understanding. It was hard. I missed him. But there were a lot of times before when he was on missions, or I was in the field, and we were out of communication."

"If you know that about the search, then you know that Strike Force is coming after Randy—they'll be just as rabid. Panther Force will be coming after me that same way. And by extension, both forces will be coming after you. Family is everything to Iniquus."

Meg sucked in a lungful of air. Randy. She pulled up the picture of him lying under the rock. He was probably, possibly, safe from the blast, but with a tourniquet on his leg…The length of time it was on came with serious ramifications. The longer it was on, the less likely he could keep his leg. That is if he even survived the night. He was wounded and outside with predatory animals looking for dinner. Of course, the explosion would have driven most of them from the area. "I'm not his real family. I'm just family of the heart."

"I know, for a fact, you're listed on Randy's paperwork as his emergency contact, next of kin. I know he has a biological family in El Salvador, but I guess he thought you'd be a better avenue for his biological family to hear any news from. As far as Iniquus is concerned, you're family."

"That makes me feel better, I guess. Whatever happened to Lynx? Suddenly Randy was back in communication, but he never answered my questions about it."

"Yeah, that was complicated. Don't feel bad. No one at Iniquus knew what was going on either, only Mr. Spencer in Command knew, and of course Strike Force."

"She was found alive then?"

Rooster chose his words carefully. "She *is* alive. She had a very rough go of it. We don't know the whole story, and I'd never pry."

Screams erupted from outside, and Meg hoisted herself up and searched for the source. She saw nothing. But from her position, she could tell the screaming was coming from the other building. Her stomach knotted into a tight ball. Every follicle of hair on her body stood at full attention.

She scrambled back to her place. "Rooster, what are they doing?"

"I'd imagine they're making videos. Remember what I said

to you. You will resist intelligently. You will swallow your panic. You will outthink them. And you will work at not getting hurt—even a little."

The screaming stopped as abruptly as it had begun. Meg took out the half-filled water bottle and took a swig, then passed it to Rooster. "The guard said he'd bring me some water, but he hasn't done it yet."

"They'll make the first few days extra hard. Right now, you've lost a comfortable bed, good food, and freedom. In a few days, that will fade, and the simple things—food and water, for example—will seem of much greater value. They mean to break your will to fight back."

"How do they learn how to do these things?"

"Sometimes they're trained by the government, their military. Sometimes they experienced these things themselves. It comes as easy as breathing to certain people. There are all kinds of ways to get there, but don't be surprised by the deprivations that you begin with. We're better off than the rest as long as your food and water aren't discovered. How many bars do you have?"

"Eight left."

"Good. I want you to get as comfortable as possible. I'm going to teach you a technique that might help you."

Meg looked around. She had no idea how to make herself comfortable in here. "Okay, ready," she said without moving from her curled-up position.

"When bad things happen, I want you to keep your focus squarely on the positive. Unless you're analyzing a situation for data that can help you, you are not to revisit a bad scene. Not to relive it. Not to question your actions or non-actions."

"That's easier said than done."

"Right. I understand that. What I need for you to do is create a box. To do that we're going to go for a walk. Are your eyes closed?"

"Yes," she whispered.

"You're walking down a garden path beside cool water. You're comfortable here. It's your place. Up ahead is a figure. As you get closer, you can make out the face, the clothes. This is your helper. She is here to give you a gift. Go up and say hello." Rooster paused for a moment. "Your helper is reaching behind her and pulling out a box. Can you see the box? Can you take it into your hands?"

"Yes."

"I want you to take some time to hold it in your hands and look it over. Change anything you want. How big is your box? What is it made from? What color is it? How does it close? Does it have hinges? Does the lid come off? It has a lock. Examine the lock. Is it secure? Do you want to change anything about it?"

"No. I like it the way it is."

Rooster coughed, and she could hear him take another swig of the water. "Good. You know how to unlock the box and how to get the lid off. That's the way the thoughts get out. How do you put them in? Is it porous? Can it absorb the thoughts?"

"There's a lever with a slit—the thoughts can go in but not out."

"Good. And what form will your thoughts be? Are they written on a piece of paper?"

"They're smoke. A light gray smoke."

"Good. Let's test out your box. I want you to think of a beach ball. Hold it in your hands. Now take that thought and turn it into smoke and put it in your box."

"It won't go."

"All right, let's get you a helper. We'll set the ball on fire, and then the smoke will go into your box. Who could help you? It's good if you can make your helper funny or cute or kind."

"It's a tiny pink elephant with purple spots."

"And what does it do?"

"He's running on the scene with a match wrapped in his trunk."

Rooster chuckled. "Okay. Good. Then what?"

"He's scratching the match on the rock. It's ablaze. The beach ball catches on fire and turns to smoke."

"Good. Press the lever and vacuum the smoke into your box. Let me know when it's done."

"Done."

"Great. Any smoke? Any smell left? Any residue from the fire?"

"No."

Rooster waited a beat. "You know, the brain can't tell the difference between make-believe and reality. It processes both in the same way. People who are in elite sports, people who are in elite operations, they go through scenarios in their minds time and again, over and over. They think through each movement— where they place their head, what their right hand is doing, where their left hand is going. They move through the same scene with various changes in scenario, and it trains the brain what to do with the body in real life. The helpers you create are real in the sense that your brain believes they are real, yeah?" Rooster waited for her response, but Meg didn't answer him. "Your brain can also believe that all the scary things you conjure up are real too. It's training your body to respond with fear. It keeps you in a state of constant fight or flight. And we talked about why that would be bad."

"Yes, okay."

"Instead, you're going to act like an elite warrior. As soon as you notice some thought, some feeling bubbling up that is not serving you, you take the time to bring in your pink elephant to burn those thoughts and put the smoke into your box. Your box will hold all the smoke you can possibly make. Yeah?"

"Yes, all right." She wasn't all right.

"I don't want you to miss an opportunity. You must fight for your own survival. If you are given a chance at any point in time, you are to escape and not try to bring anyone with you."

"But you. We've already been through this."

"You will use any opportunity to save yourself and then lead help back here to me and the others."

"You would never do that. You'd never leave the others."

"Yes, I would. I plan to. Getting all of these people out of here is going to take resources. I'd leave them, but I wouldn't leave you. I promise. I won't leave you. Will you accept my promise?

"Yes."

"Do you believe my promise?"

"Yes."

"Do you promise me in return that you will leave me, be brave, and get out on your own if you see an opening?"

Meg went numb. How could he ask her such a thing? The very thought of running through the bush, leaving Rooster in harm's way, having his fingers cut off for her chance at freedom. No. No. No, she would *not* make that promise.

"Meg, I need you to promise me. Right now."

She crossed her fingers. "All right."

"Not good enough. Say the words."

She crossed the fingers on her other hand too. "I promise that if I see the light and can escape, I will go on my own and get help for everyone else."

"Now I need you to practice that in your mind until you can own it as your strategy."

Meg didn't try. She wouldn't practice leaving Rooster.

"You're hesitating. You're thinking about how cowardly and wrong it would be."

"Yes."

"Now's the time to call in your elephant. You need to blow up all the limiting thoughts you might be conjuring. Surviving this will take limitless thoughts and limitless action. You will do whatever is necessary to carry this story to the world and get help if it's at all possible."

"If."

29

———

ROOSTER
Prison

"ROOSTER?"

"Mmm-hmm?"

"I've been thinking about what I know about being taken prisoner. And my mind keeps landing on Stockholm syndrome. Can you tell me about that?"

"It's more of a side effect than a syndrome. It's a coping mechanism. It's when someone is in a life-threatening situation —the captive bonds with the captors, and sometimes vice versa. Psychologists can't figure out why some people respond this way and others don't. But they do know that some conditions increase the potential for having this reaction."

"Yes. That's what I want to know. I want to be on guard."

Rooster thought that Meg being on guard was probably a good idea. Knowing just a little bit about her childhood, but reading even more between the lines when he saw her face after he'd suffocated the goat, she was at risk. "It depends on how long we're here, how emotionally charged things stay. If we live under the same circumstances as the hostage-takers—for example, if they have the same poor diet that they give us or live in the same physical discomfort. If they were to threaten our lives and not carry it out."

"Mock executions? Like in Iran?"

"Yes. Also, the more dependent we are on them for our basic needs matters. They gave us buckets to use as toilets, so we aren't in a position of having full and painful bladders and begging them for relief. That's good."

"We've had no water given to us. We don't need to pee."

"Not yet, anyway. If that comes regularly, water and food, that will ease some of the dependency issues—though not all of them. As long as we're locked up, there's a level of dependence. No denying that. Another component is dehumanization. They haven't done that. They didn't, for example, put hoods on us as we left the hotel."

"We've seen their faces. Is that bad?"

"I don't know. We won't know until we're out of this circumstance."

"Don't say circumstance. It's too benign. Why not call it what it is? This nightmare. This horror show."

"Does that serve you, Meg? Or does using the word nightmare make you emotional? Remember, we need to stay observers, remove ourselves from the focus as much as possible so we can see the big picture. Using words that have heat and emotion don't help you to do that."

"Fine. Then, tell me how that plays out. Did you ever try to save anyone who had Stockholm syndrome?"

"Once." It was one of Rooster's great disappointments.

"What ended up happening to that person? What did you do?"

"I left her there."

"Left her? Just…left her? She was mentally ill if she had Stockholm syndrome."

"Things get complicated sometimes. Let me tell you the story, and then you might see how limited my options were. Her family was from a small town in Ohio. They decided to take a year and give it to the Lord. They packed up and moved to Mexico to be missionaries, helping the village to build better housing. It was parents and their fifteen-year-old daughter."

"Oh, dear."

"Exactly. One of the men in the village, a forty-year-old man, worked in the city, and he talked the girl up—told her how beautiful her drawings were. That he had contacts in the city, who would love to see her artwork to put in a gallery that the tourists frequented. He thought she could make some good money. Her mother said the man was flattering Rebecca and telling her she was pretty. Her family believes that physical looks are a distraction, that real beauty comes from the soul, so they had Rebecca dress in very plain clothes. She wore her hair in a braid down her back. No makeup. No boys until they returned home, then she'd be allowed to court."

"Court? As in the old-fashioned term for finding a spouse?"

"In their culture, it's normal for a boy to be her friend and hang out with the family, no alone time. Her mother said that most girls in their church began a courtship around sixteen, and they married on or around their eighteenth birthday. Their first kiss was at the altar after they had taken their vows."

"But how would you know if you had the spark? I've gone out with guys that had me all in a flutter, but it's that first kiss that tells it. If I don't get that zing, then I know to just let things go."

"I zinged you?" Rooster smiled at the thought. She'd zapped him but good.

"All the way down to my toes. It's never felt that way before—I thought the phenomenon warranted further investigation. I was just about to draw my conclusion too," she said with a note of regret.

Rooster's mind was back in her hotel room. Her eyes closed, the drape of her long hair painting over his chest. "I'm sorry."

"Yeah." That word was heavy with meaning. He thought she'd probably traveled back to the scene too. After a long pause, she asked, "What were you saying about Rebecca?"

"Rebecca had never been told she was pretty before. She ate up all the compliments like a starving child. And one day, this guy enticed her onto the back of his scooter, and off they went to meet with the gallery people with her sketch pad under her arm. Her parents never saw her again."

"But they hired you."

"Eventually. At first, they worked with the local police. But the men were macho—from a different culture. They thought it was the right of a man to woo a girl. And in that area, fifteen would mean she'd had her *Quinceanera*. She was considered a woman. Nothing was done on the part of the Mexican authorities to bring her back. The church back in Ohio gathered enough money to send a private investigator down, but he got nowhere."

"How did you get involved? Iniquus doesn't come cheap."

"The parents visited a megachurch. They told their tale and asked for help. That church hired us. Panther Force got the job. I went down to see what I could see."

"You speak Spanish?"

"I can get from point A to point B, but my languages are

from Africa and the Middle East. I had a cultural interpreter from the region who could not only speak the local dialects, but he also helped me understand the psychology of the region. At any rate, I tracked her down, and she was about eight or nine months pregnant with this guy's kid. She said she loved him and wasn't leaving."

"How old was she by then? How much time had elapsed?"

"At that point, she had been gone for a little over two years, but she was eighteen. A legal adult in the US. If I took her, it would be kidnapping."

"But a judge could determine she wasn't in her right mind, couldn't they?"

"She was on foreign soil, getting ready to have a Mexican baby, married to a Mexican man, eighteen years old. No. No judge would get involved with that. My one and only case of Stockholm syndrome."

She said nothing.

"Are you disappointed in me?"

"I'm thinking." She sounded like she was in her rational mind, not a touch of emotion. Certainly not disappointment. "We just met. I don't know you very well. But that outcome seems antithetical to the image I have of you. You didn't just leave. You tried other things."

"When I was on that case, I talked extensively with Iniquus psychologists. You're right. We didn't just pack our bags and head on home. I was hoping there was something I could say that might change the outcome. She was living in extreme poverty in a cardboard shack with a village latrine and a common water spigot in the center of the dwellings. I didn't want to leave her there, knowing she'd give birth without proper medical attention. The psychologist told me that some studies suggest that Stockholm syndrome is an evolution that is developed from unequal power. That theory helps to explain boy soldiers, and in some cases, abused children and their parents. And if you take a group with strong patriarchal backgrounds, like the home she grew up in, then girls have already learned the coping mechanisms required to stay alive."

"My biological father abused our family, and I survived. Do you believe I'm at risk for using this coping mechanism to marry some kidnapper and have his baby in the Tanzanian bush?"

"I honestly hadn't thought it through to that point. You're actually the one who brought it up." Rooster let the silence hang between them. He was listening to the guards bring Jared back into the jail. He sounded like his footsteps were in a normal rhythm. It sounded like he was upright and walking under his own power. That helped convince Rooster that they were taking videos. When his turn came, Rooster would know if they were being held for terror or for money by the messages they wanted him to send out. A door slammed, and another shrieked open on its rusty hinges. Another man was asking. Where am I going? What do you want with me? And pleading sincerely not to hurt him, he'd cooperate. What the scientist didn't understand was that in these videos, the terrorists would want to show him being hurt and crying out in order to accomplish their goal.

The scream was inevitable.

Rooster didn't want Meg to be thinking about that. He stretched out his hand toward her. "Meghan, my hand is out. Will you reach for me, please?" After her fingers entwined with his, he asked, "Are you still thinking about Stockholm syndrome?"

"When I was little, my father used to proudly tell everyone I was a daddy's girl. I aligned with him against my mother. I was horrible to my mother. It's my greatest shame to this day, though mom always tells me it wasn't my fault, and she always understood. She blames herself for keeping us in that situation. I blame myself. Steve blames himself, and the only person who doesn't blame herself is Kelly because she was a toddler when the police came and dragged Paul away."

ROOSTER HAD COUNTED the number of times the keys had jangled in the locks. The rounds of screaming coming from the other building. And the number of people who were thrown back in their cells. The guards were bringing back number seventeen.

Meg had fallen asleep after they talked Stockholm syndrome and staying mentally healthy. She had slept the sleep of someone who'd run on adrenaline for almost twenty-four hours straight and had their last ounce of energy wrung from them. The prisoners still hadn't had food or water. He bet they'd bring water after they were done with the tapes. Humans don't live long without it—and they, at least some of them, were precious commodities, no matter the terrorists' end goal.

The three on this corridor—The Ghost, Meg, and Rooster—were the last to undergo the ordeal. In many ways, it made it that much harder as they sat anticipating their turn. The brain was a devil as it tried to conjure up images of what was happening to the others. Rooster used techniques similar to the ones he had taught Meg.

He'd been doing it for so many years, it was a reflex.

Now he wondered how to make sure he went before Meg, so he could give her some warning and maybe some more precise techniques to get through it.

The guards came for The Ghost first. One stood at the door to the cell with his rifle trained on the interior. The other two went in and hoisted him to his feet. He was able to get his legs under him. Rooster thought he was mostly unconscious; otherwise, the pain of how they were holding his arm would make him shriek—no matter his training. The Ghost never lifted his eyes, never looked Rooster's way. He had moved robotically between the guards as he left, and he hadn't been brought back in when they came for Rooster.

Rooster was cuffed for the walk. These guys were amateurs. They didn't cuff him in the back. That was information. They slipped two pieces of rope in the chain between the cuffs. One rope was looped through the cuff, then each end was tied to one of his ankles, forcing him to either squat low or bend in half. The other rope then looped through the cuffs and was held by a guard, like he was walking a dog. That image came to him, and he let it drift right on along, never resting his attention on it, just noticing it and moving it out into the distance.

Rooster scanned over the other prisoners as he made his way out.

He didn't see any visible injuries—no broken noses. Broken noses were a quick and easy way to make a point. The pain was blinding and incapacitating. It let people know you were serious. It also made a bloody mess of their face that was sure to panic the families into selling all their assets to save their loved ones.

All the scientists had screamed. Rooster assumed this meant they were attaching electric wires and sending a blast of current through their system. Yeah, that would make a very effective video. But The Ghost hadn't screamed. And he had a serious head injury. Would Momo realize he couldn't jolt someone with a concussion? Rooster didn't hold out much hope that The Ghost had lived through the ordeal.

As he had left, Rooster dipped his head under his arm, as if wiping his face on his sleeve, so he could catch a glance at Meg. He'd hoped she would still be oblivious in her cell, but she was gripping the bars and staring out at him with horror in her eyes.

Now he had to decide whether to scream and give the asswipes what they wanted or stay silent and protect Meg. He'd wait and see what was in store for him before he made that call. He was prepared for whatever they brought. Couldn't be worse than what the Delta's sprang on him in SERE—survival, escape, resistance, and evasion—school, he reasoned. *Well, yeah. It could be.* He noticed that thought and let it move on out of his consciousness and disappear over the horizon.

Rooster shuffled along beside them and reminded himself to affect the southern drawl he'd used earlier. He wondered if The Ghost had given up Rooster's identity to Momo and the role he'd played in the Bowen case.

ROOSTER CAME BACK to consciousness when they threw a bucket of water on his face. There wasn't an inch of his body that didn't ache. He knew damned well he'd gotten "special attention." Momo obviously thought there was more to him than Rooster was willing to disclose, but it was worth it. Meg should be safe.

The guards stood well back as he got to his feet. He got as far as his knees, steadying himself with his hands on the battery contraption they'd used to elicit the screams from the others. He'd been spared that part. What was a little shadow-boxing, after all? That last swing to his jaw had put him out, though. Just as well. They seemed to be done with him anyway.

Just another day at the office, he told himself. As he lifted off the ground and came to his full height, Rooster could see out the windows placed high on the walls.

Two gunmen were out digging what looked like a grave, and beside the hole was what looked like The Ghost.

The Mossad would want his body back, even if he had officially died about ten years ago.

Rooster tried to plot the point of burial in his mind, though his vision was blurry still. It was like trying to focus through the bottom of a glass. He had to concentrate carefully as he kept his balance and walked back to his cell. He hoped that they'd put him in with Meg now. But as they waved him into the same cell they stuffed him in earlier, it became evident that wasn't in the cards.

He hoped Meg still had some water. He could use a swig.

One of the guards untied his ropes, then handcuffed his left hand to the bar. Rooster made sure to keep his hand down this time, so it was on the lower panel, and he could keep his blood flowing in the right direction.

The gunmen left, and they didn't take Meg with them.

It had worked.

He stuck his other arm out in Meg's direction. He could feel the very tip of Meg's finger brushing down his arm, trying to reach for him. "Meg, I could use a sip of water, please." He wondered what he looked like. She would have seen him as he came in. He hoped she didn't think that was heading her way. Plastic pushed against his arm. He reached to take it from her, filled his mouth, let the water sit there for a moment, then he swished to get the blood from between his teeth and swallowed it down. He waited to make sure that was going to stay in before he took another gulp.

He let his head rest back against the bars. The longer he waited to speak, the longer she'd be afraid that this was her destiny. He needed another minute to catch his breath, then he'd explain.

30

MEG

    Jail

"**W**E HAVE A NEW STRATEGY. Can I have one of your t-shirts, please?"

Meg scrambled over to the corner where she had piled her extra clothes. She chose the second one of the three she'd had on —she figured it was the cleanest, and she was sure Rooster needed it to staunch a wound. Now she understood why Rooster asked her to put on so many clothes. She pressed it into Rooster's hand. "Have they chained you up again?"

"Only the one arm," Rooster said.

The gruffness in his words told Meg just how much pain he was in. She swiped away the tears that had been running down her cheeks since they took him. Abraham hadn't been brought back, and she'd been terrified that they wouldn't bring Rooster back either. She had been mentally preparing herself.

Now they'd be coming for her next. That thought sucked all the energy out of her body.

"I wasn't on their science list." Rooster said. "They needed to know if I'm more useful alive or not. And I am. Useful, that is. I'm the president of Honig International Consultation. A billion-dollar-a-year private business with deep political and industry ties. Say that name to me three times out loud."

Meg thought he was buying time to catch his breath. His last words had had no volume behind them, just air. But she did as she was told.

"Rooster Honig is the president of Honig International Consultation."

"Right. And we're married."

"*We are?*"

"Yep. Just got married. Congratulations, Mrs. Honig."

"Thank you. It was all so sudden, but you know the heart will have what the heart wants." Meg's heart squeezed down tight, and she hid her gasp of pain behind her fist. "Though you know a quick trip to the magistrate's office isn't going to take the place of a wedding. My parents will expect me to walk down the aisle with at least three bridesmaids. And Randy. Randy will be the best man."

Her attempt at a chuckle came out as a choking noise. She stopped reaching for levity. She pushed the question of her future —their future—out of the way so she could understand why Rooster would tie them together when he'd been trying to keep them separate in the eyes of their captors.

"I gave them the phone number to my business, and I told them we're covered by kidnapping insurance."

"What number was that?"

"It's a number at Headquarters. It goes to a special switchboard that keeps up with all of the employees' different doings.

Honig International is my red flag. They'll handle it. I made sure Momo knew you were covered by the insurance too. By the way, you haven't changed your last name to mine because you made your name in the field of science as Finley, so for professional reasons, you'll keep that as you travel. Socially, you're Mrs. Honig, though."

"Thank you for your understanding, darling. It took me over a decade to build that reputation."

"And I'd never ask you to do anything you didn't want to do. I think this is a good plan if it works. We'll have to wait and see how smart Momo is."

"How do you mean?"

"If he calls from here—wherever *here* is—he'll be calling the emergency department at Iniquus. My hope is that he didn't believe me, and before he does any more damage to either of us, he needs to check out the story. They have very bright people on that line. They can obfuscate with the best of them."

"You like that word—obfuscate."

"Yeah, it's a good one. Tattooed it on my left butt cheek."

Meg could tell that he, too, was trying to lighten things. But just like her attempt, his fell flat. "Stop. Tell me more about this call. They'll call to make sure that you're the president and corroborate your story, and if they confirm it, we're protected somehow?"

"Yes. With several somehows. First, it means we're an expensive chip for bargaining, so that should keep us healthy. Second, it means that Iniquus will know where we are. They'll track us on GPS, get satellite feeds from the military to keep an eye on the area, gather intel from the sky, and supply it to Panther Force, who are for sure on the ground now and on the hunt."

"Tanzania has remarkable cellphone coverage, but when I'm

in the bush, I also have my satellite phone with my SOS button, just in case. Most people who travel in the bush have them, so I assume Momo will too," she said.

"Right. Good. Because if he travels away from here, it will give the Panther's information, but the more exact the dot on the map is, the quicker the turnaround."

"Would the Panthers wait and negotiate?" Meg asked.

"That, I can't say. It depends on what intel they gather. And again, Momo might just send someone a message in a different country through the Darknet for a follow-up—then that route would be next to useless."

"In the interim, we need to get our stories straight. We should probably start with when did we get married?"

"When were you last in the United States?"

"The first week of February."

"Congratulations then, Mrs. Honig, on your Groundhog's Day trip to see the judge. Tuesday, February second at zero nine hundred hours, we were the first couple to stand before the judge that day. Tell me the day and date."

"Tuesday, February second. Nine a.m. I was wearing a cream-colored suit, and I carried sunset-colored—yellow and orange—roses. You think your company can pull this off?"

"The people who answer the red phones are very good at what they do. I trust them with this."

"Do you think they'll get in touch with my brother, Steve?"

"They'll debate it. If they think they can get resources, and it will help get those resources to us, yes. If they think that they'll be a burden and slow the movement, no. I trust them to make the right decisions there too."

Meg stalled. She'd tried to blow up the pictures, she'd tried to put them in a box, but it wasn't working. She had to know.

"How bad was the beating? What happened to you? You looked like you... It looked bad."

"Meg." Rooster stopped.

The silence between them felt heavy.

The sobs and moans echoing from around the corner gave them no respite from the fact that they were in dire straits.

Meg desperately wanted to reach for Rooster's hand, but if he'd asked her for a t-shirt, it meant he needed to apply pressure to his wounds. "You don't need to answer. I don't want you to relive it. Can you tell me why we're changing strategy?"

"I have a better handle on what's going on. Remember how I told you that we had a long row to hoe, but a good outcome if they had taken us for ransom?"

"Yes, and if we were being held for terrorist propaganda, then we were shit out of l—"

"Stop," Rooster said. It was quiet, but it was an order.

Meg felt chastened. Rooster was chained in the cell next to her, she had no idea how badly it had gone for him, and here she was chewing on her own despair. "How badly are you hurt?" she asked again.

"I'm still working on your last question. It's a bit complicated, and I'm not sure I'm fully coherent, so try to follow the best you can. I'm going to tell you a story about Momo and why I think you're safer than you might have believed. Back in Zanzibar, I asked you about Derrek Bowen. He's an oil executive, as you know. What you might not know is that he was in negotiations with the Tanzanian government. Yes, he wanted to do offshore drilling for oil, but the profits from that drill were to go one hundred percent to developing Tanzanian energy independence. All clean energy. It was taking an environmental risk in the short run in order to shift the dynamic in the long run. The Hesston Corporation has decided to become a global green energy leader. This is internal. A big secret. The reason for keeping it a big secret is politics among other oil companies."

"How does this pertain to our situation?"

"Bowen was supposed to meet with a scientist in Zanzibar."

"Okay."

"Bowen and his wife were sailing down the Red Sea to Zanzibar. Their yacht was overtaken, and they were kidnapped."

"And you were sent in to rescue them? That's why Randy said his assignment was salty? You were on the sea?"

"We were sent to Djibouti to negotiate their release. They were being held for three-million dollars. We ended up rescuing them from the Afar camp because we got word that Mrs. Bowen wasn't going to make it. She was very ill. People died. But Randy and I got the Bowens out with the help of the US Navy. We couldn't have done it on our own."

"That's how you knew about the Afar Tribe. I was wondering."

"When you went there to listen to the concerns of the Afar people, and to make sure your group made contact, since Abraham Silverman couldn't, Momo was there. He was there because he was hiding the Bowens in the village."

"That's why I couldn't go to the huts and speak with the women?"

"That's what I think."

"He could have kidnapped me then."

"No, I think that would have been counterproductive for him."

"And you think this was because…"

"The most obvious reason is that people would know where you had gone that day. If you went missing, it would put eyes on that camp. Beyond that, you were an organizer of the Key Initiative. If something happened to you, the scientists might not have come to Tanzania."

"You're suggesting that he was planning to kidnap our group all along? Why would he want to kidnap scientists?"

"I'm still making my way around to explaining that. This is going to take a little patience. The man who you knew as Abraham Silverman was actually an Israeli operative. He was in Djibouti at the same time Randy and I were. I might have thought he was a part of this, but if he was, he isn't anymore."

Past tense. He's dead. "Wait." She needed a second. She needed to deal with that. Another of their group had been killed. She willed that damned elephant into the room to blow up her feelings and help her seal them away in the box. But there they were, flowing through her bloodstream like poison. When her brain was functioning again, she asked, "Why would an Israeli operative pose as Abraham Silverman? Did he suspect there was a plot?"

"I think the Mossad picked something up in their intelligence gathering. I think they wanted to deliberately hold their scientist back. It was happenstance that the real Silverman's father died when he did. The Mossad operative—Randy and I called him The Ghost—said he was assigned to scope out the security of the situation. I have a theory that the Technion professor that Bowen was going to be meeting within Zanzibar, along with the Tanzanian government, was the real Abraham Silverman."

"He was our energy guy on the team. But that doesn't explain Israeli intelligence getting involved."

"First, Tanzania wants the safety of energy independence. And they are working on the world stage to put on a big show of their environmental stewardship. Being a green energy nation would go far in that way. Second, Tanzania loves tourist shillings. Shillings flow in, and there's no government system that needs to support that money. If the money was gained through taxes on wages, then it would have to go to educating the children, providing socially for them, healthcare, and so forth. You know this."

"Yes. But Israel?"

"They have a lot of tourist shillings to spend. Tanzanian tourism is focused on getting Israelis here. If the government could point to the good fellowship between their government and the Israelis, that would also go a far piece in encouraging good-will and tourist money. But the Israelis are ever cautious of the safety of their citizens in countries where extremism has a footing."

"If your theory is right, Momo targeted the Bowens, not for the three-million dollars, but to stop him from connecting with Abraham and the Tanzanian government."

"That's not *exactly* how I see things. As a starting point, tell me what all of these scientists have in common. What does this have in common with the Bowen kidnapping?"

Meg was squatting in front of the bars with her hands gripping the rungs by her cheeks like a monkey at the circus. "Are you sure this isn't a false positive? That these are connected?"

"Think of it as a Venn diagram. What are the overlaps in these two parts?"

Meg looked up at the ceiling and let her mind wander. "The Afar tribe. Momo. Me, but I was supposed to be Abraham Silverman. The Key Initiative scientists, Derek Bowen."

"Right, and if you take Momo out of that, what do these people have in common?"

"I don't know." She leaned her head back down and rested it on her arm. "We're here to do good things. We're here to find the win-win."

"Keep going. What's the big win here for all of these people?"

Meg shifted her eyes back and forth across the ground as if she were reading the truth in the debris. "Sustainability."

"And that would lead to…"

Meg puffed out her cheeks and exhaled with force. "I feel like a schoolgirl being led by her teacher. Why don't you just tell me?" Exasperation had edged into her words. She needed to eat. She wondered if she should use another of her precious energy bars or if she needed to ration them to one a day. Either way, she was sweating and angry and having a darned hard time concentrating.

"I'm testing my theory and seeing if you land in the same place I did." The tone of his voice was entirely too warm and patient, and Meg felt like a shithead.

"All right," she said. "Security would mean that everyone flourishes and can live better lives. Sustainability means security and a better life. A good life."

"And who could possibly be against that?" Rooster asked.

"Well, there are people who prefer chaos. People who want power. People who reap the benefits of being exploitative. If someone is desperately trying to find their next bite of food, then they don't have the strength or capacity to see, let alone fight the bigger battle. That's why we need to be here to help move everyone toward a safe existence. So, for example, girls can be educated and not get married off for the bride price as mere children to enrich and sustain the family. Are you saying Momo wants to keep Tanzania destabilized?"

"I'm testing a theory, not a fact. Panther Force has spent a great deal of time in Somalia dealing with the pirates who are taking Americans prisoner to fund the terrorism there."

"Like Momo wanted to get money from the Bowens."

"Right, but here's an interesting part of that family tree. Remember how you were telling me that Bin Laden spent time in Zanzibar?"

"It was a long time ago."

"Well, yes, but one of his close bodyguards, the man who cooked his food for him, was named Ahkmed Ghani. Ghani grew up in Zanzibar but is now serving a life sentence in the United States for his ties to the US Embassy bombing in Dar es Salaam, killing over two-hundred people. Al-Qaeda wanted Tanzania, Somalia, and Ethiopia to all become fundamentalist states. If that were true, and they had Yemen—"

"They'd control both sides of the Red Sea."

"Exactly. To do that, they are working in Somalia to attack international aid workers, civil leaders, journalists, and peace-keepers."

"But that's Somalia. That's not happening in Tanzania. The Tanzanian government is willing to bring the country forward, and the government's stewardship of the animals is the reason why the Key Initiative is centered here." Meg swiveled around and dropped her butt to the floor but kept her grip on the bars. The cement floor was dirty and cold, wicking her body heat away. But her legs were stinging from being held in a crouch. "We're focused on Tanzania, but we are reaching out to Kenya and Ethiopia, and Abraham was setting up studies for his university in Djibouti. But, yes, the three we are focusing on are Tanzania and several tribes in Kenya and Ethiopia while we get a model together. We aren't going into Somalia. I... You're suggesting that... What exactly are you suggesting?"

"Ghani's half-brother is Momo Bourhan."

"And our goals are stabilization, jobs, and a bigger place in the world community. If we are successful, then it would make the task of radicalization much more difficult, if not impossible, to establish. If they thought we were a threat, why didn't they just kill us at the hotel with all of those innocent tourists?"

"Good question. If you had to die, how would you like it to happen?"

"In my sleep," Meg whispered.

"Right. Quick, painless, enjoying life, and then on to your great reward. In the field, my buddies and I have had that discussion. Yeah, if I got my druthers, I'd pick fighting and gone. I wouldn't choose being captured and tortured and waiting to die and then dying publicly. People stand up and say, 'I'll die for this cause.' You don't often hear people say, 'I'm willing to suffer horribly for this cause.'" He paused, then dropped his voice even quieter. "I can feel you getting scared. I don't want you scared, but we do need a plan, and to get behind the solution, we have to agree on the equation."

"All right. Tell me what you think that looks like."

"I think that Momo meant to fund something big with the Bowens' ransom. He was very specific about the amount of money he needed, and in over a month of negotiations, he never wavered from that amount. That money slipped through his fingers. I think this is the timeline—Momo was planning an attack on the Initiative. He was studying each of the Key scientists. He would have had his eye on Abraham Silverman. Silverman was scheduled to go to Djibouti and visit the Afar camp with Bowen. I know that because Bowen had it listed on his calendar that was left on the yacht. If Momo had that information from tracking Silverman and looked up the name, a simple Internet search would have found Derek Bowen was in the United States news about the American companies engaging in offshore drilling. In Bowen's interview, he mentioned how much he loved boating in the Red Sea and the goodwill he had toward the people of Africa through his travels. He pushed the point by saying that he and his wife would be sailing the Red Sea to Zanzibar for the meeting and staying on their yacht. It wasn't hard information to find. We had already determined the news article was how the Bowens' were targeted. I think Bowen was the icing, not the cake."

"*We're* the cake?" That was a stunning revelation. "*Why?*"

31

ROOSTER

Jail

ROOSTER SQUEEZED THEN RELEASED Meg's hand as footfalls turned the corner onto their corridor. He didn't want them to chain his freehand too. Fear washed over him. Were they coming for Meg anyway? Were they going to make a video of her as well? Had he failed her? Anxiety effervesced on his skin. It boiled his blood. If anyone dared touch a hair on her head, he'd rip their balls off, shove them down their throats, and watch them choke. A hair. A *single* hair. He pulled himself to his full height, flexing his muscles against the pain, spreading his chest and shoulders wide. His ferocity sent waves of violence into the air. Rooster knew the danger was palpable because the guard came to a full stop. Hesitated. Then called out in broken Kiswahili, "I bring water."

The guard set a bucket down then skirted Rooster's cell as far to the right as he could get. He placed a second water bucket next to Meg's cell, right up next to the bars. A child's cup was tied to the handle.

Rooster glared at him the whole time. Made sure this piece of crap knew that despite the beating Rooster had *allowed* to happen, he was not benign. The man slithered along the cell that had once held The Ghost. He lifted the bucket intended for Rooster and crossed the hallway, out of reach. He set the bucket down next to the wall, and with his foot, he pushed the bucket to within Rooster's reach, then skittered away.

"Whatever you're doing over there, you put the fear of God into that one," Meg said. "I bet they're going to draw for the short straw to see who will have to do the next round."

"Finish drinking what's in your water bottle, then fill it from your bucket. Go look at it in the light and tell me what you think. Where did they get the water?"

Rooster listened to Meg following directions. When she answered, she was sitting at the bars next to the wall separating them. "There's no sediment. It's clear. I'd say this came from a barrel. When we were getting out of the truck, I was looking around. It's so flat here, I could see a great distance. I didn't see any signs of natural water—the kinds of birds in the sky I would expect to see if there was a body of water was close. They may have a well since this place seems to have been an established site long ago. But usually, those wells collapse over time if they're not cared for. I think this is probably okay to drink."

"Okay, put a little in your mouth and swish it around and see what you think. If you still think it's all right, then go ahead and rehydrate slowly. Then fill the water bottle from the bucket and keep it hidden in case they decide to limit water as a punishment."

"And if I think it's suspect?"

"We'll have to make more aggressive moves to get out of here. Humans need water to survive. The sooner we make that decision, the more capacity we'll have to follow through."

"Do you have a reason for not being more aggressive at the get-go? Oh wait, I already know this. Slow and steady wins the race. Can you tell me what happened when they took you away? Not in terms of what they did to you, but did you find out anything else that might be helpful?"

Rooster was reaching as far as he could toward his water bucket. His finger was just able to snag the wire handle. He pulled it carefully toward him. He filled the plastic bottle Meg had given him and used that to dampen Meg's t-shirt and gave himself a bath, washing away the filth he had been rolling in, along with the blood. Head wounds bled profusely. It probably looked worse than it was, he thought as his fingers explored the gash along his brow. After he was clean, he rinsed Meg's shirt and wrung it out as close to the far corner as he could. He noticed a snake coiled and sleeping amongst a pile of twigs and dirt. Big guy too.

Rooster drank some water and settled in to talk, now that he'd gotten his thoughts together. "What did I find out when I was visiting with our hosts? Momo was asking questions in English. They were making recordings. I saw a battery system and wires. He's been shocking the others—that was the scream-ing. They didn't shock me. I guess that part would have come at the end of the video. They punched me a few times to let me know they were serious."

"I'm so sorry."

"It's over."

Meg obviously understood that wasn't a lane he was going to travel. She went back to a pragmatic line of thought. "The questions are important. They give us information about where the bad guys' heads are."

"No one asked about contact numbers, or family, or resources. They asked me my name, my country of birth, and my country of residence. They wanted me to read a poster that said African countries are sovereign…blah-blah-blah…America is the great Satan."

"Propaganda, not ransom then. Okay." She seemed to be steeling herself. "Did you read the poster?"

"I said some of the words. I coughed through other parts. That was part theatrics, part reality."

Rooster heard Meg blow out a long breath. Her voice shook when she said, "Rooster." She cleared her throat and tried again with better control. "If they show the videos of our scientists being tortured, it will send fear through scientific communities around the world. These scientists aren't soldiers. They didn't sign up to fight and give their lives. They signed up to do science and help with scientific applications. Without knowledgeable people working on-site to come up with solutions, then the suffering will increase with climate change."

"Yes, that's right," Rooster said slowly.

"This is a real problem. This is one of the things we needed to tackle with our initiative. Young men are caught between reality and tradition. They're no longer allowed to show their strength and bravery in the ways their forefathers did. They're told it's against the law to do the very thing that gave their fathers honor. They feel denied. With their way of life disappearing with environmental changes, there aren't a lot of options when it comes to having the resources to raise a family and lead a good life. Under these circumstances, they can be convinced that it's someone else's fault they're suffering."

"Convinced that they must choose sides, and terrorists make promises that the men want to see fulfilled," Rooster added.

"Take away hope, and you have an army of desperate people willing to listen. That's true, no matter where you live. Put fear into the hearts of scientists, and they'll stay where they're safe. Not all, but most. If this theory is right, it's a worldwide setback. Potentially catastrophic."

"You can see what Momo would gain from taking you all. This will give him a great deal of prestige amongst radicals. Here's the shift in dynamic for our personal stakes—Momo needs money for something, and I offered that to him on a plate. As the president of Honig Consulting International, I have excellent kidnapping insurance. One of the problems I faced with the Bowens was that only he was covered. Mrs. Bowman was disposable. I made sure to emphasize that, as my wife, you have your own policy. You are valuable on your own. Now, as to whether they'll take you to the room to make a video, I think they'll hold off until they have a chance to verify what I said. Depending on how far we are out here, that might take a day or two. It will be verified, and the negotiations for our ransom will begin. We will be in a different category than the others."

"That makes me hopeful for us. But the others don't have this extra safety net. I feel guilty that they were beaten and I wasn't. Not that I want to be. Not that I'm not grateful. Grateful and guilty and horrified."

They sat in silence for a long moment.

"Rooster, would it be painful to hold my hand?"

"I'm reaching for you now. This is as far as I can stretch against the cuffs."

Meg touched his fingers. She ran her hand over his, up around his wrist, where he was moist and raw from his restraints. She lifted her fingers immediately. "I'm sorry, I didn't mean to hurt you." She laced her fingers with his. "I have to do something. What can I do to help?"

"You can feed me information. Let me see what I can come up with. Tell me about the goal of the Key Initiative—what was your approach to the work you wanted to do?"

"We had a framework that's starting to be implemented around the world for framing efforts. We wanted to do community building that included health with a focus on women's rights and safety. The planet—that was my bailiwick—focuses on land, water, wildlife, and sustainable green energy. And finally, the education and business enterprises would give people options for providing a comfortable life. We were coming together under a holistic management approach."

"Johnathan, who was with us in the truck, what is his specialty?"

"He does satellite imaging."

"And how will that help?"

"He, Norman Lidzt, and I were working on a project mapping migration in Tanzania and Kenya. Johnathan was watching human populations. We were correlating our data gathered from the satellite imagery. He got involved because, in his off time, he had permission to help with the chimpanzee project. In just three decades, eighty percent of Gombe's forests have been devastated. This hurt the villagers as well as the wildlife, especially the chimpanzees. The satellite images to help scientists see what they were facing. It's been a big help."

"To develop laws like those protecting the lions?"

"Well, maybe to some extent. I mean, the images help the government understand the scope of the problem and inform them when they're designing the best strategies for preservation. But in Tanzania, just like in America, survival in the moment means that they feel they can put off important changes. Fracking, by way of example, is shown to cause earthquakes in the US, but it's also putting dinner in some child's belly. In America, in Tanzania, all over the world, we need to replace long-term harmful behaviors with long-term healthful options, so people aren't being asked to suffer as we shift. It takes good policymaking."

"Right, well, we're on the same page there. What effects have those satellite images had?" Rooster wondered if some of the scientists might be kept alive to tap their expertise and others might be sacrificed to make jihadist videos that sent a global chill through the scientific world. Having access to satellite imagery—or being able to read that imagery—still stuck with Rooster as an important piece on this chessboard.

"The workers go to the villages and show them the information. They sit down with the elders and act as a resource as the elders make decisions and plans for their villages. Armed with the information and different, more effective ways to do things—ways to make life easier and better, people will choose that way. They're already starting to see the images becoming green again. It's hopeful."

Rooster's mind was churning through the information he'd been gathering since he put his foot on Djibouti soil. But now, he saw a danger to this connection. "Do you know the person running the show? Do you think if your or Johnathan's capture comes to her attention that she might pressure the Tanzanian government to come after us?"

"I don't know her. You sound like the government coming to help could be a bad thing."

"The police have a role to play, and that's to capture the bad guys. The soldiers' role is to kill the bad guys. If they are the ones who find us first, they might want to come in and save the hostages, but that's a fine-tuned skill set. You have to be focused only on the survival of the victims. We want only those with the right mindset and the right training and experience riding to our rescue."

"By that, you mean you only want Iniquus."

"I see how the playing field could get real crowded real quick. You know the phrase about too many cooks in the kitchen? The various countries, once it's known there are hostages, will be working to find their scientists and get them out. It's clever to take a group like this. There were supposed to be twenty of you. Seventeen were in the hotel. Two were from America, but the others are from all around the world. If they want the world to sit up and be shocked, they've got that covered. We're going to focus on the fact that we have the best of the best coming after us right now. Panther Force and Strike Force have a perfect record for hostage safety. We've never lost any of our precious cargo yet. You need to keep that in the forefront of all the bad thoughts that are flooding your mind."

"How did you know they were?"

"You're human."

Meg lowered her voice. "Do you think that Ahbou and Randy made it?"

Rooster had two irons in the survival fire. One was that Ahbou survived. That would tell folks that a kidnapping had happened. The second was the verification phone call that Momo was sure to make. Where he made that call was the only question. "Randy is made of steel. He'll never give up willingly. He was underneath the boulder. He was in the safest place possible to survive the blast. He wasn't losing any more blood. He was breathing. All of those things are good. If help got there quickly, he's gonna be fine." Rooster planned to blow sunshine her way until they were out of here, then they'd deal with what they had to deal with.

"There was no help to be had, Rooster. You know that."

"When they detonated the hotel, the blast must have been massive. We were miles away when we heard it. The Maasai, the rangers, people will go and investigate, I can promise you that."

"You didn't say anything about Ahbou," Meg whispered.

"It all depends on what he did next. If he stayed in the tree, he would have been thrown out of it by the blast. If he got down and was checking on Randy or he was already driving for help—"

"*Driving*?" Meg was choking on the word. She must be crying.

Rooster petted his thumb over her hand to soothe her. "He knows how to drive. It's possible that the blast happened after Ahbou had gotten away. It's also possible that Randy was in a safe position. Close your eyes."

"Okay."

"Put yourself up in the tree with Ahbou. What do you see?"

"The trucks driving away with us held prisoner."

"What do you know about the hotel?"

"There are explosives."

"As Ahbou, do you know anything about explosives?"

"No, nothing."

"Could you do anything for the people inside?"

"I don't think so."

"Who could help?"

"The rangers."

"Can you get to the rangers?"

"Yes, it's a ten-kilometer run. I can do that very fast. Oh, and the keys are in the van. I can drive."

"You're in the tree, you've seen your friends taken, your uncle is in with the explosives. What do you do next?"

"I'd go get help. Do you think Ahbou got away in time, then?"

"When I ran that scenario through my head earlier, my thought was that as soon as the trucks went down the hill, Ahbou was scrambling down the tree and running for the van. Knowing what I know of Ahbou, I think he had a chance. Either way, we can't help Ahbou and Randy until after we help ourselves."

32

———

ROOSTER
Jail

TIME WAS PASSING SLOWLY. Rooster watched the light moving from Meg's windows over to the window above The Ghost's former cell. Rooster was trying to keep track of the rhythm of the camp as they spoke. When he heard voices passing or footsteps, he marked it on his internal blackboard. From the data he'd been gathering, he thought there were about a dozen or so hostiles. That jibed with what The Ghost had said in the lobby and the kill count from their counterattacks. Something The Ghost had said tickled his mind.

A mole…

I need to know more about the people who are here. "Meg, tell me about your teammates."

"Okay." She must have been on the other side of her cell. He could hear her footsteps as she moved to their shared corner.

"Let's see. Jared Dolan was the other guy in the truck with us. He's a music educator as well as an agronomist."

"Why's he with you all?"

"Sweet potatoes."

"*Meg.*"

"I don't know why we're having this conversation. How does it help anything?"

"I just need to know what assets we have. A musical agronomist who likes sweet potatoes, not so much. An engineer? He might be able to help me rig something together."

"I'm a migrationist. Check me off your list as being helpful."

"That's your Ph.D.—what were your studies before that?"

"Still not helpful. I studied zoology in undergrad and behavioral ecology in my master's program."

"If we get out of here on our own, you'd know about the animals we'd encounter. You'd know if we should run for it or freeze like statues. You're an escape asset."

"If it makes you feel better to think that, then sure."

"We have hours and hours and hours to kill, Meg. Go ahead and tell me your potato story."

"African sweet potatoes are white and starchy, with very little vitamin A. African children are dying and going blind from a lack of vitamin A in their diets."

"So switch their sweet potatoes to orange ones." Seemed a no-brainer.

"Right. That would be a simple game-changer. But the African people are used to this other kind of sweet potato. Nobody wanted to eat the weird orange sweet potato. Imagine if someone came to you and said purple-fleshed chicken is better for you than white-fleshed chicken. It doesn't taste like white-fleshed chicken. It doesn't have the same mouthfeel as white-fleshed chicken. You don't raise these chickens the same way you raised your white chickens, but if you feed this purple chicken to your kids, they'll be healthier."

"Yeah, that would be weird."

"Would you give your kids the purple chicken?"

"Probably not until I had more evidence than your say-so."

"Who could give you this evidence so you'd believe it? Your mom, right?"

"If you mean I grew up believing purple chicken was the best chicken? Then sure. But to change my mind now? I don't know. I probably wouldn't eat the purple chicken."

"We need to convince the moms, so the next generation grows up liking orange sweet potatoes. To do that, we need to educate the moms. One of the best ways for us to do that is to hire moms from that area, native speakers, and give them the resources they need to teach. That could be picture books, but mostly it's songs and dances. The women go, and they teach the other women the songs that tell their community how good for them these orange sweet potatoes are."

"Interesting. So you're saying the reason Jared came to help you was to develop ways to educate the villagers about healthier options."

"He's our propagandist." There was a silence that followed. "What are you thinking?" Meg asked.

"Based on his physical abilities and his anxiety under pressure, if that's all Jared has to offer, nutritional science and songs, I don't think he's an asset to escape and evade."

"No. Probably not."

MEG HAD BEEN quiet for a while.

Rooster hoped she was sleeping again.

They'd had a dinner of power bars. He thought they'd probably get food the next day, or maybe the day after. He was trying to calculate how soon Panther Force would get their feet under them and when they might be coming.

That all depended on Momo.

Rooster knew Momo considered himself masterful. He liked to tout his ability to do research. It was possible he'd do an online search for Rooster—but Rooster had been washed. There was nothing anywhere that was public or private about him.

That happened years ago when he became a Delta. His friends and family all knew that he was not to be mentioned in public—especially not on social media. Not only could it put him in danger, but it would put a target on their backs as well. Given that piece of information, everyone he knew became tightlipped where he was concerned.

His red flag business had a high-dollar public face on its website.

To get in and look around, you had to put in a working email and develop a password. That turned the security system on. If the contact was routed through more than two locations, like someone who was searching from the Darknet, they'd get a failed security check message. If they took the bait and tried to enter through the Internet, then spyware was installed to track the location of the computer, to record any activity that took place on the computer, and it would even record video without the light indicating it was doing so.

If Momo took that route for verification, the Panthers had a good chance of laying hands on him.

But it would be time-consuming.

Rooster's eyes were focusing better now. He could see that the snake in the corner was waking up hungry.

The snake's head rose, and his tongue lashed the air, getting a feel for what might be around. If this was a rat snake, or something else benign, that was a-okay with Rooster.

He'd rather a snake than a rodent.

Their guard was at the corner of Rooster's visual field, and another one had just approached. They were speaking in conversational tones in Somali, probably thinking that language gave them cover to say whatever they wanted to whenever they wanted to.

"Where did Momo go?"

"He has been awake for two days. He said he was going to bed and the person who wakes him will be very sorry. He says the prisoners will cry themselves to sleep and will be too discouraged to give us any trouble tonight, except the big one. Momo said they will not break that one's spirit easily. That will take months, especially with his pretty wife here. She will make him more combative for longer. But Momo has a plan for that."

"He will move her to a different building?"

"Yes, his building. He plans to take her as his woman. But first, he needs a good night's sleep. My friend, you look upset."

"I thought she would be for all of us. If he takes her, he will not share."

"True. Perhaps he will change his mind after he has had his fill. Maybe he won't like her. We will know better tomorrow."

"What are the others doing?"

"They made a fire. You go and get something to eat. Think of me while you enjoy. I have guard duty while you dance and sing."

Momo was going to take Meg tomorrow when he woke up. That was going to happen over his dead body. He thought again of the Panthers. They weren't the only ones out there who would be scrambling if Ahbou got the word out. Strike Force, the Mossad, and the CIA would all be in that loop. Fiercer, more skilled soldiers would be hard to find. They were the elite. But they wouldn't be here by morning. The only way they could get here in time was if Momo called the Honig Consultation switchboard and Iniquus could put a pin in the map. The fact that Momo hadn't left camp made Rooster think that one way or the other, he had the resources necessary to connect to the bigger world. He'd used them. And help was already in the air. That was best-case scenario thinking. On the more pragmatic side, he had to get Meg out of here now.

"Meg? Are you awake?"

"Yeah, I'm just lying here, looking at the stars. I can see them through my window if I lie on my back."

"Could you go look out the window, please, and tell me what you see?"

Rooster could hear her move to the window, the grunt of her pulling her weight up, and then her boots hitting the ground. She moved to the second window and her hang time was considerably longer.

"They have a fire going a little distance from the second building. I count ten there. It looks like they might have a bucket of honey beer. They're passing it around."

"Could you pass me the belt, please?"

He listened as she unbuckled and slid it from the loops without a single question. He reached out his hand, and she pressed it into his fingers. "Thank you." Rooster listened to the guard's boots move to the far end of the corridor, then the scratch of wooden legs against cement. It was probably safe to do this. He popped the key out of the back and quickly released the handcuff. He rubbed his wrist and flicked his fingers to restore feeling to them. Then he staged the cuff so he could slip his hand back in if the guard made his rounds. He moved very slowly. He didn't want to excite the snake who had just found its way onto his ankle.

Rooster used the nails on his thumb and forefinger to slide into the edge and pop the flashlight from its cylinder. Miniscule in size, it was nonetheless high lumen with a head that could be twisted to broaden the range of the light or bring it down to a pinpoint.

Oh shit.

Rooster's heart picked up the pace. He could feel perspiration covering his face and chest. He worked hard to get his reaction under control. "My next question is animal-related," he said in a matter-of-fact voice.

"Good, that's my solid ground. What do you need to know?"

"I was just thinking about the movie *Killing Daylight*. Did you ever see it?"

"Um. No. I'm mostly in the bush, so I'm behind on my media consumption."

"There's a snake in the movie—a black mamba. What do you know about that?"

"That's a weird thing to think about."

"Just keeping myself entertained reviewing movies in my mind. That's the one I'm thinking about right now. The mamba?"

"Oh, that's a highly poisonous snake. Deadly. It used to have a hundred percent kill rate with humans, but they can often save the victims if they can get them to the hospital on time."

"Interesting," Rooster said as the snake moved up his leg, lifting its head and darting out its forked tongue to taste the vibrations in the air. Rooster moved the flashlight to the side, and the snake followed it with his head. While it was distracted, Rooster extended his other hand down his leg and out to the side and froze.

"It's one of the longest and fastest snakes in East Africa. It's been clocked at over five meters per second, which is faster than most people can run."

Rooster was silent.

He became a statue.

He pulled his aura in to lay against his skin. He became part of the scenery like he did when the enemy was passing by. Any move. Any move at all would pull the enemy's eyes to you and put a bullet in your head.

His eyes were mere slits, so he wouldn't need to blink. He quieted into the meditative stillness he'd practiced daily since he began his career. Everything about him calmed, like a bear in hibernation.

When he didn't say anything, Meg kept dishing up facts. "They're kind of a pewter colored. And the inside of their mouth is black, like their tongue."

Black tongue, pewter body, *check*.

"It has round eyes, and the front of the mouth is squared off, then extends outward in a slight angle."

Geometric head, round eyes, *check*.

The snake had now made its way up past Rooster's knee, onto his thigh. It stopped again to sample the air. Rooster slowly brought the light around to shine in its eyes, and with a hand as quick as lightning, he grabbed the head on either side. The snake's body struggled. It opened its mouth wide. Two bright fangs dripping with venom glowed against the black backdrop of its mouth. Rooster moved so that even the drops of venom couldn't land on him, with their potential to be absorbed into his skin and enter his system.

"Call the guard, Meg," Rooster whispered urgently.

"What?"

"Use a seductive voice. Tell him you're hungry, and you'd be willing to trade for food."

"*What?*" Before an explanation was necessary. Meg was calling out.

Rooster moved to put his left hand into the handcuff. Beads of sweat ran down his back, and his hand shook. He was holding death. If he did this right, it would be the guard who would die. If he did it wrong, the snake might bite either him or Meg. Another possibility would be that the snake didn't take out the guard. Then there would be retribution.

The guard came down the corridor. Rooster could tell by the man's newfound swagger that he thought good things were coming his way.

"Come and let me whisper to you," Meg said in Kiswahili, though the guy probably didn't understand a word she was saying. Her tone told him everything he needed to know. "I think we can be good for each other. I bet you have something I want."

The man moved far away from Rooster on the edge of their hall.

"Meg, you don't want to do this. It's not worth it," Rooster pleaded, playing his part.

"I'm hungry. I haven't eaten in two days," she returned as if she was incensed that Rooster would interfere. She really was very good at this acting stuff. The guard was parallel to her now. Rooster slipped his hand from the cuff. The snake was whipping itself into a frenzy, trying to get free. Rooster's hands became slippery with sweat. He was afraid his grip would slide, and the snake would turn its head and bite him.

"Come here. Let me whisper to you. Let's make a bargain, huh?"

The man moved to Meg's bars and reached his hands through.

Rooster used his free hand to grab the snake's tail. "Meg, jump back," he said in English. It was his command voice that blocked the part of the brain that wanted to think things over and went right to the part that wanted to survive. He trusted Meg did what he said as he said it. Rooster flicked the snake's tail and released the head.

The snake landed on the tango's shoulder. He jerked around to swat at the unknown weight. The snake lashed out and bit down hard into the bad guy's neck.

Once Rooster saw the fangs pierce the guard's skin, Rooster lifted the tail high in the air and smacked the snake's head into the ceiling, and then brought it down hard onto the concrete. Up and down. Up and down. Up and down—until the snake's skull was cracked open like a walnut, and the brain stem was dislodged, leaving a gloopy mess on the floor. Rooster tossed the snake's body into The Ghost's old cell.

The guard sat on the ground with his hand to his neck in the middle of the hall.

Rooster reached for him but couldn't quite make it. "Meg, can you reach him?"

"That was a black mamba, wasn't it?" Her voice shook in whispered horror. "You were in a cell with a black mamba."

"I got it out. It's all good." He worked to smooth down the spikes in his tone that would reveal that, yeah, that had been some scary-ass shit. Truth was, his heart was beating like a musician doing a frenzied finish on a conga solo. That hadn't been a game he liked playing. "Can you reach the guard? Can you pull him over to you? Does he have a key?"

The guard's breathing was ragged and labored. Rooster imagined from the placement of the bite that the venom had gone into his carotid artery. His death would be quick. The guy's legs swiveled, and Meg was grunting as she hauled him over. There was a clanking noise as she pulled keys from somewhere.

"Open your door, hand me the keys, and go back to check on the fire. See if there are still ten men are over there."

As soon as he had the keys, Rooster let himself out of his cage. He slid down to the end of the hall. Things were quiet. It was dark in this part of the building without the moonlight streaming into the windows like Meg had. He went back to their hallway and opened The Ghost's cell door. It had been left unlocked. He lay the guard on top of the snake and worked the snake's body into his hand. If someone came before they had a plan, they had deniability.

Meg was standing in the hall beside her open cell door. He was over to her in one step, lifted her off her feet, and crushed her against him, burying his head in her neck. "God, woman. I couldn't ask for a better partner. That was perfect. You are perfect." He set her back on her feet. "How's the party going?"

"They're stumbling around. I think one of them is passed out."

"I want you to go back into your cell, get your clothes and water, and get ready to leave. I'm going to go scope out what they have in the way of vehicles. I'll be right back." He leaned down and kissed her hard on the mouth.

She clung to his arm.

"Meg, if someone comes and sees I'm gone, I don't want them taking it out on you. I want you to pretend to be asleep. I'll be right back," he said and again punctuated it with a kiss, but this one was softer, longer, deeper. He wrapped his hands on either side of her head and rested his forehead against hers. He waited for a sign. How did she want to go forward? He could accommodate her—it just put her in a hell of a lot more danger.

After a moment, Meg stepped back, slid into the cell, and pulled the door closed.

33

———

ROOSTER

The Compound

ROOSTER WAS IN HIS ELEMENT. His body adjusted to the mission as he slid into the shadows cast by the full moon and did a perimeter walk. Off to the side, he spotted the bulk of three trucks. He had picked up the guard's rifle and checked the magazine. He could pepper the guys around the fire, but he didn't know their full number. He didn't know who, besides Momo, might be sleeping.

As he worked his way over to the vehicles, he decided that, though he had told Meg they'd be escaping alone, now that the possibility was here, she'd balk at the idea. And when he'd made that decision, he thought each person had worth to Momo in the form of separate ransom payments.

Now that he knew the terrorists weren't planning to cash in but were making propaganda films, he knew their fates would be sealed if he left them behind.

With utmost care, Rooster lifted the hood on the first truck and lay across the engine—only then, with his arm buried deep in the crevice, did he flick on his flashlight, find the distributor coil and yank it out, leaving the vehicle useless. He lowered the hood just enough that someone glancing over wouldn't see anything awry, then he moved on to the second vehicle.

The third vehicle was the one he and Meg had been brought in. He recognized the numbers painted in white on the door. He had listened to the engine for hours and knew it was in good shape. He crawled into the driver's seat and made it ready for a quick hotwire job. And lastly, he disabled the Jeep that he was sure Momo had arrived in. He took both of the gasoline containers and loaded them into the escape truck. He gave the vehicles a quick shake and found nothing that was useful. No map. No sat phone. Not even a first aid kit.

He rounded back to what he assumed would be the sleeping barracks. Momo was the ringleader. Without him, the others would be running around like chickens with their heads cut off until they could form a plan of action.

It took time for a leader to emerge. There would be a scramble for authority that might give him precious minutes. Unless, of course, they had foreseen this and had a backup plan. But Rooster doubted that was true.

Narcissists thought of themselves as invincible.

Either way, Rooster didn't know if Momo had bigger contacts involved in this who could swoop in and make things real bad real quick. Momo had to go.

Rooster moved back to the shadows of the jail and used its walls to hide as he checked on the revelry.

Things were winding down. The singing had stopped. The men were squatting around the fire, poking it with sticks. Laughter would erupt every once in a while.

The night had grown quiet.

And that was more dangerous.

He walked the perimeter of the barracks. He peered into each window opening. The panes, if they ever existed, were long gone, just like in the jail. The openings were set too high in the wall for an average pair of eyes. It was enough to bring in fresh air and light, but it kept the predators, except for the snakes and the mosquitos, out. There was only one door. If Momo was in there, Rooster had him trapped. If he went in and the hostiles returned, Rooster would be trapped.

Rooster weighed his chances. From the angles, he could see, there was only one lumpy bed. The other cots were empty. Rooster considered how he'd arrange things and decided Momo wouldn't go to sleep without a watchful set of eyes. If a guard was posted and got off a warning shot or called out, the nest of wasps would fly at him. Drunkenly. But Rooster knew, drunk or sober, just how deadly that could still be.

He walked the perimeter again, expanding his sense of hearing to search for a shuffle of tired feet, a cough, or a sniff. Reaching out with his sixth sense, he tried to take the temperature of the situation. As he crouched in the deepest shadow, Rooster made out a hostile sauntering in his direction. This was the break he needed. He'd get information here. Rooster shifted into his statue mode, calming his systems, putting himself in neutral, his foot hovering just over the clutch, his hand ready to jam his gears into go mode. He waited.

The tango was steadier on his feet than Rooster would have thought. He knocked on the door in a distinct tattoo that Rooster memorized. Another hostile unlocked the door and swung it open with a squawk. "Brother, there is still a place for you at the fire. It is my turn to guard the leader."

"You have been drinking?"

"Yes, I had two cups, but it was early in the evening. I knew I would have duty at midnight."

"The phone call did not come in as planned. Leader Bourhan says to wake him immediately. Do not answer the call yourself."

"Yes, all right."

Rooster watched as they changed places.

The new guard went into the building, and the old guard moved into the moonlight. He had a pistol at his hip, a rifle slung over his shoulder.

Rooster tracked him, moving on silent feet from the shadow of one building to the shadow of the other.

As the tango moved to pass the jail, he called out to his friend inside. "Ramo, I'm going to the fire. Is your replacement here?"

No one called back in Somali. No one called back at all.

The tango brought his rifle around and stalked toward the door. "Ramo?" he called.

As the hostile moved into the dark, open entry of the jailhouse, Rooster reached his left hand around the man's face and yanked him back, pinning the Somali against his chest.

Rooster's right hand landed on the gun barrel. He stretched his arm straight out, jerking the man's finger from the trigger.

Rooster let the rifle fall to the side, clattering and skidding across the floor.

The tango reached for his pistol, but Rooster trapped his hand in place.

The man was stronger than Rooster could have imagined. He was long and thin, but even with the power of Rooster's height and weight, it was going to be a struggle.

Rooster's ribs screamed from the earlier assault.

His left arm had lost most of its power.

He needed this to end now.

Rooster leaned backward. He could, and he would fight through this dizzying pain.

Focus.

Rooster body slammed the shithead into the cement wall, twisting the tango's weapons hand until he released his gun. Rooster dropped it to the floor. He reached out with his foot and gave it a kick.

It skittered across the hall.

Stepping back to give himself room, with a quick pull, he snapped the tango's neck.

Rooster crouched beside the dead body. He clamped his hands over his ribs. The breath he was sucking in wheezed and hissed. His knee came down hard onto the floor. He planted a hand and gasped for breath.

Mind over body.

He felt around for the guns. Then moved back to check on Meg. "You hanging in there?"

She was standing outside of her cell.

Rooster wished he could see her face and read her thoughts.

"What happened?" Her voice sounded strong. Good. He needed her.

"Tango down. I brought you a present." He ran his fingers over the 9mm, checking for safeties, feeling the weight of the magazine to make sure it was fully loaded, pulling back the slide to find a bullet already chambered. "It's good to go. Give me your hands." He moved her hands into the proper position, her finger running along the outside of the trigger guard. "Point at the bad guy's chest with this finger, then put it on the trigger and pull. Simple as that." He kissed her forehead. "Just try to remember that there are good guys here. You don't want to send bullets flying in their direction."

He felt more than saw her nod.

"You're going to stand here at the end of the corridor. If anyone comes into the opening, you shoot, then run to the trucks. They're in the northwest corner of the compound. Hide there."

She didn't move.

"Meg, you can do this. You might have to stare down a lion. But you've done that before. You made me a promise. Tell me the promise."

"No matter what, that's what I'll do. That's what I'll keep doing. I will *never* give up."

He tipped her head back and kissed her lips. "I'll try not to be too long."

ROOSTER MADE his way back to the barracks.

If there was a changing of the guard at the jail, things were about to get rocky.

At least they still had surprise on their side.

Could Meg pull a trigger and kill someone?

You never knew until you knew. Even for the battle-hardened men, he'd fought beside—sometimes the brain is a primed machine doing what it was trained to do best, and sometimes there was a stutter. No sense in debating it. It would be what it would be.

Slow and steady wins the race.

He pulled the knife from his belt and slid his index finger through the loop, making it an extension of his knuckle when he made a fist. It had an inch and a half blade, but it was razor-sharp. He stood to the side of the door and tapped out the signal knock.

The door swung open, and a head stuck out, twisting left in Rooster's direction. Rooster couldn't tell if the guy had a weapon on him or not. Either way, he'd get this done.

When the man twisted his head to look the other way, Rooster slammed his fist into his carotid artery, then grabbed his shirt and pulled him to the ground. The tango dropped his rifle as he flailed to staunch the blood. Rooster knew the man was in his last moments of life. He'd check him on the way out.

Rooster snatched up the rifle and moved farther into the building, checking each room before he moved to the man still sleeping in his bed. Rooster simply wrapped his hand around the man's trachea and squeezed.

Momo came awake fighting for his life, but Rooster pinioned him under his knee, leaning the full bulk of his near three-hundred pounds onto his chest.

After a minute, Momo fell unconscious.

Rooster used his knife to exsanguinate him.

Momo was dead.

Rooster went to the door to read the compound. All was as it had been. Rooster used the micro-flashlight to go over the place, and he found a sat phone sitting next to Momo's bed.

He dialed.

"Nutsbe," he gasped into the receiver, calling Iniquus Headquarters. "This is Honey. I'm in need of an assist."

Gunfire exploded the silence.

34

———

MEG

  Jail

INSIDE THE JAIL, on the corridor with the other scientists, it was black as pitch.

They had hissed at her. "Let me out!" "What are you doing?" "What's going on?"

Rooster hadn't said to let them out. He must have had a reason.

She wouldn't do anything that he didn't tell her to do. Guard the jail. That was her task.

"Shut your mouths and keep them shut." Words like that had never been uttered by Meg before. She'd never used that tone of voice before. And she'd never raised a gun toward somebody's chest before.

She couldn't make out much, but a figure had moved toward her, framed in the doorway.

He stood out, barely, as a silhouette against the night sky, the full moon illuminating the ground around him.

Meg knew she was invisible until she moved. That's how animals reacted. They sensed movement. Her finger stretched along the gun.

As the silhouette came closer and closer, she brought her hand up farther and farther. Now that he was in the doorframe, she was pointing directly at his chest. Her finger curled back without an acknowledged command and squeezed down on the trigger.

Her hand jumped in the air.

For a moment, she stood there, staring wide-eyed at the space that had been filled by the tall, thin shape. Now it stood empty.

Shouts came from the other men over at their fire. She knew they'd be scrambling for their weapons. Meg's brain still hadn't fully engaged, but her feet didn't seem to need special instructions.

Rooster had said shoot and run. And that had been the mantra she had chanted until the shot rang out.

Now all she had left was *run*.

Run. Run northwest.

She pivoted.

Her teammates behind her were screaming for her to *let them out*! *Let them out*! They rattled their cage doors. But she bolted from the jail. She ran in the direction she had been given, out into the night, searching for the trucks.

Find the trucks. Hide there. Hide. Hide in the trucks.

She crawled under the middle one and curled herself into a tight ball up against the inside wheel, pulling her black windbreaker over her head. If they had a light, it might get absorbed by the dull finish of the fabric.

The night exploded. Rifle fire and screams—some in agony,

others in desperation. Calls in English and Somali. Another scream. Another shot. Silence. A long, long, long silence. She held the coat tight against her and supported her body weight with her forehead against the ground.

"Meg?" It was Rooster's voice. He wasn't disguising his tone. This wasn't a clandestine whisper, but a bellow. "*Meg!*"

"I'm here." Meg lifted her head and called back through chattering teeth.

His hands reached under the truck and grabbed her under the arms, dragging her out. Rooster fell back from his crouched position and pulled her between his legs, wrapping his whole body around her.

She could feel him trembling.

He brushed the filth from her forehead and kissed her hard. He tucked her head into him and stroked a hand down her hair. "I couldn't find you."

"I did what you said." She spoke into his sweat-soaked shirt. At least, she hoped it was sweat. She pushed her hands up and massaged his chest and arms, looking for open wounds. "What's happening?"

"The threat's been eradicated for the time being. Panther Force is in the air. We'll have an exfil soon."

"Eradicated? We're safe?"

"We're watchful until we're in the air."

"The others?"

"Safe. Injured from their video shoots. Nothing permanent."

Meg squeezed her arms around Rooster.

He sucked in a pitched gasp and tapped her arm. She instantly loosened her hug.

"You're hurt."

"I might need a look-see when we get back to civilization."

"What should I do?" She gripped at his shoulders, feeling

desperate. "What can I do?"

"Just lie still in my arms for a bit. I need to feel you—to know you're safe." He pulled her back to him and dropped a kiss into her hair. "I've been in and out of situations like these for almost twenty years now. I can tell you for certain, I've never felt as scared in my life as I did when I heard that gun go off." His hand rubbed down her back and drew her hips tighter into his body. "It blows me away that we just met two days ago. It feels like a lifetime." He tipped his head back, scanning the night sky, then brought another kiss down on her hair. "I saw Randy's picture of you laughing, and I knew." He stalled, then whispered, "I just knew."

Meg felt his stomach muscles contracting under her hand.

"When you fired that gun, and I wasn't sure if you were shooting or getting shot. Thinking in that second that someone had hurt you…" He shook his head.

Meg put her hand over his heart. It beat fast and hard against her palm. She leaned her head back and kissed him on the stubble of his unshaven chin. He tipped his head down to kiss her. It was tender and sweet. She felt his lips spread into a smile against her mouth. "I do believe I've fallen in love with you, Meghan Finley. Who knew that could happen to this rusty old heart?"

"Wonderful, brave heart." She put her head back on his chest. "*My* heart."

THE SEARCHLIGHT on the helicopter took in the compound. Rooster and Meg didn't move from the cocoon of each other's arms as they leaned against the truck tire. The scientists, though, were out waving their arms and screaming, "Here! Here!"

Meg could see the feet of the men sitting on the runners, and she knew Panther Force had their rifles aimed. Rooster was on the phone with them. He shielded her as they were pelted by flying debris from the helicopter wash for the second time in as many days. As soon as the helicopter landed, before the rotors had stopped, the Panthers swarmed out the doors, dropped to the ground, and spread out. Rooster tapped her, and they stood. They would be flying back to the hospital in Arusha. Nutsbe let them know in their last update that Randy was in surgery, and Rooster said that's where Meg needed to be.

The Panthers would drive the scientists back to safety in the trucks. There were too many to fly out.

Rooster took Meg's hand and put another on her head to make sure she didn't stand up. They scooted to the door. Without letting go of her, Rooster reached out to shake the pilot's hand. "Honey," he said. "Appreciate the lift."

"Ripcord. Glad to find you in one piece."

Meg saw the American flag on his helmet and reached out to run her fingers over the symbol that always meant freedom to her but took on a special significance in that moment. "Thank you," she said.

"Glad to be of service, Dr. Finley." He turned to look forward, calling information into his mouthpiece. She and Rooster strapped in for the takeoff.

"Ahbou, wait here for a second." Meg walked into the orthopedics suite, where they were finishing up a cast on Rooster's arm.

"It's broken?" Meg asked, thinking back to everything he had done with that arm since he'd been taken to the other building to make the video. Now that he was shirtless and under a light, she could see the horrible purple streaks crossing his arms and torso.

"Just a hairline. It'll mend quick."

Her eyes traveled along the bruises, trying to read what had happened. Long and thin, they must have been beating him with some kind of stick. She felt nauseated. Horrified.

"Meg." He held out his free arm. "I'm fine. A few cracked ribs and a hairline fracture. I'm *fine*. Tell me about Randy."

"His commander, Striker Rheas, is here. There's a lot of damage. But Striker promised they'd get him the best help possible. They've arranged for a private jet to take him back to the States. Iniquus has some crackerjack surgical team on their way from London to meet Randy when he deplanes. We'll have to wait and see. The concern right now is that Randy lost a lot of blood. They're not sure how that's going to affect him."

Meg felt Ahbou moving up beside her.

"There's the hero." Rooster smiled.

Ahbou ducked his head to hide his grin.

"Tell me what happened after we left, young man."

Meg went over to draw two chairs closer to Rooster. She and Ahbou sat down. Meg chose the chair where she could hold hands with Rooster.

"As soon as the truck lights went over the hill, I jumped from the tree to check on Mr. Randy. He was not awake. I thought that to find the helpers and to bring them back, it might be too much time. I drove the van over to him, and I put him in the back."

"You did that, Ahbou? All by yourself?" Rooster asked, reaching over to squeeze Ahbou's biceps and give him a nod of approval.

"My mother always told me that when you are scared, you will either have the strength of an elephant or the weakness of a sick calf." He put his hand on his chest. "I was scared like an elephant. I dragged Mr. Randy up the back, where there is a ramp for the dolly. I shut the doors, and I drove very fast. When I was too far away from the hotel to see it in the mirror, there was the explosion. I kept driving all the way to the clinic. They called the helicopter just like for Mr. Robert. I got to fly with Mr. Randy here to the hospital."

"Rooster, I talked to them about Robert, and he's doing fine. They're releasing him in the morning."

"Good to know." He sent her a questioning look then slid his eyes over to Ahbou.

Meg shook her head and mouthed, "No survivors." She put a hand on Ahbou's shoulder. "Did the doctors check to make sure you were okay? You ate? And slept?" Meg asked.

"Last night, they let me sleep on the couch, and they gave me some food. In the morning, Mr. Striker was there with me. He is a very nice man. He asked me about what had happened, and I told him everything about the bad men in the hotel. I told him about you going away in the trucks. And Mr. Rooster putting me up in the tree, then the explosion. He said thank you for taking care of his friend and wanted to know if my family knew where I was, but I have no family. My uncle was the last one."

Meg pulled him closer. "I'm so sorry about your uncle, Ahbou."

Ahbou nodded.

Meg waited for a clue what to say. She needed to make sure that Ahbou would be taken care of. That he'd be okay. "We need to make plans for what happens next for you."

"Oh yes, the hospital was sending word to my school. But it is not an orphanage. They will look for an orphanage that might have room for me. Mr. Striker said I should not be afraid. He would make sure I was all right. Just like Mr. Rooster said to me when I was in the tree. And I am." Ahbou stroked his hands down the hospital gown they must have given him since Ahbou's shirt went to stop Randy's bleeding. "Mr. Striker said first he was going to find you and Miss Doctor Meg, then he would find a good school for me."

"For certain, we will find a good school for you. But you also need a home and someone to love and take care of you. As brave and strong as you are, you are still a child."

Ahbou looked at his feet.

Meg took his hands. "Ahbou, will you come and live with me in Dodoma? I bet we can find a very good school for you there. One that will teach you all about engineering and water systems."

Ahbou blinked at her.

"You gave my brother love and protection. You saved his life when you could have only thought of yourself. In that moment, you became my *family*." Meg didn't know if it was the right thing to do in Ahbou's culture. But she gathered Ahbou into her arms to hug him.

Ahbou leaned his body into Rooster's leg.

Rooster lowered his hand to Ahbou's head and pressed a kiss into Meg's hair.

With the three held still in that tight circle, a silent promise was made and accepted.

A seal.

An unbreakable bond.

The End

Please follow Ahbou, Meg, Rooster, and the Iniquus family as they continue their fight for the greater good.
The next book in the Uncommon Enemies Series is ***THORN***.

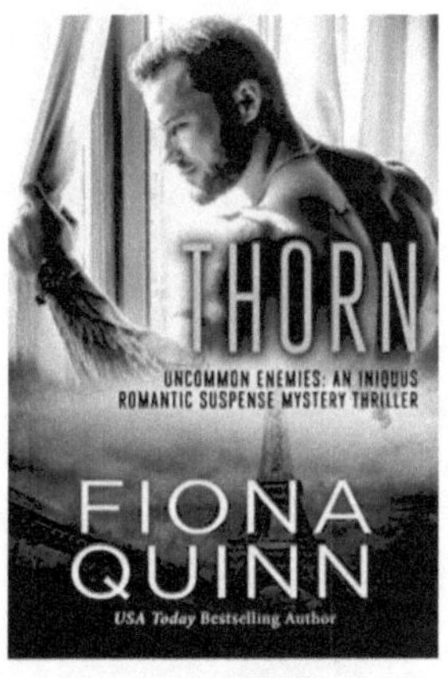

Would you like a sneak peek at the next book in the Iniquus chronology?

Keep reading for sneak peek of ***InstiGATOR***.

Readers, I hope you enjoyed getting to know Rooster and Meg. If you had fun reading DEADLOCK, I'd appreciate it if you'd help others enjoy it too.

Recommend it: Just a few words to your friends, your book groups, and your social networks would be wonderful.

Review it: Please tell your fellow readers what you liked about my book by reviewing DEADLOCK on Amazon and Goodreads. If you do write a review, please send me a note at hello@fionaquinnbooks.com. I'd like to thank you with a personal e-mail. Or stop by my website, FionaQuinnBooks.com, to keep up with my news and chat through my contact form.

INSTIGATOR

Not even his psychic visions prepared him for her…

Retired Marine Raider Gator Rochambeau is struggling. He *should* be focused on his mission. Instead, he's distracted by bizarre psychic visions—and by the beautiful asset the CIA is using to stop a billion-dollar coup that could devastate the world helium market. All he knows now is that he better get his head on straight, or people could die…maybe even him…

Special Ops pilot Christen Davidson is out of her comfort zone. All she wanted was to fly a rescue mission and save some fellow operators. Instead, she's playing dress-up for the CIA while trying (and failing) to ignore her attraction to a man she has *no* business fantasizing about. This is *not* why she joined the military…

. . .

For Gator and Christen, there's nowhere to run and nowhere to hide—not from their mission, and not from their feelings. They'll have to trust each other implicitly if they want to survive. But what if trust is a luxury they just can't afford in this high-stakes international game? Only time—and maybe fate—will tell…

1

CHRISTEN

TUESDAY, FORWARD OPERATING BASE, IRAQ

"SCRAMBLE. SCRAMBLE. SCRAMBLE."

The PA system's bright, tinny voice yanked Lieutenant Christen Davidson from her curled-up sleep. She found herself standing on the unfinished planks next to her bunk before her eyelids could even pry open. As her feet hit the floor, she criss-crossed her arms and jerked her t-shirt up over her head. Her flight uniform lay draped over the headboard in such a way that there would be no fumbling as adrenaline, Christen's drug of choice, shot excitement through her system.

She scratched her fingers through her short pixie-cut hair, the most she would do to make herself presentable. Vanity was a time suck. Christen's time was spent piling special forces operators into the back of her heli and flying them into the fray. They depended on her. Missions and lives were at stake – *they* were her priority.

Perched on the edge of her cot behind the makeshift privacy

curtain formed from a queen-sized striped sheet, Christen pulled on her clothes, yanked the laces of her flight boots, and quickly looped a bow. With a shove of the door, she shot herself into the daylight. The sun glared in her eyes as she ran full-tilt toward the command tent to get her orders.

Christen wasn't normally awake this time of day and didn't normally fly in sunlight. She was a member of the Night Stalkers, the Army's 160th. She was one of the only female pilots in what had been, up until very recently, the only special forces unit that allowed women to apply. She'd earned her place. Anything the male pilots could do, she could do too—maybe better, maybe not. Everyone had their strengths *and* their weaknesses.

Christen's strength was flying low altitude flights in the black of night, hugging the terrain, glossing over its surface, scaring the hell out of the people below her while hiding her customers from any enemy eyes that might be scanning the midnight sky. She'd trained long and hard, year after year. She'd logged hundreds of hours — every hour she could possibly fly, any *thing* she could find to fly.

These last five years, she had flown in every kind of weather, terrain, and impossible-to-survive scenario her commanders at the 160th SOAR(A) at Fort Campbell could contrive. Before this last deployment, she'd received her change of status. She was fully mission qualified. She could go on any assignment required of her – bar none. But daylight? —Christen looked up at the sun as she reached to pull the command tent door open— that's not what Night Stalkers did. This was odd. Something was off.

Christen stopped short when she saw her commander barreling toward her.

"Let's move it, Lieutenant." The colonel growled as he strode through the door, she held wide. He thrust a clipboard of papers at her, then pointed toward the Little Bird helicopter across the field getting fueled. The tanker truck was positioned far enough away that if an enemy combatant wanted to set it on fire, it wouldn't explode the whole Forward Operating Base, situated just this side of enemy-held territory.

A line of Delta operators formed to her left, with their long hair and bushy beards. The "quiet professionals"—latent death and destruction. Each one laden with weapons, fully geared up in their battle rattle. Christen wondered when they'd flown in. They weren't on base when she'd gone to sleep. The Deltas stepped, one at a time, onto a bathroom scale, and one of their group noted each man's weight on their clipboard. Weight mattered to the speed and the dexterity of a helicopter's maneuvers. If they were being that precise, this wasn't a taxi ride.

Christen looked down at her flight plan and blinked. What the… "What?" She held a hand up to shield her eyes and read her orders again. She flipped to the waypoints marked on her map, and the GPS coordinates she knew were already loaded into her flight computer system. *Wow.*

"I'm not sending you out on a Sunday picnic." Colonel Martin stabbed a finger into her shoulder. "You're our precision flier. Guts forged out of steel, I told 'em. And now, you're going to make sure I don't regret putting my reputation behind you."

It was uncharacteristic of the colonel to point to any one pilot — to lift them up or set them apart in any manner from the rest of the Night Stalkers. Christen didn't like it. She was a team player, period. She didn't seek out and didn't want flattery or recognition. She just wanted to do her job.

And with or without any added pressure, this was going to be one hell of a trick-shot. Christen's gaze scanned down the fuel calculations. With her tank filled to spill--depending on the weight of the Deltas and the opposing wind speeds--she had a little over a two hundred sixty-mile range. With the calculated hover time... Yeah, this was shaving it close. She turned the page to find the weather read-out, then glanced up again at the bright sunshine, not a cloud in the sky. Of course, here in the desert, that could change in the blink of an eye – no matter what the weather report said. Haboobs came when they wanted to. These violent winds carrying blinding dirt and debris could choke an engine and put a bird nose down in the sand quicker than quick. Sunlight, though, totally sucked. She wished they'd let her do this at night when she was in her comfort zone.

Like a vampire, Christen thrived after the sun went down. The 160th Night Stalkers loved the pitch-black of moonless nights. With their FLIR—forward-looking infrared systems—and their night vision goggles along with some rad computer systems, she could sweep over the terrain, almost undetectable, to deliver her customers to the required spot, arriving on time and on target in plus or minus thirty seconds. It was the precision that her customers demanded. The Night Stalkers were the air support for the United States Special Operations units.

The 160th had flown the Osama bin Laden mission, which had been planned and trained for to the Nth degree. Even with the technical problems, that mission could only be seen as a success of vital importance. The 160th had also been the team that zoomed their way into the Hindu Kush Region of Afghanistan when the call was made for an immediate extraction after a SEAL team came under heavy fire during Operation Red Wings. The Night Stalkers in their CH-47 Chinook helicopters took off without a gunship escort, hoping against hope to extract the team in time. The Taliban shot down one of the Night Stalker's helicopters with a rocket-propelled grenade, killing the eight Navy SEALs and eight special operations aviators on board. The second helicopter was forced to leave the scene. It was a soul-crushing horror of a day. It was the day Christen swore she'd become a Night Stalker, dedicating her work to the memory of those fallen warriors.

Christen chewed on her upper lip, reading over her orders to fly straight into the center of a populated city. She visualized the scene in her mind. This kind of challenge was exactly what she'd signed up for. She reached around and hooked a hand behind the back of her neck as she processed the schematics. The road width with the apron of sidewalks and parking lanes on either side was marked on the satellite photo as thirty-one feet five inches. Her rotor diameter was twenty-seven feet, four inches. Could she trust these calculations?

Whew! This was going to be one hell of a hairy mission. She'd never trained for this. Never imagined it. Wasn't completely convinced it was possible. But damned, she was glad *she* was given the opportunity to try.

Typically, they'd sit down and plot this out meticulously. They'd practice, practice, practice until go-time, working to find any holes and plug them. But this time, she didn't get to sit down in the wooden chairs and participate in the mission planning. They were spooling up with the pressure of some undefined time constraint. Papers slapped into her hands. There must be an imminent threat—a small window of opportunity.

Christen turned as her stick buddy, Nick Campbell, moved up beside her and read their paperwork over her shoulder. A low whistle blew between his teeth. "How many customers are we taking in our bird?"

"We have four. The Deltas are checking their weight now to make sure we're well below the max takeoff load. The Black Hawk will have the rest of the customers and the heavier firepower."

"I guess we're glad they've got our backs." His gaze scanned over to the Black Hawk. "I hope they have all the firepower they can cram on there. I have a feeling we're going to need it." He tucked his helmet under his arm and grinned. "It's a good day to die." He raised a hand toward their clients and went to do his pre-flight checks.

Finish reading InstiGATOR

THE WORLD of INIQUUS

Chronological Order

Ubicumque, Quoties. Quidquid

Weakest Lynx (Lynx Series)

Missing Lynx (Lynx Series)

Chain Lynx (Lynx Series)

Cuff Lynx (Lynx Series)

WASP (Uncommon Enemies)

In Too DEEP (Strike Force)

Relic (Uncommon Enemies)

Mine (Kate Hamilton Mystery)

Jack Be Quick (Strike Force)

Deadlock (Uncommon Enemies)

Instigator (Strike Force)

Yours (Kate Hamilton Mystery)

Gulf Lynx (Lynx Series)

Open Secret (FBI Joint Task Force)

Thorn (Uncommon Enemies)
Ours (Kate Hamilton Mysteries)
Cold Red (FBI Joint Task Force)
Even Odds (FBI Joint Task Force)
Survival Instinct - (Cerberus Tactical K9)
Protective Instinct - (Cerberus Tactical K9)
Defender's Instinct - (Cerberus Tactical K9)
Danger Signs - (Delta Force Echo)
Hyper Lynx - (Lynx Series)
Danger Zone - (Delta Force Echo)
Danger Close - (Delta Force Echo)
Fear the REAPER – (Strike Force)
Cerberus Tactical K9 Team Bravo

Coming soon, more great stories from the ex-special forces security team members who live, work, and love in a tightly knit family.

FOR MORE INFORMATION VISIT
WWW.FIONAQUINNBOOKS.COM

ACKNOWLEDGMENTS

My great appreciation ~
To my editor, Kathleen Payne
To my publicist, Margaret Daly
To my cover artist, Melody Simmons

To my Beta Force, who are always honest and kind at the same time, especially M. Carlon and E. Hordon

To my Street Force, who support me and my writing with such enthusiasm. If you're interested in joining this group, please send me an email. **Hello@FionaQuinnBooks.com**

Thank you to the real-world military and CIA who serve to protect us.

To all the wonderful professionals whom I called on to get the details right. Please note: This is a work of fiction, and while I always try my best to get all the details correct, there are times when it serves the story to go slightly to the left or right of perfection. Please understand that any mistakes or discrepancies are my authorial decision making alone and sit squarely on my shoulders.

Thank you to my family.

I send my love to my husband, and my great appreciation. T, you are my happily ever after. You are my encouragement and my adventure. Thank you.

And of course, thank *YOU* for reading my stories. I'm smiling joyfully as I type this. I so appreciate you!

ABOUT THE AUTHOR

Fiona Quinn is a six-time USA Today bestselling author, a Kindle Scout winner, and an Amazon All-Star.

Quinn writes action-adventure in her Iniquus World of books, including Lynx, Strike Force, Uncommon Enemies, Kate Hamilton Mysteries, FBI Joint Task Force, Cerberus Tactical K9, and Delta Force Echo series.

She writes urban fantasy as Fiona Angelica Quinn for her Elemental Witches Series.

And, just for fun, she writes the Badge Bunny Booze Mystery Collection with her dear friend, Tina Glasneck.

Quinn is rooted in the Old Dominion, where she lives with her husband. There, she pops chocolates, devours books, and taps continuously on her laptop.

Visit www.FionaQuinnBooks.com

COPYRIGHT

Deadlock is a work of fiction. Names, characters, places, and incidents either are the product of the author's imagination or are used fictitiously, and any resemblance to actual persons, living or dead, business establishments, events, or locales is entirely coincidental.

www.ingramcontent.com/pod-product-compliance
Lightning Source LLC
Chambersburg PA
CBHW061311190726
48288CB00002B/451